ARGENTUM

The Adventures of a Silver Piece at Great
Moments in History

James Leslie-Melville

The Book Guild Ltd

First published in Great Britain in 2023 by
The Book Guild Ltd
Unit E2 Airfield Business Park,
Harrison Road, Market Harborough,
Leicestershire, LE16 7UL
Tel: 0116 2792299
www.bookguild.co.uk
Email: info@bookguild.co.uk
Twitter: @bookguild

Argentum is a work of fiction. The events portrayed in it, while based on historical figures,
are the product of the author's imagination.

Typeset in 12pt Adobe Jenson Pro

Printed and bound by CPI Group (UK) Ltd, Croydon, CR0 4YY

ISBN 978 1915352 682

British Library Cataloguing in Publication Data.
A catalogue record for this book is available from the British Library.

To MDW,
J & G & R

Prologue

My name is Argentum, my number forty-seven, but most people just know me by my colour Silver.

I am about five thousand years old.

I have been beaten into many shapes and sizes over the years. I have been stamped on, melted, moulded, embossed, tarnished, ribbed, fused, ionised, alloyed, oxidised, compounded, electrolysed.

I have been bought; I have been sold, stolen, buried, sacrificed, wagered, hoarded, spun, lost and found.

I have marked exploration, invasion, revolution, plague, genocide, eruption, inferno, famine, faith, greed, humility and folklore.

I have witnessed births, marriages, deaths, good deals, bad deals, sporting excellence, bankruptcy, romance and betrayal.

I have aided the advance of medical care, art and culture, communication, entertainment, photography, space travel, energy storage, weapons of mass destruction.

I am beautiful, ductile, precious, cleansing, lustrous, conductive, malleable, rare.

I am Silver: this is my story.

'A word fitly spoken is like apples of gold in pictures of silver'

– Proverbs, chapter 25, verse 11

One

Discovery

c. 3000 BCE – Western Anatolia

Lugal trudged wearily up the small hill towards the seam, his tall, thin frame stooped against the incline. The afternoon sun beat down relentlessly on the baked earth, with no shade to be found in the shallow valley. The respite of darkness was a long way off and the guards' whips would ensure that all the slaves continued to work at full pace until the light failed. The alternative was to be beaten unconscious in front of the work team, as an example to others, and left to recover or die by the latrine beyond the night shelters. He had seen it happen often enough to his men and doubted whether he would be strong enough to survive such treatment. There had been a time when he was one of the fittest members of his tribe, but at the age of thirty-eight he no longer had the energy and resilience of youth. Life at the mine had taken a heavy toll, and his body already harboured a daily list of mild aches and pains.

It was three years now since the shame of capture and imprisonment. Lugal still winced at the memory of the raid on the village and his failure to protect the tribe. The humiliation of being marched away in shackles and reduced to slave labour with the other able-bodied men was an irrelevance when he thought of his family, slaughtered in front of him together with the rest of the women and children. As headman he should have set regular pickets and organised his people to prepare for just such an event. The tribe had prospered in the previous few years thanks to a series of good harvests and little interruption from the nomadic groups roaming the land. There had been neither need nor curiosity to venture beyond the grazings close to the village, and he recognised too late that their peaceful existence could never have lasted. Now he was failing again; the men had looked to him for leadership within the harsh confines of the slave camp, and in all the time they had been there he had been unable to form a plan to break out. Yes, he had organised the provision of clean water and basic food, arguing with the guards that the mine would simply cease to function without reasonable living conditions. But men still died from mysterious diseases and the occasional fatal beating, and he could see no end to their enforced labour as long as the earth continued to offer up the glinting metalled rock. Moreover, he knew that once the seam was fully dug out, the nomads would move on, and the slaves would be left to starve.

Although Lugal had never seen rock formations like this before, and did not know what purpose the metal extract served, he could not help but share the nomads' excitement for it. Even from the distance of a long stone's throw, a glittering horizontal band stood out on the bare face of the mine, measuring seven hands in depth and running level across the hill for some four hundred paces. To his left were the scattered remains of rubble already excavated, the metal from the seam having been removed and loaded onto mules for transport to the coast. To his right the band came to an abrupt end as the hill sloped down towards the valley floor: another year's work at the rate the slaves had achieved since their capture. He guessed that the seam would probably be his destruction and yet it mesmerised him, a deadly trove sparkling in the sunlight, willing him to touch it, own it, treasure it. He remembered the women in his village fashioning necklaces and thought how they would have enjoyed adding pieces of this strange rock to their collections of stones and beads. But more than being just a thing of beauty, he knew intuitively that the metal carried a value which could be traded with the merchants on the shoreline. It was a passage to freedom and safety, if only he could find a way to escape.

Lugal's grasp of the slaves' position was more accurate than he realised. Having swept across Anatolia from the east as one of many roving groups seeking new feeding grounds for their livestock, the nomads had settled on an area close to the western sea with a good supply of pasture but limited fresh water. In setting up camp they had chanced upon an underground stream, whose source they had located several days' walk towards the rising sun. There they had found the low hill and the glinting rock face, open to the elements and easily accessible. Like Lugal, they had recognised immediately the importance of the discovery, the older members of the group having seen similar mineworks many years earlier on their travels across from the Caucasus. The only settlement nearby was Lugal's small village which they had easily overrun, taking the surviving menfolk as slaves to dig out the precious rock which could then be sold to the coastal merchants. Unlike Lugal, the nomads were disinterested in the use of the metal as decoration, but they understood its potency as an article to trade for food and other provisions.

Looking up at the rock face, Lugal could see the slaves working, some kneeling on the bare hilltop scraping away the earth down to the seam, others digging out the metal that had already been exposed. He had left a third team down at the night shelters, sharpening stones and branches for use at the mine and weaving panniers for the mules to carry the precious metal away in. The digging tools were woefully basic, and often the slaves' hands were reduced to bloody shreds as they clawed at the rock. Many also suffered from crushed feet and flayed backs as they heaved the metal into the panniers under the guards' sharp gaze. Only by regular rotation of the three teams around the mine had Lugal been able to ensure that bodies could recover and the work rate be maintained. He knew that he was fortunate to have escaped much of the hard labour in his role as slave driver but was well aware of the resentment it caused amongst the men. This, together with his failure to protect and liberate them, meant they no longer saw him as their leader, and he had come to the reluctant conclusion that any attempt to break free would need to be a solo effort.

A guard's whip flicked at his calves, and he realised that, lost in his thoughts, he had come to a standstill. At that moment there was a loud cry, and he looked up to see a flurry of activity at the seam. A large mound of earth and loose stone had been dislodged from the hilltop, and in falling down the front of the rock face, it had hit one of the men. Lugal began to run up the track, as workers and guards gathered round the injured slave. Even from a distance he could see the damage done – a heavy stone had landed squarely on the man's head, staving in the front of his skull and smashing his nose. He lay sideways on the ground, his legs twitching and blood running freely into the earth around him. Despite the daily brutality of life in the camp, all those around him seemed frozen by the scene, and it was not until Lugal reached them that a babble of noise began. His role as headman was instinctive, and he forced his way through the throng, ignoring the guards and shouting over the hubbub:

'You, Kashid, run to the night shelters and get a mattress. Mashda, give me a strip of cloth. Everyone else, step back and keep the dust off him. He's alive, and we may be able to save him, but only if we can keep the wound clean.'

One of the slaves standing at the front of the knot of onlookers tore a cuff off his shift and thrust it into Lugal's hands. He knelt by the body, thinking privately that it would be a miracle if the man survived, and reached under the head to lift it free from the ground. With the cloth he was able to staunch the flow of blood, winding it in a tight knot across the temples. Above him the guards were at last galvanised into action, shouting at the watching slaves to return to work and sending one of their number scurrying down the path after Kashid to report the accident to the nomads' chief. Lugal insisted that he remain with the injured man, and to his surprise they agreed, dispersing to their posts around the mine and leaving him crouched at the base of the seam.

After several minutes Kashid reappeared with a straw palliasse, placing it on the ground and kneeling to inspect the man's broken nose. Lugal moved down the body, rolling it gently onto its back and feeling for any other injury on the torso and hips. Suddenly his hand pressed against a rough object the size of a large pebble hidden under the man's buttock. He pulled it out, his back to Kashid, and stared in amazement at what he held in his palm. It was a small lump of the precious rock, a piece of almost entirely pure metal, which the injured slave must have torn from the seam just as the falling stone hit him.

Lugal had never seen a nugget of such quality before. It gleamed in the shadow of his frame as he bent over the injured man, out of Kashid's view. Even in the dull light, it seemed to radiate a strange power, and he knew instantly that this was his salvation, if only he could avoid being caught with it.

The whole structure of the mineworks was set up to ensure that the slaves could not conceal any of the rock they hacked from the seam. Every labourer was overseen by at least one guard, and every chunk of loose rock was inspected, either to be loaded into the panniers or discarded as rubble. At the end of each day the slaves were strip-searched as they returned to the night shelters, and in three years no one had managed to steal anything. Those who had attempted to do so, and had inevitably been found out, had been flogged to death.

Lugal feigned an itch on his stomach and tucked the nugget into a fold of the belt around his waist. Rising to his feet, he turned to Kashid, gesturing brusquely towards the palliasse with one arm and shielding the front of his body with the other. 'We'll use this to carry him to the night shelters. It's touch and go whether he'll live, but it's the least we can do. Take his shoulders.' He wondered whether Kashid heard the tension in his voice as they lifted the body, now unconscious and inert, and placed it roughly onto the makeshift stretcher.

Carrying the injured man down the hill behind Kashid and an accompanying guard, Lugal considered what to do next. Any search at the end of the day would immediately reveal the nugget; he had to find a way of concealing it until he had formulated an escape route. Somehow the fog of helplessness and indecision that had bedevilled him since enslavement fell away, a plan taking shape in his mind as he walked. The little lump of metal was precious not only as an item to trade, but it was also a charm, a catalyst; he knew how he could break out, and he would do it later that night.

*

The night shelters in the base of the valley were a rudimentary construction of straw roof on wooden poles, with ten men to each hut. The sides to the huts were of thin reeds, doing little to keep out the keen breeze that blew towards the sea after sunset each evening. There were numerous holes in both ceiling and walls where rats had forced their way through in search of food, and the slaves were used to disturbances during the night as wind and rodents interrupted their sleep. Outside, two guards patrolled the entrance to each shelter, and more were posted around the stockade enclosing the mules. In the early days of imprisonment there had been several attempts to escape, but over time a lethargy had overcome the slaves, due to a combination of the strip searches, beatings, exhaustion and a lack of awareness for the surrounding area beyond the village where they had used to live. Now, with no hope of food and water outside the mining camp and no precious metal to steal away with, the slaves were easily corralled, and the guards were less alert after dark than they were when watching over the daytime labour teams.

Lugal lay on his bed listening to a rat scratching at the roof and waiting for the new moon to sink below the horizon. Since the others had fallen asleep, he had been silently working at the reed wall beside him, enlarging a hole close to the earthen floor. It was a painstaking process if he was to avoid attracting the attention of his neighbours or the guards at the front of the hut. At last, the sliver of moon disappeared, and it was time to act. He slipped off the straw mattress and began to wriggle head first through the opening in the wall, his determination to escape finely balanced against a gut-wrenching fear of detection. He froze as he heard a man stirring across the room, but it was only a moment before the snoring resumed and he could worm his way into the blanket of darkness outside.

It was a starlit night, and despite the lack of moon, Lugal was able to make out the shapes of the other huts and the latrine trench fifty paces to their rear. The guards had insisted that the injured man be left there, as if he had been the subject of a beating. Lugal crawled towards him, stopping repeatedly to listen for voices or footsteps, but none came. It seemed to take an age, but eventually he was able to lie alongside the supine body, partially out of the guards' view should they glance in his direction, and reach for the man's left arm lying curled across his torso. The fingers were clenched into a fist, and it was no surprise to confirm that he was dead.

When Kashid and Lugal had placed the body there that afternoon, Lugal had pretended to comfort the man, kneeling over him and arranging his arms neatly across his stomach. Kashid and the guard had walked away, disinterested in what they both knew would soon be a corpse. Lugal had been able to transfer the nugget from his belt to the man's hand, squeezing the fingers round it and guessing that the stiffness accompanying death would keep it hidden there. In the unlikely event that the guards checked the body before sundown, they would not think to inspect a cold, lifeless palm. Now he prized the fist open, and the nugget rolled out onto the ground. Once again, Lugal experienced a flare of astonishment at his good fortune, quickly quelled as he thought how much more luck he would need for his plan to succeed.

He looked across at the mule stockade beyond the night shelters and considered whether to dare stealing an animal. It was tempting. He knew that the route westwards to the coast would be easy to follow and that riding offered a chance to put good distance between him and the guards before sunrise. Furthermore, the coast was the obvious place to aim for if he was to lose himself amongst crowds and trade the nugget for onwards escape by boat. But he also suspected that the nomads would waste no time in pursuit once they found him missing. Even though they were unaware of the theft from the seam, they would want to make an example of him as headman to deter further breakouts and would guess from the loss of the mule which direction he had taken. There was also the problem of the guards at the stockade.

Reluctantly, he discarded the idea and returned instead to his original plan. He remembered from his time with the tribe that there was a little-used caravan route southwards beyond the village. No one in the tribe had ventured far along it, but rumours had circulated from time to time that it led to another coastline, many days' walk away. It was in the opposite direction from the nomads' main camp, and he suspected they would be unaware of its existence. The chances of being followed were low, even if it was a journey into the unknown. He had half the night to get away from the mine, and he had his metal charm – it was a risk worth taking.

Clutching the nugget, Lugal crawled round to the far side of the latrine and on into the darkness. Thirty paces further, he hugged the ground in terror as two guards came to urinate in the stinking trench he had left behind him, but they were too busy exchanging crude boasts to look carefully into the shadows. He watched them return towards the huts and waited for a long moment before summoning the courage to start moving again. Stones and thorny scrub tore at his clothing as he crept stealthily up the side of the valley, stopping over and over again to ensure that outlines in the darkness around him were not sentries. At last, in the glimmer of dawn, he was able to look back at the mine and night shelters, now over a thousand paces away. There was still no time to lose, and he slipped over the horizon just as the seam began to glitter once more in the first rays of the sun.

Finally, he was able to stand up and begin to run. He imagined the consternation in the huts as his empty mattress was discovered and the guards began their search. They would have no reason to suspect that he had visited the body of the injured man, and he was confident that his trail would not be visible on the broken and stone-strewn ground. The obvious place to look for him was westwards, on the mule path to the coast, but nonetheless he worried that they would send men to check every ridge around the valley. He plunged down the slope towards some low trees and dared not look back, fear of recapture spurring him on towards the familiar countryside around his ruined village. There he would cut across the old caravan route and head south.

*

Four days later, Lugal was all but finished. He had found the path, almost abandoned but still distinct enough to follow without trouble, and had made good time at first as he jogged determinedly towards the midday sun. He was used to the heat, and although it would be more unobtrusive to travel at night, he wanted to put as much distance as possible between the mine and himself in the early hours of his escape. In any case, he could not risk losing the trail in the darkness. By dusk on the first day, he reasoned that the likelihood of being caught was now limited and that sleep and water were greater priorities. He found a small watercourse off the side of the track and slumped down beside it. Over the next two days he repeated the pattern, running again as dawn rose and halting, exhausted, each evening as his belly rumbled in hunger. He encountered no one on his journey and estimated by nightfall on the third day that, although his pace had begun to slow, he had now covered more than five days' walk. However, he had noticed that the countryside was becoming more arid, and without food and water he wondered as he lay under the stars how much longer he could go on. On the fourth day he was able only to stumble along the path, his throat parched and his energy spent. By mid-afternoon he had lost all sense of direction in the blinding sun and finally collapsed on his chest into the dust. He lay there unconscious, the nugget still clasped in his hand, not even the cool air of night being enough to resuscitate him.

A sharp prod in the ribs and the sound of high-pitched voices roused him. He rolled onto one elbow, squinting up at a small boy blotting out the morning sun and poking him again with a thin stick. Gathering his senses, he counted six other children, all with sticks and chattering excitedly. It was evident that they were responsible for a herd of stringy goats that milled about him. More importantly, the boy nearest him carried a bulging waterskin across his spindly shoulders. Lugal realised suddenly that he still grasped the nugget in the hand beneath his body, so he gestured to the waterskin with his free hand, hiding the precious metal under his belt as he shuffled to his knees. He tried to speak, but no words would come from his dried and swollen lips.

The waterskin was thrust towards him and after a long draught he was able to think more clearly. The children appeared to be more curious than dangerous and presumably belonged to a tribe nearby. It was mid-morning on the fifth day of his escape, and he guessed he had wandered off the caravan route in his delirium the previous afternoon. He was lost and debilitated and would have to risk the tribe taking him in rather than killing him outright or selling him back to the nomads. He stood up shakily and found his voice, weak and tremulous. 'I mean you no harm. I am lost and hungry. Take me to your village.' He knew he sounded piteous, rather than commanding as a headman should, but it was the best he could manage before dizziness overwhelmed him again.

Sometime later, Lugal was wakened by a rhythmic bumping and men's voices ahead of him. He looked up to find himself strapped to the back of a mule which was being led into a village in the gathering dusk. The same child that had jabbed his ribs that morning straddled the mule's neck, twisting round to observe him as he struggled against his bonds. It occurred to him that it must have taken much of the day for the boy to summon help, lead the men back to Lugal and then bring him in. It suggested that these people were friend rather than foe, otherwise they would simply have left him to die.

The mule came to an abrupt halt; the straps were loosened; and rough hands lifted Lugal down. Looking about, he could make out a circle of tents and goat pens constructed around an open area some forty paces wide. At its centre was a firepit tended by several women. To one side of this was a knot of men inspecting him as he was pulled, half walking, half carried, towards them. His stomach cried out at the smell of cooking meat wafting across the camp from the firepit. But he knew that any offer of food or water was dependent on the interrogation he was about to undergo.

An elderly man carrying an ornately carved crook stepped out from the group by the fire and addressed him. 'You are lucky to be alive. If the children had not found you, you would have been dead by sundown. Who are you, and why are you on our grazing land?' The voice was stern but not unfriendly, and Lugal thought again that these people seemed inquisitive rather than aggressive. He realised that this must be the headman and that the others beside him would be the council of the tribe. He breathed deeply, acutely aware of the nugget concealed at his waist, and began his story.

Lugal had indeed been fortunate. The tribe was similar to his own, farmers of crops and goats leading a peaceful and isolated existence in the interior of south-west Anatolia, indifferent to the outside world. From the tales of occasional travellers passing by on the caravan route from which Lugal had strayed, they were aware of the coast several days' walk to their south but had no reason to venture there. They had also heard of the nomadic groups marauding the land to their north but had been left untouched due to the poor quality of the pasture and semi-desert on which they lived. Choosing his words carefully, Lugal was able to outline his escape without mentioning the nugget, and from their reaction to the description of the mine, he could tell that they had no interest in the precious metal dug from the seam. Despite his ragged and filthy appearance, his tale clearly impressed them, and after a few more mild questions, food and water were brought to him. The goat stew was the best he had tasted in three years, and he ate ravenously.

Over the next few days, Lugal talked at length with the members of the council, discussing the management of the tribe and the farming methods used on their crops and livestock. From his knowledge and natural air of authority, he was able to convince them that he too had been a headman. They were eager to test some of the ideas he introduced and therefore happy to share their meagre resources of food with him. After the malnutrition of slavery and the ordeal of his escape, his body was slow to recover, and it was not until the passing of two full moons that he felt fully restored. Even then, he was conscious of a residual nagging pain in his stomach and occasional numbness in his hands and feet. He remembered men in the slave camp complaining of such things, a few going on to become so ill they had eventually died. But there had been so many different ways to die there, he gave it little thought.

Lugal knew that the time had come to leave his rescuers and resume his journey to the coast. As an uninvited visitor it was unreasonable to take any further advantage of the tribe's kindness, and in any case he still worried that the nomads would find him if they swept south in search of more grazing. He had some misgivings about leaving the safety of the village, but he reasoned that the continuing weakness of his body was the last legacy of his collapse and would gradually disappear. Equipped with fresh clothes and plentiful supplies of food and water, he finally set out, escorted back to the caravan route and bidden farewell by the headman himself. His final act before leaving his tent was to check for the nugget lying wrapped in cloth beneath the provisions in his shoulder bag.

Three days later, Lugal halted at a crest on the sandy path and gazed down at the sea for the first time in his life. He had heard it described once or twice by visitors to his village, but nonetheless he looked in awe at its shimmering vastness stretching out over the horizon in front of him. In the foreground was a cluster of buildings many times bigger than the villages he had seen, with numerous boats bobbing on the water beyond. His stomach quailed in a bout of rising pain; his limbs trembled with weakness; and his head throbbed. With trepidation, he advanced into a world different to anything he had previously experienced.

*

Lugal's escape plan had always been to reach the coast and use the nugget immediately to buy his way onto a boat heading across the sea, in case the nomads had spies seeking him at the waterfront. He had no way of knowing the metal's true value but assumed vaguely that it would be sufficient to give him passage and food to another land where he could find work. However, a more pressing issue now presented itself, as he staggered down towards the shoreline. His body seemed to be falling in on itself, his lungs gasping for breath, his stomach churning in agony and his legs threatening to buckle at every step. He could not understand what was happening to him, but he knew he was seriously ill and needed medicine before attempting to board a boat.

Hobbling to a stop in an open square amongst the buildings, he looked around for assistance. Men, women and children were everywhere, shouting and haggling and gesturing to piles of goods laid out on the ground or spread across vertical racks and trestle tables. Goats tethered to stakes bleated noisily; chickens and ducks flapped at their reed cages; and beggars cried out at passers-by. Lugal's head swirled at the apparent chaos of the market, and he wondered despairingly what he should do. A wave of nausea forced him to sit, and he waited in the dust for someone to notice him. Distinguished from the vagrants lining the square by his fresh clothing, he attracted attention soon enough.

A large, fleshy man came over from a stall and stared at him. Gasping with effort, Lugal raised his head and spoke weakly. 'I am ill. I need medicine quickly. I can pay for it, but please...' His voice trailed away, and he squirmed again from a contraction in his stomach.

The man laughed and pointed to his stall where numerous phials and small dishes were set out on a table. 'Look no further! I am a physician – see there, I have solutions for any problem. Come with me, my friend.' He hauled Lugal to his feet and helped him across to the table. 'You have a bad head? Yes? This is perfect for you. Or pain in your body? Then this.' He waved a hand at one of the phials, and then at a muddy paste in a saucer.

Lugal was in no state to notice several other merchants in the square offering similar wares. He lent on the table and tried to describe the swirling pains assailing his head, lungs, stomach and limbs. The man claiming to be a physician nodded sagely at the list of ailments, and his eyes lit up when Lugal reached into his bag and began to unwrap the cloth-bound nugget. Glancing sharply at his market neighbours, he said in a low voice, 'My friend, I will give you medicine for all these troubles. But what you need first is shade and rest. Come to my home, and we can discuss payment there.'

The merchant beckoned to a young girl sitting behind him. 'Arinna, look after the stall while I help this man.' Then he swung Lugal's arm around his shoulder and walked him quickly away into the shadows of an alley running out from the square. Such was the bustle of the market, no one took an interest in the two men's departure.

Beyond a corner in the alley, the merchant turned into a low house of mud walls and thatched roof. He propped Lugal into a sitting position on the floor and squatted in front of him. 'Show me again what you have in your bag.' Lugal unwrapped the nugget in full, and the merchant turned it over in his hands. Even in the poor light of the room he could see the glint of the precious metal and guessed what it was. He was a greedy man – and certainly not a physician – but not entirely without scruples, and he decided he should at least offer some remedy in return for the lump of rock. 'Wait here,' he shouted as he ran out of the house to fetch one of the phials from his market table.

Lugal barely heard him. His breathing was increasingly laboured, and he was drifting in and out of consciousness. He did not know it, but he was dying. Through the fog in his mind, he was convinced that he had exchanged the nugget for real medicine and that the merchant was also helping him in his quest for onwards escape by boat. He believed the precious metal, known by others as silver, had been his saviour, when in truth it and the seam from which it was dug were his downfall. He was dying of lead poisoning, the mysterious disease to which some of his fellow slaves had succumbed from digging out the mine face and which would afflict many more silver mine workers in the centuries to come. He sighed deeply; his head sank onto his chest; and he was dead by the time the merchant returned.

*

And then...

The silver nugget changes hands many times over the next thousand years, finding its way through traders and travellers to Ur, the capital of southern Mesopotamia (modern day Iraq).

In Ur, it is acquired by Abraham, leader of a tribe which would come to be known as the Jews, around 2000 BCE. He carries it on his travels up the Euphrates river valley to Haran (south-eastern Turkey), to Sechem in Canaan (southern Levant) and on to Egypt where he trades it for supplies with which to feed his family and followers.

In Egypt, the nugget falls into the hands of a metal worker in Memphis (close to the modern-day city of Cairo) where it is melted down and fashioned into an ebony and silver-lined cup.

*

Author's Note

Silver was first recorded as being mined in Anatolia (modern Turkey) around 3000 BCE. By 483 BCE, large scale mining was underway at Laurium (near Athens) in Greece, with captured enemy soldiers being used to dig out the silver following the discovery that the lead content in the ore was highly toxic.

In ancient Egypt silver was scarcer than gold, making it a very valuable commodity. In the second millennium BCE the Egyptians found a way to separate silver from its ore, allowing pure silver articles to become more widespread. It would be unlikely for the nugget to be large enough to allow a meaningfully sized cup to be made entirely of silver. I have therefore added the Egyptian wood black ebony, much prized in the ancient world, to the construction of the cup, plated by silver beaten into thin sheets.

Two

Joseph, Son of Jacob

c. 1700 BCE – Memphis, Egypt

Unsurprisingly, the Vizier's house commanded one of the best views in the city, second only to that of the Pharaoh's palace. From the rooftop parapets it was possible to see the full sweep of the kingdom's capital, the maze of streets running all the way to the city walls and the muddy, blue waters of the River Nile beyond. Further to the east, a heat haze hung over the desert, with land and sky blending into each other in the far distance. Today, though, the Vizier saw none of this. Instead, he looked down onto the central marketplace below, where a huge crowd was assembled in front of a phalanx of guards. There was no sign of unrest, but the Vizier knew it took little to ignite a mob driven by hunger, especially when only a thin line of soldiers separated it from the grain stores.

For over a year now, this scene had been repeated each day in the market. When the drought had first struck, families had been able to rely on their own supplies of grain left over from the previous year's abundant crop. The Vizier had issued instructions throughout Egypt at the time for stores to be hoarded, but after seven consecutive years of exceptional harvests, his pleas had fallen on deaf ears. People's memories were short, and they had forgotten the hardship of famine. Their stores were quickly exhausted, and soon they were coming from all parts of the country to buy grain from the Pharaoh. Even foreigners from neighbouring lands where the crops had also failed were beginning to appear in the capital.

Joseph stood on the roof thinking back to the extraordinary events over the last twenty years that had brought him to this place. Sold as a lowly slave to Potiphar, captain of the palace guard, he had risen rapidly through the ranks of his master's household to become his principal steward. He had earned each step of his promotion through a combination of hard work, quick wits and complete trustworthiness, and he had relished his job. But all that had changed with Potiphar's marriage to Zuleika. Even after all this time, he still flushed at the memory of how, only months after the wedding, she had flaunted herself at him, seeking to seduce him into sleeping with her and then taunting him for his refusal. He could hardly complain to his master, and in the end, she had done so herself. He knew he had been lucky to escape with his life after her accusation of rape and that it was God's will for him to have been flung instead into the Round Tower gaol.

The memory of his imprisonment was still vivid, the dark and stinking cell shared at first with the Pharaoh's cup-bearer and his baker. Like him, they had been torn from senior positions of power and trust as a result of jealous rivalries in the palace hierarchy, though not, he smiled wryly, the charms of an oversexed temptress. They had protested their innocence loudly and often, but he had always wondered whether the claims of poisoning had not had an element of truth and whether perhaps that was the underlying explanation for the dreams they had asked him to interpret. Joseph had foreseen death for the baker and restoration to his previous rank for the cup-bearer – each within three days – and so it had been. After their removal, Joseph had languished in that cell for a further two years, until the strange morning when he was escorted up to the palace with no explanation, told to shave and change into fresh clothes and ushered into a room where the Pharaoh and his cup-bearer were waiting impatiently.

'I've had a dream,' the Pharaoh had stated flatly, 'and my servant here tells me you can interpret it.' Joseph had taken a deep breath and said, 'Of course, Your Majesty, tell me.' All his good fortune since then had flowed from that moment, with the Pharaoh's story of fourteen ears of corn, the first seven fat and ripe, the second seven thin and shrivelled, revealed to him as an augury of seven years' bountiful harvests, followed by seven years' famine. The Pharaoh had been so impressed with the explanation, and Joseph's suggestions on how to prepare for the food shortages, that he had immediately appointed him as his minister of agriculture.

There was no denying it had been hard work. During the run of unusually good harvests that followed the Pharaoh's dream, Joseph had purchased huge quantities of grain in his master's name from all corners of the country, arranging for it to be stored in vaults at the capital. After five years, the Pharaoh had promoted him to his chief of staff, or Vizier, in recognition of the accuracy of his predictions, commenting tartly that the real test would come in three years' time. When the crops failed in the eighth year, Joseph had been able to sell grain back to the people, saving them from starvation and making a tidy profit for the Pharaoh's treasury. He had been rewarded with a new vizier's residence, constructed over the grain vaults running along one side of the capital's marketplace, and, as a personal token of the Pharaoh's gratitude, he had been presented with a small ebony chalice, lined with silver and engraved with the Vizier's crest, seven ears of corn on a single stalk. As a modest man, Joseph was more pleased with the cup than his lodgings, but he was careful not to show it.

And now, after another year and a second disastrous harvest, people were streaming into the capital in ever greater numbers to find food. The vaults were still well stocked, and the palace guard were able to keep control of the crowds queuing to buy the Pharaoh's grain, but Joseph had a fresh problem to wrestle with. As he gazed out over the city, his mind turned again to the ten men now imprisoned in the Round Tower. He had thought of little else since they had arrived in Memphis three days ago, and yet he was still unsure what he should do with them.

Ten men, each one a brother to him – only half-brothers, admittedly – and it seemed scarcely believable that not a single one had recognised him. He, on the other hand, had spotted them the moment they arrived in front of the vaults to tell his granary staff of their long journey from the neighbouring country Canaan to buy food. They did not look so different; more mature, naturally, their features etched with the passing of twenty summers; less cocksure than when they had thrown him into that pit in the wilderness and then sold him to the passing slave gang; now stick-thin from famine and pleading for help. He realised that, by comparison, he had probably changed much more in the transformation from their seventeen-year-old little brother to Vizier of all Egypt, and of course the one who had known him best, his full brother Benjamin, had not travelled with them. He would dearly have liked to see Benjamin again and was delighted to have learnt that he and their father were still alive. Suddenly a scheme came to him.

Joseph turned abruptly and ran down the steps from the roof terrace to his office, shouting to his steward, 'Rehu, those men in the Round Tower, bring them to me.' It was so tempting to send them away empty-handed, to give them a taste of the desperation and hopelessness that he had felt all those years ago when they abandoned him, but he knew it was not for such base retaliation that God had delivered him from death, slavery and imprisonment. A more subtle reaction was called for, in keeping with his eminence as Vizier. He reached for his official robes and headdress, the freshly laundered khat shrouding his hair and neck and fastened across his forehead by a broad gold band.

The men filed into the room and stood in front of his desk, avoiding his eyes as he spoke. 'You claimed when we first met that you are not here to spy on our city defences, that you are the sons of one man in Canaan who is being tended by your youngest brother and that you wish to take food back to them. I do not believe you. Normally spies here are executed immediately, but I am a God-fearing man, and I will give you a chance to prove your honesty. You will fetch your brother to me, and in the meantime this one will stay in gaol here as a hostage.' Joseph gestured to his brother Simeon. 'Now, leave me and pay my staff downstairs for the grain you wish to buy.' Little did he know the effect this would have on his father Jacob, already mourning one son presumed dead all those years ago, when he was told that a second was being held in prison and that his youngest, Benjamin, must be taken from him too.

*

Six months later a group of ten men presented themselves at the Vizier's residence, nine of them familiar with the heaps of grain lying in the adjacent vaults and the corn-eared crest on the entrance door, the tenth looking in astonishment at the demonstration of wealth surrounding him. The steward ushered them into Joseph's office, where he stood in silence, once again dressed in the full regalia of his position. Their spokesman Judah began nervously:

'Your Excellency, you will remember that you agreed to spare our lives if we brought our brother to you. We have had great difficulty persuading our father, but he accepts that if our other brother Simeon is to be released, then Benjamin here must be presented to you.' Judah pulled Benjamin to the front of the group and went on hurriedly. 'But you must understand that another brother of ours called Joseph was killed many years ago, and our father is now very concerned that he will have lost three sons. We have promised him we will return Benjamin and Simeon to him, and as a gesture of good faith, we have brought these humble gifts.' Four of the brothers now stepped forward with small wicker baskets. 'Our country is famous for each of these goods: balsam, honey, myrrh, almonds. We have larger packs in our bags outside.' His voice trembled, but he pressed on. 'As well as collecting Simeon, we would also like to buy more food for each of our families. The famine is still raging in Canaan, and we have finished the supplies that you so kindly sold us on our last visit. Our father has insisted that we pay twice the market price this time.' He stopped uncertainly, as Joseph stared grimly down the line of brothers.

Beneath his fierce scowl Joseph was battling to contain his emotions. Unbidden, the true horror of his brothers' callous behaviour twenty years before had come rushing back to him, the humiliation of being stripped of his clothes and left to die in the pit, of brother Reuben's intervention on his behalf and the decision instead to sell him like a beast to the slavers. Despite his rise to power and riches, he had assumed he would never see his family again, least of all his favourite brother Benjamin, yet here he was, standing in front of him and clearly terrified at what the Vizier would do next.

Joseph strode out of the room, barking to the steward as he went, 'Rehu, let the prisoner join his brothers; get the kitchens to feed them; and then report back to me.' The ten brothers watched his retreating back in silence, relieved that Simeon was to be released but confused by the harsh response to their gifts and offer of money. Only when they had been reunited with Simeon and were eating in the staff quarters did they start to believe that they would all be permitted to return to their father in Canaan.

At the same time, back in the Vizier's office, Joseph was giving fresh instructions to his steward. 'Let these people buy as much grain as they can carry, at the price they're offering, and tell them they must pack up their donkeys and leave at dawn tomorrow. But while they are asleep tonight, I want you to put this into the top of the pack belonging to the one they call Benjamin.' Joseph pushed the ebony and silver chalice across the desk.

'But, My Lord, I don't understand. Why give them all this food when we should be saving it for our own people? And worse still, your cup? I know how much it means to you, and the Pharaoh will be furious when he hears you have given it away. I promise you, my lips are sealed, but someone here is bound to tell him.'

'Rehu, how long have we worked together? Six years now? Trust me, I know all about palace gossip, and you are right – the cup is one of my most favourite possessions. But you know me better than anyone else, and you know I wouldn't risk losing it. Tomorrow morning this is what I want you to do.' The steward listened carefully as Joseph talked, nodding in agreement, although privately he was still mystified by the Vizier's plan.

*

As day broke the next morning, the eleven brothers guided their donkeys out of the marketplace and down the quiet streets towards the rising sun. The animals were loaded high with grain packs, and the steward had given them several days' food for their journey. They had needed no encouragement to leave at dawn. They were still confused by the Vizier's reception and sceptical of the ease with which they had retrieved Simeon and kept Benjamin safe. But with every step their suspicions lessened, and by the time they passed through the city gate, they had begun to relax, chatting easily amongst themselves about the prospect of the journey ahead and their father's pleasure at their homecoming.

It was as they queued for the ferry over the river that they heard shouts from behind. A cloud of dust heralded the approach of a group of horsemen, and as the riders came closer, the brothers could make out the Vizier's steward in the lead. There was no way to escape, and, in any case, they had no reason to do so; they had done nothing wrong.

The steward reined in to a halt and snarled at them. 'Thieves and spies, all of you. I suspected as much, but my master is too kind. He has given you as much food as you can carry, even though the famine is raging all around our own country, and this is how you repay him? Where is the cup?'

The brothers looked up at him in bewilderment, Judah's voice rising above the others. 'Sir, what are you talking about? We know nothing about any cup. All we wanted was to collect our brother and take food home to our families. We paid handsomely for the grain. God forbid that we should steal from you. Search our bags, we've nothing to hide.'

People in the queue around them looked on in amazement, and the brothers could hear the word "thieves" being repeated down the line to the waterfront. The steward spoke again, his tone no less stern. 'Very well, let's see. But understand this, the silver cup is one of the Vizier's most prized possessions, a present from no less than the Pharaoh himself. If we find it in any of your packs, then all of you will come back to hear judgement from my master.' He waved to his men, who dismounted and began to inspect each of the donkeys.

As pack after pack was unloaded and opened, the brothers began to breathe more freely. They had seen the chalice the steward spoke of on the Vizier's desk, but none of them would have been foolish enough to steal it. With only Benjamin's pack still to be searched, they began to look towards the ferry which was coming in to dock for the next intake of passengers. Suddenly, one of the steward's men cried out excitedly and held up the chalice in his fist. The steward walked his horse across to Benjamin and towered over him. 'You foreigners can never be trusted. You, of all people, should have known better. Now your father has lost another son.' He looked at each of the brothers in contempt, then wheeled his horse about, shouting to his men to round up the group and bring them back to the city.

Two hours later, still aghast at the discovery by the ferry, the brothers were once again shepherded into Joseph's office by the steward. Benjamin had wept inconsolably all the way back into the city, sobbing to his siblings that he knew nothing of the cup. They believed him; after all, why would any of them have jeopardised the trip home when they had rescued Simeon and secured enough grain to feed their families until the next harvest was gathered? But none of them could explain what had happened, and they faced the Vizier with dread.

Joseph sat studying each of them in turn, his expression beneath his headdress unreadable, and after a lengthy pause, he spoke. 'Rehu, you have done well. I wish to speak to these people alone. Please leave us.' The steward looked astonished but knew better than to question his master. As he left the room, the brothers started to plead their ignorance of the theft, but Joseph interrupted them curtly. 'Be quiet! Gentlemen, you have sinned, all of you, and you will be judged. However, first I wish to tell you two stories.' The brothers shuffled their feet miserably, utterly bemused at where this was leading, and Joseph went on.

'The first story concerns a boy who grew up amongst a large family in a foreign country. They were herdsmen, and he used to help his brothers tend the sheep and goats. The boy was his father's favourite, which irritated the brothers, and they were even more annoyed when he told them about a dream he had had where all of them were in a field gathering corn into sheaves. He claimed that his sheaf had risen up to stand on its end, and all his brothers' sheaves had bowed down in submission. They were so resentful of his airs and graces that they decided to kill him, and it was only the intervention of one of them that saved him. Instead, they stripped him and threw him into a pit in the wilderness and then sold him to a group of passing slave traders.'

By now, the brothers were gaping at him. Judah burst out: 'Your Excellency, how can you possibly know this? He was called Joseph. It was our family, and we have carried the guilt of what we did to him ever since that time. We took his coat home covered in goat's blood and told everyone he had been killed by wild animals. Our father was heartbroken and now perhaps you can understand why it is so important for us to return our brother Benjamin to him.'

'Wait!' Joseph said firmly. 'I have still to tell you the second story. It is about a young man here in Egypt who is taken on as a slave by the captain of the palace guard. He proves trustworthy and hard-working, but nonetheless he ends up in prison convicted of a crime that he didn't commit. It is only thanks to his ability to interpret dreams that he is released into the Pharaoh's service, where he gains his favour and rises to a position of power and influence. Now, if you can tell me the link between the two stories, then you are all free to go. If you cannot, then the thief will be kept here as my slave, and the rest of you will be deported from the country.'

The brothers looked appalled. It seemed likely that the second story was about the Vizier, but none of them could see a connection to the story about themselves, and they were still horrified that their brutal treatment of Joseph so long ago was common knowledge. Even Judah was lost for words.

After another long silence, Joseph pointed to the ebony and silver chalice, safely restored to his desk by Rehu a few minutes previously. 'I believe my steward explained to you that this is one of my most precious possessions. It was a gift from the Pharaoh, and it bears the crest of my family. Look at the engraving. Wasn't one of your brother Joseph's dreams about sheaves of corn? And if you were to ask the Pharaoh's cup-bearer, he would tell you that one of the Pharaoh's dreams that I interpreted for him was about ears of corn, seven of them fat and ripe, another seven shrivelled.' He stopped, surprised that even now the brothers had still not recognised him under his formal robes and khat, and Judah spoke again, his voice more measured.

'Your Excellency, we know nothing of your background, but I am guessing that the second story is about you. None of us can see how this relates to the story about our brother Joseph,' he gestured to the others, 'but I beseech you to believe me when I say that we did not steal the silver cup. We are so grateful to you for the grain you have allowed us to buy, and we desperately need to feed our families – why would we do anything to endanger that? But there is something else as well.

Everything you described about Joseph is right – we did sell him to the slavers and told our father that he had been killed by animals. Not a day goes by that we do not face the wrath of our God for what we did. Our father has never recovered from losing Joseph, and our shame is as intense now as on the day we told him. If we go home without Benjamin, the shock will kill him. If any of us is to be a slave, let it be me. I could not bear to see the misery that my father would suffer.'

Joseph could no longer control himself. Tears poured down his cheeks as he stood up, unclipping the gold band of his headdress and shaking his hair free. Suddenly Benjamin exclaimed, 'Dear God, can it really be true? Joseph, you are Vizier?' The other brothers looked at him, astounded.

'Yes, it's me. How could you not recognise your own brother?' He came round the desk, arms outstretched, and hugged them, one by one, as they inspected him in a rising babble of excitement.

Eventually, the noise subsided, and they looked at one another more calmly. 'Brothers, there is much to say, but first we need a toast.' Joseph turned to a sideboard where eleven cups and a pitcher of wine lay ready, prepared in advance for this momentous occasion that he had looked forward to every day for the last six months. With his back to them, the brothers glanced silently at each other, residual suspicion still pricking them at whether this was another trap to punish them after their shameful behaviour all those years ago.

Joseph passed a filled cup to each of the brothers and then poured wine into the chalice sitting on the desk. With a broad smile, he raised it to his lips. 'To forgiveness!' He took a deep draught. The eleven brothers repeated the toast with whoops and cheers, secretly relieved to see that Joseph was drinking from the same pitcher. Once more, Benjamin was the first to address him, framing the question in every brother's mind.

'Dear Joseph, this is just incredible. My own full brother, you have no idea how much I have missed you. How can you have risen to such power and wealth, when we left you to the slavers in the wilderness? Like Judah said, we have lived with our guilt every single day since then and deserve no mercy for that. But, truly, we did not steal the chalice. As God is our witness, we are not thieves, whatever else we have done to you.'

Sitting back on the edge of the desk, Joseph smiled again and held up a hand. 'Much has happened since we were last together. The first story was of course about me, and you were wrong to treat me, and our father, the way you did. But I look back and think how insufferable I must have been as a brother, describing dreams where you were subservient to me. As for the second story, Judah was right, that was also mine. I was falsely accused of rape, just as you have been falsely accused of theft. But it was my gift of understanding dreams that brought me into the Pharaoh's favour and gave me all this.' He gestured at his robes, the headdress on the desk and his chalice. 'Don't you see, it was God's will that I was brought to Egypt as a slave, that I was sent to prison where I met the Pharaoh's cup-bearer, that I was able to foretell the seven great harvests and the famine that has followed them. Our God is a god of love, not wrath as Judah suggested earlier. It is thanks to God that we are reunited and not for me to judge you now. This chalice is the emblem of His forgiveness, and we should drink to that again.' He drained the chalice with gusto and beamed at them.

*

And then…

Joseph's family remain in Egypt, multiplying rapidly over succeeding generations and continuing to occupy positions of power. However, they fall from favour on the ascent to the throne of a new king, Pharaoh Rameses VIII, who acquires the ebony and silver chalice. On his death in 1129 BCE, the chalice is entombed alongside his body in the Valley of the Kings at Thebes (modern day Luxor).

The tomb remains undisturbed for the next eight hundred years, the chalice lost to the world above.

*

Author's Note

The well-known story of Joseph, son of Jacob, is recorded in Genesis, the first book of the Old Testament in the Bible. Although I have pared the story down to its basics, a silver cup is indeed used to frame Joseph's brothers for theft. The final chapters of Genesis describe how Joseph urges the brothers to collect their father and their wider families from Canaan and how the Pharaoh grants them land in Egypt. The book of Exodus goes on to describe how, many generations later, the Israelite nation has risen in size and power throughout Egypt and how its people are reduced to slavery after a new pharaoh feels threatened by them.

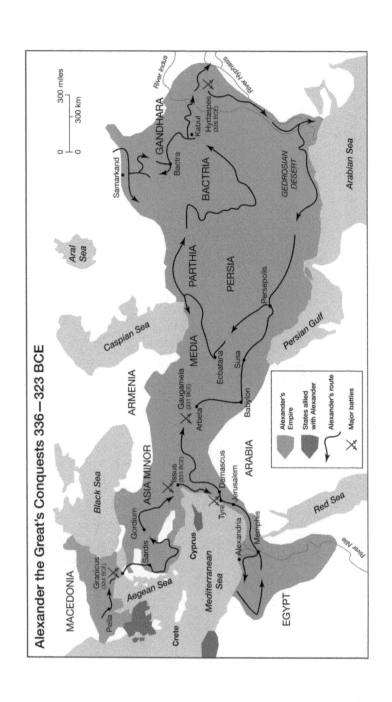

Alexander the Great's Conquests 336—323 BCE

Three

Alexander the Great

332 BCE – Thebes, Egypt

The high priest rose from his knees and turned to face the visitors, gesturing towards the doors behind them. In the gloom of the great hall, the Macedonians were able to hide their expressions of relief after the interminable ceremony and began to reach for the armour and weapons they had been encouraged to lay aside on their arrival. Nonetheless, they were careful not to show their impatience; they knew better than to show disrespect to the gods, even the gods of foreigners, and the king's orders to his generals had been clear. Homage at the age-old temple, rather than brutal suppression, would be a much more effective means towards consolidating their rule over the Egyptian people.

As they emerged, blinking, into the mid-afternoon sunlight, Alexander looked about him at the immense construction of the temple complex. Notwithstanding a childhood in the royal circles of Macedon, and several years spent campaigning against rich and ancient cities on his journey to the south of the Mediterranean, he had never seen a building to rival this. The temple of Amun, creator and sun god, had stood on the bank of the Nile for over fifteen hundred years, embellished by successive pharaohs, ravaged by invasion, repaired and renovated to suit changing religious beliefs, but always central to Egyptian power. From the hall at the temple's centre, steps led down to a large square, paved in huge stone slabs and framed by colonnades on three sides. Beyond the pillars was a series of satellite chapels to lesser gods, each decorated with statues and obelisks to commemorate their founder king. The scale of the place was breathtaking, and from an earlier inspection of the various buildings, Alexander was aware it also housed enormous wealth. Even if his strategy for invasion had been one of coercion rather than partnership, he would have baulked at desecrating such an historic expression of devotion and splendour. But it would be a sign of weakness to try to explain this to his army, which expected to be allowed to enjoy the spoils of war.

Alexander led his staff out of the temple gates to where their horses were tethered in the shade of some acacia trees. As they mounted, a rider clattered up to the group, panting with exertion and coated in dust. The nearest officer, Ptolemy, caught the man's reins and spoke brusquely, 'Stop. Explain yourself.'

The rider looked nervously at the stern faces, seeking out the king and answering in a rush, 'Your Highness, I come from the other side of the river. Our company have been foraging for supplies there, and we've found something you ought to see. My troop captain said it's urgent and you should come immediately.'

The king looked at the sun. 'We have around three hours' light left. There's little time to do much else today, and we may as well see what this fuss is about. Ptolemy, you will accompany me. The rest of you, back to your units and start preparing for the journey north. We've done what we needed to do here, and I want to return to Memphis as soon as possible. We must spread the word of our tribute to Amun while it is fresh in the priests' minds. Come, Bucephalus.' He reached forward to pat his horse's neck, nodded to the messenger and Ptolemy to follow him and the three of them set off at a canter towards the river front.

Standing on the ferry platform as twenty oar blades dipped in unison into the Nile water, Alexander studied the far bank and the dry, undulating landscape beyond. There was nothing unusual to attract his attention, and he turned instead to the messenger, a boy in his mid-teens who was clearly overawed by the presence of his king. 'Tell me what has happened and who sent you,' he said mildly.

'We crossed the river from the city this morning, Your Highness. Our patrol has been out looking for food each day since we arrived in Thebes, but this is the first time we have been over the river. There's been a rockfall on the other side of that hill,' he pointed to a ridge on the near horizon, 'and some sort of building has been uncovered. My Lord Nearchus is with us, and he said you would want to give orders for what to do.' Alexander raised an eyebrow in surprise. Why a half-buried building should be of such interest was beyond him, but Nearchus was one of his most experienced officers, fully capable of making his own decisions, so there must be more to the discovery than the boy knew. He grunted non-committally and returned his gaze to the splashing oars.

Several minutes later, the ferry bumped to a halt, and Alexander walked his horse onto the jetty. He motioned the messenger to lead the way, and they rode the short distance to the ridge. Looking down into the hollow beyond, he could see the result of the landslide, little more than a tumble of sand and small stones probably caused by the fierce desert winds that had been blowing ever since the army's arrival. Embedded in what remained of the low cliff was the gable of a sizeable, man-made structure, the stone masonry rough-hewn and chipped but solid and intact. What appeared to be a door below the gable was surmounted by a huge lintel bearing a carved inscription of some sort. Alexander guessed immediately why he had been called for.

Guiding his horse slowly down the sandy path to the floor of the little valley, he was greeted by Nearchus in front of a score of soldiers. 'Your Highness, I think this might be—' Alexander cut him short with a glare and a shake of the head. 'We will discuss this in private. Come with me.' He dismounted, handed his horse's reins to the messenger and waved for Nearchus and Ptolemy to accompany him out of the soldiers' earshot.

'A pharaoh's burial chamber.' It was more of a statement than a question. The king and his generals had all heard the rumours, even at home in Macedon, of Egyptian royal tombs filled with riches but lost in the sands of the Nile. There had been whispers in Memphis too, but unsurprisingly, the priests and city leaders had said nothing. It was not in their interests to boast of treasure to the invaders. Alexander had been sceptical of the stories, but he had recognised the carving on the front of the building as a royal insignia similar to those visible on the chapels at the Amun temple.

'We need to tread carefully here,' he said to the two officers. 'Raiding a pharaoh's tomb will be seen by the priests as a sacrilege. It could undo all our efforts to gain control of the country, and then we may struggle to take all the taxes and plunder from these people that I'm hoping for in the years to come. In any case, I don't want to upset the gods, theirs or ours!' He grinned boyishly to his subordinates, both several years senior to him, and went on. 'So what we'll do is this. We're running out of time today. Place guards on the building overnight, and say nothing to the priests about what we've found. Tomorrow we will bring your men back at first light with tools for a full day's digging. Whatever comes from that, we will tell the priests that the men acted out of curiosity and ignorance. That way they will be appeased, and if there is anything worthwhile inside, we can take it without them knowing. But,' his voice hardened, 'tell the men that if any of them breathes a word of this, I'll have his eyes and tongue cut out in front of the whole army.' Despite his sensitivity to the priests, Ptolemy and Nearchus knew it was no idle threat – they had seen their king in action too often to doubt his savagery when it was needed.

By mid-morning the following day, the soldiers, equipped with spades and pickaxes, had dug the end of the tomb clear and hammered grappling hooks into the seams of the great stone doorway. Chains led from the hooks to a harness spanning a team of four mules, which were now being whipped into movement with shouts and curses. As Alexander and his two generals watched, the stone was slowly dragged away from the tomb wall, eventually toppling on its side to the men's raucous cheers. A gap wide enough to squeeze through had been opened, and the top of a steep staircase cut into the rock floor could be seen in the dark interior. Holding a burning torch in front of him, the king advanced into the gloom and descended hesitantly. He had faced many foes without fear in the eight years since his first battle but never the ghosts of the ancient dead.

At the bottom of the steps, the torch illuminated a second doorway, sealed by mud plaster. Thumping on it with his fist, Alexander quickly broke open a hole big enough to thrust the torch through. In the flickering light, he could see a large, vaulted room, a rostrum in its centre and several painted clay urns on the floor to each side. Once he had widened the hole so that he could lean his head and torso in for a better view, he could also make out the ceiling decorated with a glittering golden moon and scores of stars, some of whose constellations he recognised from his schooling in the night sky many years previously. On each of the four walls, traced by shells and semi-precious stones, was the same design that adorned the external lintel, topped here with a painted gold coronet. There could be no doubt that the stone sarcophagus sitting on the rostrum was that of a pharaoh.

Climbing back up towards the sunlit doorway, Alexander shouted to Ptolemy and Nearchus to join him with pickaxes and braziers. In the improved light they were able to break down the remainder of the mud door and climb through into the burial chamber to inspect the sarcophagus. Standing on the rostrum, they prized up the lid and peered inside, with considerable apprehension. They looked down on a wooden coffin and an extraordinary collection of objects stacked against its panels, ranging at first sight from a small bronze spear to a golden trumpet, oil jars of clay and glass, brightly painted animal and bird sculptures, a miniature ebony boat and innumerable gems and other items of jewellery. They looked up at each other in astonishment, each man reluctant to breach the tomb's final secret, the coffin itself.

After a long pause, Alexander raised his pickaxe and forced its point under the lip of the coffin. The wood splintered loudly in the sepulchral silence, and he wrenched the top panel aside. Again, the three men looked down, this time onto a mummified body adorned with an ornate golden headdress. The only other item to be seen was a small ebony chalice, lined with silver and engraved with seven ears of corn on a single stalk, wedged into the cloth bonds across the body's stomach.

Alexander gazed at the cup, mesmerised by its simple beauty and the mysterious crest. Then the three men stepped down from the rostrum and, after glancing briefly into each of the urns around the room, the king spoke.

'What we have discovered here must remain between us. We will take everything of value from the sarcophagus except the headdress, the wooden boat, the trumpet and the spear. When we tell the priests about the tomb, they will believe that those items were there to carry their pharaoh into the next world, to herald his arrival and to protect him. We will leave the urns too – they seem to be empty and are presumably just for decoration, to please the gods. I will keep the chalice from the coffin, and you will share the rest of the booty between yourselves and the other generals. Not a word to anyone else. Maybe there are other graves nearby, but we will leave them undisturbed. As I said yesterday, we can justify this pillage, but we should not antagonise the gods any further.' Ptolemy and Nearchus nodded in agreement, their natural greed overridden by fealty to their young king and a shared fear of the gods' vengeance.

*

326 BCE – The Hyphasis river in northern India

Alexander watched as the wooden platform was rolled on logs down to the river's edge, the massive black carcass lying on thick rush matting and attended by flaming beacons on each corner, as if in state. Two soldiers waded deep into the water, pulling the heavy raft towards them while four more pushed forcefully from the bank. Suddenly it was plucked from their hands by the current, swirling into the centre of the fast-flowing river and moving rapidly downstream. The king looked on in silence until it finally disappeared from view, then turned his back, muttering a final goodbye under his breath as he walked towards the tented encampment where his staff waited for him in the emerging dawn.

He knew this sentimentality must appear odd to them. But with all that had happened in the recent months, the death of his great horse, his companion for the last eighteen years through innumerable campaigns, had touched him in a way he had not anticipated. It was unclear what the cause of death had been, probably a failing heart after such a long and eventful life, but a proper send-off had been entirely appropriate. He thought again of that first encounter with the wild stallion brought for sale to his father's royal court in Macedon. No one had been able to control it, until the twelve-year-old prince had stepped forward to claim it for himself, taming it with soothing words, firm hands and a will of iron. He had named the horse Bucephalus, meaning Ox Head, in honour of its strength, and it had never failed him. Like a bursting dam, the memory of those campaigns came flooding over him once again. The early wars against Thrace and Illyria; the consolidation of his power as newly anointed king in conflicts and diplomacy across the Peloponnese; the invasion of Egypt; the battles of Issus and Gaugamela, both so crucial to his conquest of Persia; the four-year-long sweep eastwards across central Asia, beating down old enemies and overwhelming new ones. And over the last year, marching through the mountain passes into a land hitherto unknown to western armies, crossing the mighty Indus river, defeating King Porus of the Paurava people and advancing still further east to this point. Bucephalus had borne him every step of that way, shrugging off battle wounds, impervious to the extremes of desert heat and mountain ice, a fellow adventurer in the creation of the greatest empire ever known… and now he was dead, alongside Alexander's dreams of further exploration towards the rising sun.

Striding into the camp, he saw the expectant faces of his generals and knew the time for a final decision had arrived. Never before had his word been questioned, his strategy challenged, in such a way, but the tone of last night's war council had been unmistakeable. Despite emerging victorious, the army had suffered its biggest losses ever at the recent battle against the Paurava, and after ten years' constant campaigning, the soldiers were weary and disillusioned. They wanted to return to their homelands and families, and the promise of rich plunder in the princedoms of the Ganges valley, his next target beyond the nearby river, was not enough to dissuade them. Even the generals had made little attempt to argue against a retreat. Already distressed by the death of his horse earlier in the day, Alexander had raged at them for their timidity, sorely tempted to kill their chief spokesman, Coenus, there and then as an example to the rest. But he was reluctantly aware that without their unwavering support he was lost, and perhaps therefore the time had indeed come to turn back. Now, despite the growing morning light, his dark mood surged once more, and he pushed past them into his pavilion without speaking.

Sitting on his camp bed, he looked around the tent, simply decorated with some of the spoils of his campaigns. Always on the move, he chose to travel light, but a certain level of royal pomp was required, and he had collected various mementos over the years. Embroidered rugs from the capital cities of central Asia hung from the canopy; a carved headstone of his most implacable enemy, Darius of Persia, stood on a pedestal by the door; various weapons torn from assailants' hands leant against the rawhide walls. On an intricately carved rosewood table in the centre of the room stood a single object, the ebony and silver chalice taken from the Pharaoh's tomb in Egypt. The wood was cracked and brittle from constant storage in his saddle panniers over the last six years, and it was useless as a drinking vessel. But the silver lining still shone brightly thanks to his servant's polishing, and even though it was of little value compared to the thousands of treasures his army had won, the cup remained one of his dearest possessions. Ever since plucking it from the coffin in that darkened burial chamber, he had considered it a token of his earthly power on his journey across the world.

As he brooded, a bleak thought came to him. Bucephalus was dead and, simultaneously, the expansion of his empire into the east had come to an abrupt halt. Two of his driving forces had abandoned him, without warning, on the banks of a little-known river in a distant foreign land. Was this a sign that the gods had also deserted him, those gods whose rage he had dared to invoke by stealing the chalice so many years before? Had the Pharaoh's ghost finally come to haunt him? He was not a man given to self-doubt, but the fates did seem to be conspiring against him.

He shook his head roughly and stood up. There was a way to cap such dangerous notions, to mark the outer limit of his conquests and to commemorate his beloved horse, all at a single stroke. He would have the chalice destroyed and the silver remoulded by a local craftsman into an amulet in the shape of a rearing stallion. He would wear it every day around his neck, as a constant reminder of the far-flung river to which he and Bucephalus had stretched a Macedonian realm. And when his time came to die, he would take the amulet with him to his grave, just as the Pharaoh had taken the chalice, and return it to the gods in the next world. He swept open the door of the pavilion and shouted for his servant to summon a metalsmith from the nearest town.

It took two days for a jeweller of sufficient skill to be found and the amulet to be fashioned to the king's satisfaction, during which time he remained in his tent, drowning his sorrows in wine, surly and alone, refusing to communicate with any of his officers. The generals waited for a decision on the proposal to retreat, uncertain of the reason for the delay and increasingly anxious that a full-scale mutiny would flare up amongst their men. On the third day, Alexander finally emerged, a new piece of silverware around his neck shining in the bright morning sun, and gave orders to strike camp. The army was heading back home across the Indus at last.

*

323 BCE – Babylon

He had seen it in his mind's eye for so long. A triumphal return to the city he had first captured eight years previously; enthronement in a palace once occupied by the fabled Nebuchadnezzar; a royal court of faithful warriors whose allegiance and counsel he had enjoyed since his boyhood in Macedon; a time of peace and stability throughout his empire; a chance to rest, to dwell on his achievements, to plot his next assault. But instead, it was turning out so differently.

True, he was back in Babylon's palace, selected as his seat of government long before his expedition into the east, but his army was restless, his subjects rebellious and his imperial strategy in tatters. The journey back from the Indus had been slow and arduous – a two-year struggle to maintain his soldiers' goodwill as they died in the heat of the southern desert, followed by mistrust and mutiny as he criss-crossed Persia to suppress fresh uprisings amongst vanquished foes. Even his generals, friends and mentors at his side through countless struggles, seemed uneasy now. He knew that Antipater was incensed at the prospect of losing his position as Macedonian viceroy, a role he had held since Alexander's father's reign but which Alexander was now offering to Craterus. Furthermore, Coenus had never forgiven him for his rage on the banks of the Hyphasis river; Ptolemy had made his desire for outright rule of Egypt clear on the retreat through Asia; and he suspected that Nearchus nursed similar hopes for parts of Persia after his successful voyage mapping the ocean's coastline back from the Indian campaign. Worst of all, his closest friend and confidant, Hephaestion, had died earlier that month in what was rumoured to be an act of poisoning.

In his thirteen years as king, Alexander had uncovered innumerable plots and had developed an extraordinary ability to thwart them, sometimes by sudden and brutal bloodletting, sometimes by quiet diplomacy. Now, however, he felt listless and uncertain, for once ill-equipped to assert his authority and in no mood to face the evening's banquet with his staff. He sat in the throne room, idly twisting the amulet at his neck for inspiration and wondering how to deal with Ptolemy and Nearchus.

Two hundred paces away, in a dusty street hidden from the palace gate house and battlements, a tall, expensively dressed man was giving instructions in a low voice to a kitchen girl. 'So you will definitely be serving the royal table at tonight's dinner?' The girl nodded, not daring to speak. 'And you are sure you will recognise the king?' She nodded again, blurting out, 'I've been working here ever since the army returned. I know which all the generals are.' The man glowered at her, and she lapsed into silence.

'Listen carefully. Once the main meal is over, the chief steward will order extra flagons of wine to be brought out. You will make it your business to serve the king, and when you get to him you will accidentally knock over his goblet. Even if it doesn't break, you will say the glass may be cracked and that you should replace it. You will leave the flagon on the table, bring the goblet back to the kitchen and find a replacement, which you will put this into.' He opened a small leather pouch that he was holding and showed her the contents. 'You will take the new goblet out to him and fill it from the same flagon you carried out before.' The girl looked at him in horror as he pressed the pouch into her hand, and he smiled grimly. 'Don't worry, they will all have been drinking like fish, especially the king, and no one will take any notice of you. It will be easy. Just make sure you are the one serving him, and tell nobody what you have been asked to do.' He stood back from her, reached into his pocket and held out a handful of coins. 'If all goes well, meet me here at the same time tomorrow, and this will be your reward.' He paused, then added in a fierce tone, 'But if I hear even a whisper of my name in connection with this, I will know you have been talking, and you and all your family will be dead within days. Now go.' He watched her as she scurried away, clutching the pouch and glancing fearfully over her shoulder at him before she disappeared from view.

Three hours after sundown, the banquet was well underway, the king deep in conversation with Nearchus beside him and the other generals at the top table chatting animatedly amongst themselves. Antipater was the centre of their attention, having only recently arrived from Macedon and evidently with many a story to tell of their friends and family there. As the food platters were being removed, Alexander looked up and shouted for more wine to be brought. It was standard practice for all food and drink to be tasted prior to being served at court, and there was a brief delay while the steward performed the usual ritual. Then the servants emerged from the kitchen with fresh flagons and began to top up the diners' cups. There was a sudden crash as a young maid knocked the king's goblet over, wine and shards of glass spilling across the table. Visibly shaken, she set the flagon down, picked up the broken drinking vessel and rushed to the kitchen to fetch a replacement. For a few vital seconds the steward was distracted by the operation to clear up the mess, and then the girl had reappeared to fill the new goblet up from the waiting flagon. The king chuckled drunkenly at the chaos and shouted a toast to the generals. They drank dutifully, only Antipater continuing to look at the serving girl as she backed away.

The drinking session ran on into the night, and Alexander could barely walk when his steward finally ushered him to his bed. The following day he woke to a thumping hangover and did not leave his room. After a further three days his headache had still not abated, and he had developed a high fever. He gave instructions to his steward for court business to be suspended, and the palace hummed with rumours as to what was wrong with him. After the fate of Hephaestion, there was inevitably talk of poison, and numerous names were aired as possible assassins. None of the generals escaped the gossip, but Antipater's name seemed to arise more than most. For his part, he had left Babylon the day after the banquet, announcing that he was needed back in Macedon to quell an uprising. In a back street across the city, the dead body of a young girl had been found, beaten beyond recognition, but no one connected the discovery to a missing serving maid at the palace.

On the twelfth day, the king lay on a divan that had been set up for him in the throne room, scarcely able to speak as he listened to his generals bickering. He realised that they were arguing over the spoils of his empire as if he no longer existed, and he knew there was nothing he could do to defy them. He summoned his last reserves of energy to sit up and wave Ptolemy across to him. 'My friend, you have been with me all the way. I have one last request of you. Remember the chalice in the Pharaoh's tomb, which I had turned into this after Bucephalus died?' He bowed his chin towards the silver amulet around his neck. 'You must ensure it goes with me in my coffin to the next world. The gods will bless you and your family for generations to come if you do that.' Exhausted, he collapsed back into the divan's cushions.

Later that afternoon, Alexander died, ruler of the greatest empire ever seen and still only thirty-two years old. In the heat of the summer, his body was quickly embalmed and placed in a coffin, the general Ptolemy presiding over arrangements for its transport in a golden sarcophagus to Macedon where it would receive an emperor's burial. Just as the ebony and silver chalice had followed the Egyptian Pharaoh into his tomb, so the reworked amulet of the rearing stallion would accompany Alexander the Great on his final campaign.

*

And then...

On its journey to Alexander's birthplace in Macedon, the golden sarcophagus is seized by Ptolemy, who takes it to Egypt where he has been appointed governor in the break-up of Alexander's kingdom. Initially buried in Memphis, the sarcophagus is moved to Alexandria by Ptolemy's son, who opens the coffin and extracts the silver amulet during the transfer. The amulet is retained by the Ptolemy family, who go on to rule Egypt for the next three centuries.

*

Author's Note

Alexander III of Macedon, commonly known as Alexander the Great, invaded Egypt in 332 BCE, founding a Mediterranean port on the Nile delta which would come to be known as

Alexandria, occupying the city of Memphis (close to modern-day Cairo) and visiting the ancient royal capital Thebes (modern-day Luxor), some five hundred kilometres to the south. The tomb of Pharaoh Rameses VIII in the Valley of the Kings across the Nile from Thebes has never been found, but it is possible, in theory at least, for Alexander's army to have discovered and ransacked it. Certainly, there is evidence that looting of graves was widespread prior to the recorded excavations that have taken place over the last two centuries.

From Egypt, Alexander's army swept eastwards through central Asia, crossing the Indus river into the Indian subcontinent in 327 BCE and defeating Porus, leader of the ancient Paurava kingdom (a region in modern-day Punjab) at the Battle of the Hydaspes River in 326 BCE. Alexander's favourite horse Bucephalus, which had accompanied him on his travels all the way from Macedon, died around this time, prompting him to found a city on the river with the name Bucephala. His intention to continue to the Ganges valley and beyond was frustrated by a mutiny amongst his soldiers, who were exhausted by ten years of constant campaigning and eager to return to their homelands. Alexander reluctantly turned back, the Hyphasis (modern-day Beas) river in northern Punjab marking the furthest extent of his conquests.

After a slow homewards journey through Persia quelling numerous uprisings that had arisen in his absence, Alexander died in Babylon (in modern-day Iraq) in 323 BCE, possibly from poisoning. His body was placed in a golden sarcophagus, and in common with the burial rites for other monarchs and leaders of the time, it is likely that precious items were added to his coffin, to accompany him into the next world. The intention was for the sarcophagus to be transported to his birthplace in Macedon, but it was seized by his long-standing general Ptolemy and taken instead to Egypt where Ptolemy had been appointed governor. There Alexander was laid to rest, initially in Memphis but with the sarcophagus later being transferred by Ptolemy's son to Alexandria.

Ptolemy declared himself King Ptolemy I Soter (or "Saviour") in 305 BCE, establishing a dynasty which went on to rule Egypt for almost three centuries. One of his successors, Ptolemy IX Lathyros, is said to have replaced the golden sarcophagus with a glass substitute so that he could melt the original down for coinage. It is reasonable to assume that any items of value from the coffin would have been extracted and retained by the Ptolemy family. For simplicity, I have merged the actions of Ptolemy's son and Ptolemy IX Lathyros, in moving and raiding the sarcophagus, into a single event.

Four

Cleopatra and Julius Caesar

48 BCE – Alexandria, Egypt

'Explain to me exactly why I should be pleased about this,' Caesar's voice boomed around the courtyard, his face contorted with fury. Ptolemy XIII, King of all Egypt and proud descendant of a three-hundred-year-old dynasty, backed away quailing at the unexpected response and raised his hands in apology. The sack containing Pompey's severed head, stained with dried blood and buzzing with flies, lay open on the ground between them, the hair matted and filthy, the lips set in a death snarl.

'But he was your enemy. After you defeated him at Pharsalus, he came to me looking for help to raise a new army. Surely you wanted him dead?' Ptolemy spoke plaintively, uncertain how to handle this first encounter with the consul, now absolute ruler of Rome after the victory over Pompey. He was also acutely aware that, since his father's treaty with them ten years ago, the Romans regarded Egypt as little more than a province of their republic, giving them the right to dictate matters in his country. He needed Julius Caesar to support him in his civil war against his sister and co-regent Cleopatra, and the last thing he had wanted to do was offend him.

'My dealings with Gnaeus Pompey are my affair, not yours. He was a good servant of Rome, and he was married to my daughter. Even if we had our differences, it was not for you to kill him. You have dishonoured my people, and worse still,' Caesar pointed to the sack, 'you have dishonoured him in the manner of his death. I will not forget this.' He turned and strode towards the side door of the palace, his aides following him out of sight.

King Ptolemy stood alone in the stifling late summer heat of the courtyard. He had not lied in what he had said to Caesar. Pompey had arrived in Alexandria a week ago seeking to use the city as a base to rebuild his forces. From the reports Ptolemy had received of the rout at Pharsalus in Greece, and of the lack of support offered to Pompey in his flight through the islands of the east Mediterranean, it had been clear to the king that the ageing general was no longer the man to back for Egypt's future. Ptolemy's chancellor Potinus had been emphatic in his advice that killing Pompey would win favour with Caesar, who would then bring troops to help the king oust Cleopatra from the jointly held throne once and for all. The war between them had been smouldering for more than a year now, his sister proving a tenacious adversary, and he needed to bring an end to it. He had genuinely believed that both Caesar's and his own causes would be served by Pompey's death, and he had wasted no time in ordering the assassination. Evidently it had come as a complete surprise to Caesar, who had appeared in Alexandria only yesterday in pursuit of his rival, demanding a meeting with the king. Perhaps, on reflection, presenting the man's head in a sack had been unnecessarily vulgar, but Ptolemy remained mystified by the Roman's reaction.

Inside the palace, which he had occupied immediately the previous evening in order to assert his position as head of state, Caesar was also reflecting on what he had discovered. Pompey's murder was of course beneficial to him, since it resolved the matter of who should govern Rome without placing the blame for the killing on him. But they had been friends and allies for many years before their quarrel for power began, and Caesar had always sought, where possible and politically expedient, to harness the support of his opponents. Pompey's sons were already a thorn in his side, and he would have preferred to have their friends at the senate in Rome behind him rather than against him; there was a constant need to bolster his position there. However, the first thing to tackle was this weak Egyptian king. Caesar called for a scribe to take down orders. 'Write to the king and to his sister Queen Cleopatra telling them I have read the will of their father, Ptolemy XII Auletes, which clearly stated that they should rule as co-regents, and that I will enforce its enactment. Tell them that they must both lay down arms to end this absurd civil war and demonstrate their allegiance to Rome. This is by my decree as consul and thereby supreme governor of Egypt.' He waved the orderly away and began to consider instead how best to use his time in Egypt, a country he had never visited before and knew little about other than the stories of its ancient pharaohs and their fabled riches. There was political advantage to be had here in his quest for domination in Rome, not to mention the use of Egyptian ships and armies to control the east Mediterranean seaboard, and he did not intend to waste his opportunity now that Pompey was out of the way.

Over the next three months, Caesar continued to base himself in the palace, taking command of the entire city of Alexandria as he waited for evidence that the war between Ptolemy and Cleopatra had ceased. As the weeks passed, autumn giving way to winter, no such news emerged. Instead, Ptolemy's eunuch Potinus made repeated attempts to negotiate terms to ensure the king's supremacy over his sister, which Caesar ignored, while the queen sent several emissaries to him from her stronghold in Thebes thanking him for his interjection in their affairs and suggesting ways in which their countries might work together. The more Caesar learnt about the history and wealth of Egypt, the more curious he became about Cleopatra, who appeared to have a strong grasp of government – more so than her poorly advised and faint-hearted brother. Finally, however, an answer to his decree arrived, though not in the form he had hoped for. Ptolemy's army was at the gates of the city, pressing to attack, and Caesar found himself under siege. There was no danger of defeat, since the city was well supplied from its port, and the strong walls were easily defended by the small force he had brought to Egypt in his pursuit of Pompey. But Caesar was unable to break out until reinforcements arrived, which he had summoned from Rome but which might take several weeks to muster.

One evening, as he sat mulling over the situation in the private quarters of the palace, he thought ruefully of Alexander of Macedon and the vast empire he had created by the tender age of twenty-nine. Caesar was now fifty-two and although his conquests had taken him from Gaul to Persia, and even to that wild land Britannia across the northern sea, he was not an emperor in the way Alexander had been. No emperor would have been foolish enough to find himself besieged by a dolt like Ptolemy, caught in the crossfire of a ridiculous family dispute whose outcome was largely irrelevant to his ambition. Caesar had dared to liken himself to Alexander as a younger man, and he wondered now whether the fates were mocking him for such a presumptuous claim. His reverie was interrupted by a tap on the door, and his senior aide entered.

'Sire, you have a visitor, a woman. She is insistent that she sees you and won't take no for an answer. We've searched her for weapons, and there's no danger.'

Caesar looked up moodily. 'How did she get in here? You know well enough that if I want to talk to the Egyptians, I'll go out onto the streets. I don't expect them to be running free in the palace.'

The aide took a deep breath and replied, 'She seems to have smuggled herself in amongst the kitchen staff, but she's no servant. I wouldn't have disturbed you if I didn't think it was important. She says she has information about the king's army, which she will only give to you personally. Short of torturing her, I wasn't sure what else to do.' He trailed to a halt and waited nervously for Caesar's reaction to his mild joke.

'OK, bring her in. And since you find it all so amusing, get some food and wine for us – for two, mind you, not three.' He stared dourly at his assistant, who retreated quickly, telling himself never to test Caesar's sense of humour again.

A few minutes later the aide reappeared with a tray and a small amphora, which he placed on a table close to the door. Then he ushered in the visitor and left the room. Caesar rose from his desk and inspected the woman standing in front of him. She was a head shorter than him, a veil obscuring her face and neck. She wore a plain white dress with no jewellery, and on her feet were simple brown sandals. However, he noticed that the shoes were of soft, high-quality leather and that the skin of her forearms, hands and ankles had a smooth lustre to it. As he had been told, this was certainly not a kitchen servant, and he suspected she was of noble blood. There was a presence about her that he could not explain, and he had a sudden urge to pull up the veil, to put an end to this mysterious entrance. Before he could move, she spoke in a firm but mellifluous voice.

'My Lord, thank you for receiving me. I had to come here in disguise in order to slip past the king's soldiers outside. I pretended to be a kitchen maid and joined the servants entering the palace this afternoon for the evening shift. I hid for a while and have been arguing with your staff ever since to be allowed to speak to you. I promise it will be worth your while.' She paused and then lifted the veil with both hands in a dramatic sweep. 'Queen Cleopatra, at your service.'

Caesar was transfixed. He had seen drawings of the queen and knew this to be her, but he could scarcely believe she had been bold enough to pass through the lines of her brother's army or humble enough to pose as a servant girl. She might well have been killed outright if she had been discovered outside the palace walls or humiliated in the kitchens if she had been spotted as an imposter there. The pictures did not do her justice, he thought, continuing to look her up and down. Her black hair was coiled on her head above a strong jawline, an aquiline nose and wide, sensuous lips. Her eyes were a midnight blue, set in a face lightly tanned and oiled but with no other make-up. Free of the veil he could see that she was wearing one piece of jewellery after all, a necklace with a silver amulet in the shape of a rearing horse, which Caesar found oddly beguiling. She was not pretty in the traditional sense, but there was a dignified beauty about her that the modest clothes could not hide, and she emanated authority. She gazed steadily back at him, and Caesar realised he was staring like a teenager.

'My Lady, forgive me, you have caught me off guard!' He laughed to hide his embarrassment and went on, 'Your arrival here is remarkable, and we should celebrate it.' He went to the amphora and poured two glasses of wine. 'I have read your messages over the last few months with great interest, and I am delighted to meet you at last. It is very brave of you to come here and, as you say, I think it will be worthwhile.' He handed a glass to her and raised his. 'To our mutual benefit.'

They talked over dinner, and deep into the night beyond, on a wide range of subjects, from her war with Ptolemy to Caesar's position in Rome following Pompey's death, to the history of the pharaohs, the state of the Egyptian economy and her ambitions for her country. To his surprise Caesar found himself treating her as his equal, astounded by her education, her eloquence and her knowledge of Mediterranean affairs. They talked of the stars, of the gods and of the ancient Greeks, from whom she reminded him solemnly she was descended. It was only then that she pointed to the amulet round her neck. 'This was once owned by the great emperor, Alexander, and he gave it to my ancestor on his deathbed. The story goes that it was made in India, at the furthest reach of his empire, and that the animal is his favourite horse Bucephalus.' Caesar examined it across the dinner table, a fierce longing for it and the woman wearing it engulfing him. It was five days before Cleopatra let him take her to bed, by which time she had extracted a promise from him to chase Ptolemy out of Egypt, restore her to her throne and adjust her country's status in the eyes of Rome from that of vassal to partner. Julius Caesar, commander of armies across the western world, dictator and consul of the mighty Roman republic, was in love.

By early spring of the following year, the affair between the queen and Caesar was common knowledge. He was well aware that news of it would have reached the senate in Rome and no doubt his wife Calpurnia too, but that had only ever been a marriage of convenience. In any case, matters in Egypt had moved on, and the fates were smiling on him once again. His reinforcements had arrived to relieve the siege; the king's army had been crushed in a battle on the Nile; Ptolemy himself had drowned in his attempted escape; and Caesar had appointed Cleopatra as co-regent with her younger brother. Most importantly, the queen was carrying his child, the baby due in midsummer, and when the morning came to tell her he must return to Rome, he was uncertain how she would react.

'My darling, I have to address the senate. I simply cannot delay any further. You must understand, I am consul only until the end of the summer, and although they are just a gaggle of tired old men now that Pompey has gone, I still need to remind them who they should re-elect. Sending a messenger is not enough. A little personal encouragement is required.' Caesar smiled bleakly at the thought of all the pompous windbags on the senate benches and what 'encouragement' might be necessary to ensure their continuing support. Virtually none of them had ever led troops into battle or known real hardship in stamping Rome's imprint onto foreign soil. They were timid and fickle, and he would deal with them just as he had done after crossing the Rubicon river to challenge Pompey two years previously.

The queen lay on their bed, the outline of her rounded belly showing clearly under the sheets. She studied him in silence, hesitating long enough to allow a pang of guilt to wash over him, then spoke. 'Of course you must go, my love. I know you only expected to be here briefly last year, and there will be much to do back in Rome. But don't you dare forget me once your back is turned.' In what appeared to be an unwitting gesture, she folded her arms across her stomach, then added innocently, 'And of course you will need to tell your senators of the revised treaty with Egypt.'

'Yes, yes,' Caesar said hurriedly. 'That is one of the first things to discuss. And I will arrange for you to join me there as soon as the baby is born. You shall be Queen of Rome!' He knew perfectly well that was an impossibility, not least because he was leader of a republic, not a kingdom, and also because of Calpurnia. But as usual he found himself making promises to his mistress that he had not intended. He had better leave, he thought, before he made an even bigger fool of himself. 'I will sail on this afternoon's tide. Three legions will remain here to protect you, and I will think of you every day that we are parted.'

Cleopatra contrived to look sad, although in secret her heart sang at this culmination of her plans ever since she had first presented herself to Caesar during the siege. Her country's future was assured; her baby would be publicly acknowledged as the child of the most powerful man in Rome; and she would be lauded as queen of not one realm but two. She sat up against the pillows and said gravely, 'In that case, you must have a token to remind you of your pledge.' She lifted the necklace with the silver amulet over her head and held it out to him. 'My betrothal gift to you. Wear it well, my king.' Then she grinned mischievously and reached forward. 'Now come back to bed with me one last time.'

*

The Ides of March, 44 BCE – Rome

With the river Tiber at his back, Julius Caesar walked quickly through the city streets, accompanied only by a handful of wretched beggars trailing in his wake. He wondered why they bothered – he had never given them money, and he certainly was not going to start today. He stopped and turned sharply to snap at them, 'Piss off, you miserable bastards. If I see any of you behind me after a hundred paces, I'll call the guard out on you, and you'll be gutted from gizzard to groin before you can blink.' As a statesman he seldom used a soldier's vocabulary these days, but he was never shy of falling back on it when necessary. The bedraggled group scattered, and he was able to concentrate again on the morning ahead.

There was much to think about, and it was little wonder that he was preoccupied. He was due to meet his generals that afternoon at the Field of Mars to make the final preparations for a campaign in Thrace and Parthia, which would take him away from Rome for at least a year. They would sail from the port of Ostia in three days' time, and aside from the military arrangements, there were numerous other matters to be resolved before then. Changes to the tax system, land reforms, plans for a new library to bear his name in perpetuity, all things that he had been working on ever since his return from Egypt and now needed to force through the senate in a final vote that morning. But in particular, he needed to close off this ludicrous business with the diadem.

It had happened at the festival of the Lupercalia a month before, and as he walked, he remembered with rising irritation how badly it had turned out. After three years tiptoeing round the subject in private discussions with his associates, and with Cleopatra never missing an opportunity to remind him of his promise to her, he had decided to test the level of public support for him to be crowned king. In a pre-arranged scheme, co-consul Mark Antony had placed a simple diadem on his head at the festival, and Caesar had then removed it in a show of false modesty, hoping that the crowd would urge him to replace it. Not only was their response muted, but those who did support him now seemed to despise him for such a crude and poorly calculated display. Since then, his spies had reported that the senators were talking openly about his vanity, claiming that he had lost respect for the republic, that he lusted only for his mistress queen and a crown to match hers and that he needed to be brought back to heel. However spineless the senators were as individuals, his address that morning to them in assembly would need to be finely balanced, reassuring the doubters, reminding them whose generalship allowed them their lives of comfort and ease and at the same time leaving the door open for monarchy at a later date. Cleopatra and their son Caesarion were waiting in the villa across the Tiber, having joined him in Rome only a few weeks before, and he did not relish having to confess that the prospect of her being anointed Queen of Rome was dead. Neither the senate nor the people had ever accepted her, as if his marriage to the dreary Calpurnia was something worth cherishing, but he would find a way to honour his commitment, for the sake of Caesarion as much as her.

As he drew nearer to the Senate House, he spotted the seer Spurinna sitting at a street corner, the same man who had accosted him a few days before, claiming his life would be in danger until the Ides of March. Passing in front of him, Caesar said mockingly, 'Well, Spurinna, today's the day, and I'm still alive and kicking!'

The seer called out to his retreating back, 'True, it's come, but it hasn't yet gone.' Caesar broke his step momentarily, a chill of foreboding running through him, then he laughed and walked on. Rumours of assassination were always circulating, indeed Cleopatra claimed to have heard some sort of conspiracy theory from the villa staff only a few days ago, but they never came to anything. In any case, he was a soldier amongst soft politicians, admittedly not armed today because of his visit to the Senate House, but no one would be foolish enough to attack him in such a hallowed place. Nevertheless, he fingered the amulet at his neck for the gods' blessing. He was not superstitious, but he always wore it in appreciation of his beautiful queen and the fates that had led him to her. He would be a king one day, just as the amulet's creator Alexander had been.

Turning his mind again to his forthcoming speech, Caesar was pleased to see the magistrate Tillius Cimber waiting for him at the top of the Senate House steps. Cimber was a friend and long-standing supporter who he had recently awarded governorship of two provinces in Asia Minor, and it would be reassuring to have him at his side as he entered the lion's den of Roman politics. 'Good morning, Tillius,' he said heartily. 'Good to see you before you head off. When do you leave?' Cimber did not answer but thrust a rolled petition into Caesar's hand, muttering that it was to do with recalling his exiled brother to Rome. Caesar tried to brush past him through the open doorway, annoyed at the lack of civility, but Cimber blocked his path bodily this time, grabbing him by the shoulders and forcing him to a halt.

'What in the name of Jupiter are you doing?' Caesar growled at him. 'Get out of my bloody way, you fool.' Only then did he look beyond the magistrate, at last registering a group of twenty or more senators pressing in behind Cimber to confront him with what looked like other petitions. Flushing with anger, he steeled himself to remain calm and forced a smile as he tried again to move into the main chamber. Cimber seemed to turn aside and, as he stepped forward into the crowd, Caesar felt a glancing blow under his chin. He reached up to his neck and felt blood running through his fingers and down onto his tunic. In astonishment he looked round to see the senator Casca beside him holding a dagger, poised for another thrust.

Caesar bellowed, more in rage than pain, and launched himself at the throng, still struggling to comprehend what was happening. Casca tumbled back and others led by the legate Cassius Longinus took his place, baying like dogs now the first blow had been struck, daggers raining down as they jostled to get at him. Caesar fought them all, taking cuts to his arms and head as he lashed out with his fists, but finally he tripped and fell to the floor, blood streaming from his wounds. Still they came for him, one after another, stabbing down on his writhing body. Barely conscious, the last person he saw bending over him was Marcus Brutus, Pompey's general whom Caesar had pardoned after the battle at Pharsalus. 'You too, Brutus?' he gasped at the man he had considered his friend, and then the dagger slashed across his throat in a final death stroke.

As Brutus stepped back from the corpse, dark blood pooling on the white marble paving stones of the chamber, there was a terrible silence. The conspirators had plotted Caesar's death for weeks, fed up with his dismissive approach to the senate, the final straw being his clumsy effort at the Lupercalia festival to win the people's approval for kingship. However, now that the deed had been done, they seemed appalled at their own brutality, many of them being unused to the horrors of war. Brutus was the first to gather himself, and he climbed onto the speaker's podium to address them. But as he began to speak, the men nearest the door turned to flee, and before he could marshal them the rest of the senators were pouring out into the street. Brutus was the last to leave, not daring to look back at the blood-strewn scene behind him.

The news spread like wildfire, and the streets of the city quickly emptied as people cowered indoors, fearing a backlash from Caesar's soldiers. Across the Tiber, Queen Cleopatra hugged her son Caesarion, knowing immediately that he was in more danger than anyone and that Egypt's alliance with Rome was finished. It was not until noon that the magistrates' servants came to clear the aftermath of the assassins' work, and in the intervening hours Caesar's body remained on the Senate House floor where he had fallen, abandoned by friends and foes alike. Only one person attended to him, a soldier who had been talking to the seer as the conspirators fled past them.

Unseen in the chaos, he slipped into the empty chamber to rob the dead man, as if on a battlefield. He rifled through the tunic pockets to no avail, but then his eye fell on the silver amulet, all but hidden in the gory mess under Caesar's neck. Reaching in, he tugged it forcefully towards him to break the necklace on which it was suspended. Then he crouched on the floor for a few moments to inspect the gleaming ornament in his blood-streaked palm, scarcely believing his luck. He would never know that he was holding the marque of an ancient emperor, the love token of an Egyptian queen, but he knew he was rich, and there was no time to lose in hiding his treasure from prying eyes.

*

And then...

The amulet is taken by the thieving soldier onto the back streets of the city where it is reworked into a silver coin to avoid being traced. In accordance with usual practice at that time, the coin is stamped with the initials RR to denote the Republic of Rome.

Over the next seventy-five years the coin changes hands many times within Rome, eventually coming into the possession of another soldier who takes it with him when he is posted to the province of Judaea, in the army reporting to the procurator Pontius Pilate. There it finds its way into circulation in Jerusalem.

*

Author's Note

Queen Cleopatra VII was the last of the Ptolemaic dynasty to rule Egypt, a direct descendant of Ptolemy I Soter and the granddaughter of Ptolemy IX Lathyros. Her father Ptolemy XII Auletes had recognised that Rome was becoming the region's strongest power and had allowed the Romans to annex Egypt in order to ensure he remained on the throne. When he died in 51 BCE, Cleopatra and her brother Ptolemy XIII were named co-regents, but this soon descended into civil war between them. Cleopatra is said to have been both forceful and intelligent, speaking several languages and educated in maths, philosophy and astronomy.

The story of Pompey's death at the order of Ptolemy XIII, Caesar's appearance in Egypt, his intervention in the war between Cleopatra and Ptolemy and his love affair with the queen, is based on fact. Despite their differences, Caesar was horrified at the underhand manner of Pompey's death and sided with Cleopatra in her dispute with her brother. The queen communicated with Caesar initially by emissary but then arranged for herself to be smuggled into Alexandria, allegedly inside a roll of carpet but more likely in veiled disguise, in order to win him round to her cause personally. Caesar was said to be entranced by her bold arrival. Historians are split on whether the impression she made on him (and subsequently on another Roman leader Mark Antony) was due to her beauty and sexual appeal or her political astuteness as queen of a rich and influential country. In Roman eyes the couple did not marry, since Caesar already had a wife, Calpurnia, and there is no record of him divorcing her. As for Caesar's interest in Alexander the Great, he is reported to have seen a statue of the emperor in Spain in 69 BCE, when he would have been thirty years old, and expressed frustration at how little he had achieved compared to Alexander at a similar age.

Caesar left Cleopatra in Egypt before the birth of their child, Caesarion, but she visited him in Rome in 46 BCE and again in early 44 BCE. The story of the diadem at the festival of the Lupercalia is true, and one of the reasons for the plot leading to Caesar's death was said to be his desire to be crowned king. His assassination took place at a senate meeting in Rome on 15 March 44 BCE, a date known in the Roman calendar as the Ides of March. He was aware of a plot, having been warned by a soothsayer that his life would be in danger until the Ides. Following the attack, the assassins fled, and the local population took refuge indoors for fear of riots once the rumours of the murder began to emerge. As a result, Caesar's body lay unattended on the floor of the Senate House for several hours before it was removed. It is therefore possible for his personal effects, such as the amulet, to have been stolen by a soldier during the chaos.

Five

Judas Iscariot

33 CE – Jerusalem, Judaea

The twelve apostles watched from the back of the crowd as Jesus of Nazareth drew his sermon to a close. He stood at the top of the steps leading up to the temple, looking out over a sea of heads below him, his voice firm and strong, clearly revelling in the chance to share his teaching with so many. He had barely drawn breath all morning, and his listeners had been captivated from the start, drinking in the stories he used to illustrate his message and nodding amongst themselves in agreement. The apostles noticed with amusement that even the priests had remained silent, mesmerised by his eloquence even though they hated him for it.

At least things were calmer today, compared to the agitation of the previous forty-eight hours. It had been a tumultuous journey into Jerusalem two days ago, a mob of supporters cheering Jesus wildly all the way to the centre as he rode through the streets on a donkey. He had made only a brief visit to the temple that afternoon, shaking his head in dismay as he observed the money lenders trading noisily in the shadows of the bays there. On his return yesterday, however, he had walked unhurriedly up to the entrance hall, then moved rapidly amongst the lenders, flipping their trestle tables upside down one by one. Pandemonium had broken out as piles of coins sprayed across the stone floor, dealing slates smashed and traders and clients alike exploded in rage at the disruption. Several priests had come scurrying from the inner rooms of the temple to find the source of the commotion, adding to the clamour of exasperation. The apostles had been as surprised as anyone, and they had needed to move quickly to stop their master being assaulted. They had hustled him out of the hall and down the steps, astonished at the abrasiveness of a man they had hitherto regarded as the picture of composure and tranquillity and somewhat embarrassed at the chaos he had unleashed. Out in the sunlight he had simply shrugged their hands off him, smiling broadly, and shouted back into the temple, 'This is a house of prayer, not a robbers' cave. Shame on you all!' Then he had turned to the throng that had gathered in response to the excitement, picking out individuals and chatting animatedly with them as he laid hands on crippled limbs and blinded eyes with that extraordinary touch the apostles had seen so often. The priests had watched in silence then too, maddened as much by his gift of healing as by the way his words undermined them in front of the people.

This morning, though, it was very noticeable that the money lenders were nowhere to be seen. They had evidently taken the view that, with the mob so clearly on the side of Jesus, it was not worth their while setting up in the temple again while he remained in the city. And that was the real question for the priests – how to be rid of him from Jerusalem with his subversive attitude and his sly parables. Stories abounded that he claimed to be the saviour of the Jews, and the priests could not let that pass. They longed to arrest him but were afraid of how the people, so recently *their* people, would react to that.

With the sun at its zenith, Jesus concluded his address with a blessing and invited the audience to join him in the same place again the following morning. As they clapped loudly and began to disperse, he signalled to the apostles to stay where they were while he answered questions from a group of priests who had detached themselves from the crowd to intercept him on the temple steps. Above the hum of enthusiastic discussion amongst the departing throng, the apostles could hear the accusing tone of the priests' voices and the calm responses offered by Jesus. At last, he was able to extract himself, rolling his eyes as he walked across the street.

'I'm sorry, my friends, you've been very patient. But in a way, talking to the priests is as important as my sermons. They see me as a threat, sowing dangerous ideas in the minds of their flock, challenging their leadership and control here in the city. If only they would actually listen with an open mind… but I'm afraid that is never going to happen. They haven't quite worked out what to do with me yet!' He gave a short laugh, and then said in a more sober voice, 'Remember what I told you before; in three days' time it will be Passover, and I will be handed over for crucifixion. That should satisfy them.' He looked round at the twelve men and added brightly, 'Cheer up; it's my destiny, but in the meantime, we need some lunch.'

Six hours later, Jesus's fate was being discussed again, this time at a gathering of senior temple and city officials in the palace of the High Priest of the Jewish faith, Caiaphas. Some forty men were squeezed into the palace dining hall, all keen to express their views on the charlatan preacher with the temerity to say he was a healer, a Messiah or, worse still, the Son of God. Feelings were running high, and accounts of his words and deeds over the last few months were becoming increasingly extravagant. Seated on a dais at one end of the room, Caiaphas listened to the strident voices for several minutes and finally thumped the table for order. 'Gentlemen,' he shouted as the noise began to subside, 'I think we all agree in our opinion of this man. He is dangerous, and we can't let him continue to undermine us, or our teaching, anymore. He must be stopped. What we do not seem to have agreement on is how to deal with him. Let me be clear; there is no point simply putting him and his followers in prison. The people won't stand for it – there would be rioting in the streets, and we would look even more foolish than he's making us appear already. So we need to arrest him on a charge which carries the death penalty. I need hard evidence to support that, and I need you to bring it to me before the Passover festival. You have two days. Now, go, and find us a way to stop this nonsense once and for all.'

While the meeting in the High Priest's palace was taking place, Jesus was at a house just beyond the city walls attending to a leper. The apostles were waiting outside in the street, speculating on what the next few days might bring and how they could dissuade their master from walking openly towards his own death. They were a curious assortment of men, from a range of backgrounds and trades, with no obvious similarities other than their belief in Jesus and a deep-seated desire to help spread his message. The most recent arrival had been amazed to find that fishermen like the brothers James and John were prepared to mix with the tax collector Matthew or that Peter, the most headstrong amongst them, had been ready to accept the teaching of a simple carpenter from Nazareth. But, the new man kept reminding himself, they had all welcomed him with open arms, a vagrant with no firm job and no family who had scratched a living on the coat-tails of the Roman army occupying Judaea and was ostracised by most people on account of it.

The new apostle was too shy to contribute to the debate in the street, even though he was as committed to their master as any of the other eleven. A thin, wiry man of similar age to Jesus, with a mild stutter and a naturally hesitant manner, he squatted on his haunches at the back of the group, listening to the conversation running back and forth and wishing he could think of something useful to add. After a lifetime in the dust of rural Galilee, scavenging food and craving company other than drifters and vagabonds, he was unused to anyone paying attention to him and could not really believe his good fortune at being accepted into Jesus's little band. He longed to be taken seriously by them but seldom plucked up the courage to speak.

At exactly the moment that Caiaphas was delivering his instructions, the apostle felt a peculiar sensation run through him. There was a loud humming in his ears, blocking out his colleagues' voices, and his body seemed to fizz with new energy. From the darkest pit of his imagination a terrible scene welled up, Jesus stretched out on a cross, a crown of thorns on his head and a stab wound in his side, and he saw in a sudden flash of clarity what he must do to stop the crucifixion. He would not tell the others; they would not understand, or if they did, they would shout him down with alternative plans. This was for him alone, his opportunity to prove his worth to his new friends and their remarkable leader. Quietly, he slipped away from them, muttering his excuses to the man nearest him, Thomas, and headed back through the city gates. His absence went unnoticed as Jesus emerged from the leper's house, the man whom he had been treating thanking him profusely through an open window for his help.

Night was falling as the apostle walked through the streets, and after so many years living rough, he half expected to be stopped by patrolling soldiers. However, no one challenged him, and with unaccustomed boldness, he climbed the steps to the temple entrance hall from which Jesus had ejected the money lenders the previous day. Stopping to listen for a moment, he was considering which of the various doors facing him to open when a wheezing voice came from behind him, 'Where do you think you're going? We don't want tramps like you skulking about here.'

The apostle jumped at the noise and turned to find an old man looming out of the darkness carrying a broom and a bucket. He guessed this was a cleaner or caretaker, rather than one of the men he sought, and said tersely, 'I have an important message for the chief priests. Please take me to them.'

Unused to people doing what he asked, not to mention his newfound self-assurance, he watched in surprise as the man put down the bucket, jerked a thumb at him and gasped, 'This way.'

The old man shuffled over to a low door on the left-hand side of the entrance hall, opened it and pointed down a short corridor. At the far end the apostle could see a room lit by flickering oil-lamps, and as he stooped to pass through the doorway, he could make out the murmur of several voices. Straightening his back, he advanced into the room, and the conversation ceased abruptly. Five sets of eyes inspected him, and after a long pause the figure nearest him barked, 'How dare you interrupt us? This is a holy place. Beggars are not welcome.'

Rather than being overcome with nerves, as he would have expected, the apostle felt himself suddenly infused with that same energy he had experienced outside the leper's house. Almost trance-like, he stepped forward and spoke, with no trace of his usual stutter. 'Gentlemen, I am not a beggar. I believe you are looking for a way to arrest the preacher, Jesus of Nazareth, and I may be able to help you. What would you give me to betray him?'

The five priests seated around the room, senior members of the temple who had all been at the meeting in Caiaphas's dining room, looked at him in astonishment. They had been discussing how to apprehend Jesus when the apostle walked in, and however appealing the proposition might sound, they had certainly not expected an offer like this to be thrown into their laps. The man who had spoken first leant forward, his hands raised to the others in caution, and said, 'That is an interesting suggestion, but you can't simply walk in here and expect us to take you seriously. You look like a tramp, and you smell like one too. Tell us who you are and what you have in mind. If you sound believable, we might give you something for your trouble, but if you are wasting our time, I promise you will regret it.' Glaring menacingly to enforce his point, he sat back in his chair.

The apostle met his stare, conscious of the strange calm that had descended on him. 'I am one of the preacher's twelve assistants. We accompanied him into Jerusalem two days ago, and you will have seen us here at the temple yesterday and today. His intention is to continue delivering his sermons and faith healing over the next few days until Passover. Most of the time he is surrounded by well-wishers and supporters, so arresting him during the day without provoking a riot is virtually impossible. But in the evenings, I and the other apostles are the only people with him. That is the time to arrest him, and I will alert you when the opportunity arises. Provided of course that you make it worth my while.'

The priests looked round at each other, still wary of this turn of events so soon after the exhortation from Caiaphas. Nonetheless, they had been sharing their frustrations regarding Jesus only moments before, and here was a possible way to solve the problem. It was not simply that the preacher was mocking them, he was a danger to their entire livelihood, and on that basis a modest sum of money was surely worthwhile if this assistant could deliver him to them. One by one, they nodded their assent in response to the spokesman's questioning glance, and he rose from his chair to reach into the drawer of a desk behind him. Turning to the apostle standing in the centre of the room, he held out a small leather pouch. 'I don't know your name, but I recognise you from the hallway here yesterday when your master upset the money-changers' tables. You have forty-eight hours to bring him to us. Here are thirty silver pieces in payment. That's a great deal of money to scum like you, so understand that if you let us down, you will die. Make no mistake – you are being watched, and we know where to find you.'

The apostle took the bag of money and picked out a coin at random. Even in the dim light he could see that it was an old silver piece, embossed with the initials RR. He weighed the bag in his other hand, his expression impassive, and replied, 'My name is Judas Iscariot. I will not fail you.'

*

Two days later, on the eve of the Passover festival, the apostles were gathered with Jesus in the upstairs room of a house in the outskirts of Jerusalem, eating supper together following a long afternoon amongst the crowds of the city. The apostles were tired, and the conversation around the dining table was fitful, each of them preferring to dwell on the successes of the past few days rather than the nagging memory of their leader's prediction for the day of Passover itself. As they ate, Jesus interrupted their thoughts, 'Friends, I must tell you, one of you is going to betray me.'

The apostles looked at him in horror, Peter speaking for them all as he blurted out, 'Master, this surely can't be true. None of us would do such a thing. How can you say this?'

Jesus pointed to a serving bowl in the centre of the table and gave a gentle smile. 'Someone who has dipped his hand into that bowl with me will betray me.'

There was uproar as all the apostles leapt to their feet and began to speak at once, each one professing his innocence. Jesus patted the air in front of him for quiet. 'It is written in the scriptures. I've already told you what will happen at the day of Passover. You must accept it and learn from it. Now, sit down and help me finish our supper, because there is more to do this evening before we can get some rest.' He lifted a bread roll out of the serving bowl, broke it into several pieces and raised his wine glass. 'Take this bread and eat it. Imagine it is my body. And drink from this cup, for this is my blood, shed for the forgiveness of sins.'

Reluctantly, the apostles took their seats again, and the remains of the food and wine were shared out and quickly consumed. A buzz of conversation started up as they rose to clear the table, leaving Jesus musing in silence at the far end of the room, and Judas broke away from the others to join him. 'Rabbi, can you have meant me when you talked of betrayal?' he asked quietly.

Jesus looked at him and replied in a level voice, 'The words are yours.' Then he turned to the others and said loudly, 'Gather your coats, everyone, we are going to walk up to the Mount of Olives to pray.'

By the time the small group had walked through the city gates and onto the hill overlooking the city, night had fallen. Bathed in the light of a full moon, Jesus led the apostles to an orchard where they sat down to pray. Under the fruit trees, no one noticed that the men now accompanying Jesus numbered only eleven. Judas had detached himself as they left the house where they had dined, disappearing into the shadows and heading towards the temple. One by one the apostles succumbed to sleep, exhausted by the events of the last few days and the new worry that they might inadvertently betray their master. Only Jesus remained awake, praying for the courage to follow his chosen path.

Around midnight, the silence in the orchard was broken by the sound of excited voices. Jesus stood up and shook the apostles awake, and they watched the torches held by a file of men running up the hill path towards them. As the crowd came nearer it was evident that they were armed with a mix of swords and clubs and that the person at their head was none other than Judas. Standing squarely in front of Jesus, he pointed at him and shouted to his companions, 'Grab him.'

The other apostles moved to form a protective circle around Jesus, but he waved them back, holding Judas's gaze and saying calmly, 'Friend, do what you are here to do.' The apostles could only look on, aghast, as their master's hands were bound behind him, and he was manhandled roughly down the path towards the city.

*

In a quickening dawn breeze Judas made his way to the High Priest's palace and crouched in the lee of a low wall opposite the main entrance. He knew the mob that he had assembled the previous night to arrest Jesus had taken their captive to the palace for trial, and he wanted to hear what the outcome was. A month or two in gaol, and perhaps expulsion from the city with an edict never to return, would surely satisfy the priests. Anyway, he had played his part in saving Jesus from himself, arranging the arrest so that his master would come to no worse harm than a prison sentence. Most importantly, there would be no more talk of crucifixion and death, and once Jesus was released, Judas and the other apostles could take him back to Galilee to resume his preaching and healing work there. Judas felt confident that he could explain his role in all this to his colleagues once the dust had settled, although he missed that giddy sensation of assurance that had borne him through the last few days. He waited and watched patiently as the sun rose in the sky, oblivious to hunger and thirst and even to the leather pouch tied to his waist band.

At last, the palace gates swung open, and men flooded out into the street, a mixture of city officials and priests, a handful of whom he recalled from his interview at the temple three days previously. Then a detachment of soldiers emerged, a figure in chains stumbling behind them. Judas recognised Jesus, dirty and bruised from the journey into Jerusalem after the arrest in the orchard, but otherwise unhurt, it would seem, from his night's detention in the palace. The chains came as no surprise to Judas if, as he assumed, Jesus was being taken to the main city gaol, and he fell in at a discreet distance behind the soldiers to check that this was their destination. As the squad moved through the streets, he could hear observers shouting abuse, directed mainly at the soldiers rather than their prisoner, and it was only when a voice asked what was happening that he paid more attention. The officer in charge shouted over his shoulder, 'Don't ask me. All I know is, he's been sentenced to death. It's up to the Governor what happens next, but my money's on a crucifixion.'

Judas stopped in his tracks, appalled at what he had heard. The death sentence… that was unthinkable. Jesus was a teacher and a healer – how could he possibly be killed for that? He turned back towards a group of priests that had halted outside a shop and repeated the question put to the soldiers. The priests eyed him with distaste, and one of them spoke, 'That's the preacher, Jesus of Nazareth – the one who caused all that trouble at the temple the other day. He's been found guilty of blasphemy, and the sentence for that is death. You'd do well to remember it. The Governor, Pilate, will decide how he dies, but die he will.' Judas sank to his knees in the street, speechless with dread at what he had unwittingly set in course. The priests looked at him in contempt and then turned their backs to begin bartering with the shopkeeper, as if he did not exist.

Shortly after midday, having wandered aimlessly through the city streets for several hours, barely aware of his surroundings, Judas sat alone in an alley behind the temple. He still could not quite comprehend what had happened. But the story was all over the city – the preacher had been arrested on a tip-off and would die that afternoon. The most recent person he had talked to confirmed it would indeed be by crucifixion, though how he knew, Judas was uncertain. What was crystal clear, however, was that Judas had lit the touch paper to this tragedy. He had betrayed his master in the worst possible way, just as Jesus had predicted.

Judas shuddered in despair at his own foolishness. Arrest and the relative safety of imprisonment, that was all he had sought to achieve for Jesus, and now he was a murderer in all but name, with a bag full of silver to remind him of it. He tugged the pouch out from his belt and tipped the contents onto the parched earth next to him. The thirty coins gleamed at him accusingly in the harsh light, and he noticed the old one with the RR stamp at the top of the pile. He picked it up and examined it more closely. Recently minted Roman coins carried the head of the emperor, but he remembered Jesus explaining once that in years gone by the empire had been a republic, and he guessed that the initials were a throwback to those days. The sight of the money brought him to a final decision, and he scooped the coins back into the bag, putting only the one he had been holding into a pocket.

Rising to his feet, he walked swiftly round the temple

building to the familiar front entrance and headed directly to the inner door he had passed through three nights before. Once again, he could hear voices at the end of the corridor, and before his nerve failed, he burst into the room where the same five priests were sitting. Throwing the bag onto the floor between them, he sobbed, 'I have s-s-s-sinned. I have brought an innocent man to his d-d-death. Keep your filthy money.' Then he turned and ran back up the corridor, tears streaming from his eyes as the priests watched in silent astonishment.

Out in the open air again, Judas walked to the shop where he had heard the charge of Jesus's blasphemy that morning. Without delay he asked to buy the coil of rope he had spotted on display behind the counter earlier. He handed over the single silver piece from his pocket and left the shopkeeper inspecting the curious old Roman coin. He knew he had overpaid, but he felt a weight lifting from his shoulders now that he was rid of the last of the blood money.

Two hours later, Jesus was led from the cells below the residence of the Roman Governor Pontius Pilate and taken to the place of crucifixion. The fate he had foreseen, that his apostles had struggled to contemplate, had come to pass. They huddled in their lodgings, all too aware of their failure to save him from arrest and unable to bear the prospect of watching him die. Only Judas Iscariot was insensible to their teacher's final suffering, his body swinging from a rope high in an orchard tree on the Mount of Olives.

*

And then...

The coin continues to circulate in Jerusalem, ultimately coming back to Rome in the pocket of a soldier returning with the army from Judaea.

In the ensuing years it finds its way to the outskirts of the city of Pompeii where it is buried under ash during the eruption of Mt. Vesuvius in 79 CE. It lies there undisturbed for over three centuries until it is dug up by a craftsman who has fled to the Bay of Naples following the sacking of Rome by King Alaric's Visigoths in 410 CE.

The craftsman transforms the coin into an elaborate silver ring, which he retains as a good luck token, only selling it in Rome forty years later, shortly before his death there.

*

Author's Note

The role of Judas Iscariot in the days leading up to the death of Jesus of Nazareth is recorded in the gospel stories of the New Testament in the Bible. All four gospels (Matthew, Mark, Luke and John) cover his act of betrayal on the night of the apostles' final supper with Jesus, but the details vary. Only in Matthew is there mention of money actually being given to Judas by the priests – the thirty silver pieces – although Mark and Luke refer to the priests' offer to pay him an unspecified amount. Similarly, only Matthew describes Judas returning the silver to the priests in remorse and going on to hang himself, and even the narration of those actions is limited to a couple of brief sentences.

Little is known about Judas beyond the events of Holy Week – for instance his background, what he did for a living, how he came to be an apostle. Apart from the reference to money, no motivation for his betrayal of Jesus is provided in the gospels. Luke and John state simply that he is possessed by Satan. In retelling the story here, I have cast Judas as coming from a life of extreme poverty, a man of no self-esteem to whom financial reward would be highly compelling if his mind had been temporarily clouded by the devil of temptation. The further suggestion that his behaviour was driven by a misguided attempt to see Jesus arrested and imprisoned but thereby saved from death is also a fiction. It is fair to say, however, that Judas's reasons for betraying his master have been the subject of debate for centuries, and my interpretation of his actions is at least a possibility.

Six

Attila the Hun

April 450 – Ravenna

Valentinian sighed loudly with exasperation and flopped into his ceremonial chair, head in hands. As if he did not have enough to worry about, with barbarians on every border, his chief minister Flavius Aetius scheming to usurp him and the delicate balance of power between Ravenna and Constantinople under threat since his cousin Theodosius's riding accident. And now a court scandal which, although minor in comparison to his other concerns, needed to be resolved swiftly if he was to avoid looking foolish. That meant facing up to his sister, which he had spent a lifetime trying to avoid. He fluttered a hand at his steward to summon Honoria and steeled himself for her arrival. He had been putting it off since the previous day and had decided it would be best to hold the conversation here in his official chamber, to impress upon her the impact of her stupidity.

For all his melodrama, the situation was certainly dire. Valentinian III, ruler of Rome's western empire for the last thirteen years, had spent all that time watching his territories under attack from foreign tribes. The lucrative province of Carthage had been lost to the Vandals; the Suebi and Franks were a constant scourge in Hispania and Gaul; and the Burgundians were massing on the banks of the Rhine for renewed invasion, despite having been crushed only a few years previously. That war, a brutal campaign conducted in an unlikely alliance between Rome and the Huns from the East, had allowed an uneasy calm to be established on the empire's north-west frontier, but Valentinian did not trust the Huns under their fearsome leader Attila. They had wrought havoc across Rome's eastern empire for two generations, and King Attila had a reputation for bringing other tribes under his banner when it suited his strategic purposes.

The pressure from the barbarians was nothing new; what had changed in recent weeks was the situation in Constantinople and the rumours about his subordinate Aetius. Since Theodosius, commander of the empire in the east for over thirty years, had cracked his skull falling from his horse, civic and military control in his domain had begun to unravel. Although this was not directly Valentinian's concern, it threatened to destabilise the split in the empires between Ravenna and Constantinople that had been successfully maintained since being established by Valentinian and Theodosius's grandfather. Normally, Valentinian would have looked to Aetius to assist him in defending his empire, whether by military action against the barbarians or by political manoeuvring against the new agitators in Constantinople. But now the word across Ravenna was that Aetius was no longer content with being Valentinian's chief minister and field marshal and yearned to be emperor himself. The man had been at Valentinian's side for as long as he could remember, chief minister in name but, in reality, the driving force of the western empire for the last two decades. If ever there was a moment for the emperor to assert himself, this was it, which was why the news about Honoria was so badly timed.

The double doors to the chamber opened, and Valentinian looked up to see his sister sweep into the room. His immediate thought, as usual, was how much she resembled their formidable mother Galla Placidia, and how unfair it was that he had not inherited the same traits. She stopped in front of him, a haughty and impatient expression on her face, and he realised that he was already on the defensive. He cleared his throat and launched into what he hoped would be a suitably imperial dressing down.

'Honoria, word has reached me about your affair with your clerk. What in heaven's name were you thinking of? You are the emperor's sister; you cannot behave like a common prostitute. It brings shame on the family, and I won't stand for it.' He faltered, and she cut in with a scornful voice.

'Little brother, why should I care what you think? Look at you, sitting in your big chair, surrounded by all this pomp and glory.' She glanced round the richly decorated room. 'And what have you done to earn any of it? At least Eugenius is good at his job, and if I want to lie with him then it's none of your business. Not that you would understand about taking anyone to bed. From what I hear, you can't even manage it with the women on the streets.'

Valentinian blushed with embarrassment at her jibe but chose not to respond to it. He stood up and tried again to inject a tone of severity. 'Don't speak to me like that. I would remind you that I am emperor, and therefore anything you do concerns me. I will not have you debasing yourself here in the capital, and especially with a servant.' He hesitated for a second time, then added plaintively, 'It discredits both of us, not just here in Ravenna but amongst our people throughout the empire and even our enemies.

Do you really want to be known around the world for your sexual exploits?'

'I couldn't care less,' Honoria replied. 'No one bats an eyelid when men behave like that. You talk about *our* people, but they aren't *my* people. You know perfectly well that I am better suited to being emperor than you ever will be. Maybe I should team up with Flavius Aetius to see what we could do together. What would you say to that?'

The reference to his chief minister was enough to rouse Valentinian to real anger. Thankfully, he had a course of action ready, devised over the course of the last week since news of the scandal had come to his ears. 'Be quiet, blast you,' he shouted. 'I know well enough this is not the first time you have bedded men, but this time it's different. If you insist on sleeping around then you should at least have the sense to be discreet about it. As it is, everyone here at court seems to know, presumably thanks to Eugenius going around boasting about his conquest. I have tolerated your behaviour for too long, and this is the last straw.' He sat down again, breathed deeply and continued.

'To stop you dishonouring our family any more, I have made arrangements for you to be married. The senator Bassus Herculanus has agreed to be your husband, and you will live with him at his villa in Rome.' Valentinian chose not to mention that it had taken a sizeable sum of money to persuade the senator to accept Honoria, but the cost was more than worth it to ensure her removal from Ravenna. 'As a sign of his goodwill, he wishes to offer you a betrothal gift.' The emperor reached into his pocket and then held an upturned hand out to his sister. She looked at the intricately worked silver ring in the centre of his palm in utter horror, for once reduced to silence.

At last, she found her tongue. 'You cannot be serious!' she hissed at him. 'I will not be disposed of as if I'm your personal property. I know Bassus Herculanus. He's old and fat and one of the most boring men in Rome. I will not leave Ravenna, and I'll decide who I'm going to marry.' Her voice rose as the full implications of her brother's words began to dawn on her. 'You've done a deal with him, haven't you? How much am I worth? Who paid for this absurd ring?' She snatched the ring out of his hand and shook it at him in fury.

Valentinian shrank from her but steadied himself sufficiently to retort in a neutral voice, 'Too late, Honoria. It's done. The senator bought the ring in Rome and sends it to you in good faith. He will be a fine husband. You will be married in the summer, and until then you will be confined to your quarters in the palace here. If you disagree, you will go to prison. The dishonour of that is less than the damage caused by your disgraceful behaviour. Once you leave this room you will be taken to your apartment, and I do not expect to see you again until the wedding.' He paused, and then added sarcastically, 'Where I will give you my blessing.'

'By God, you will regret this,' Honoria raged. 'You have no idea what you have unleashed.' Then she turned on her heel and stormed out of the room, the ring clasped firmly in her fist.

The emperor watched her depart, two guards beyond the doors falling in behind her as she headed towards her suite at the other end of the palace. All in all, he felt, the meeting had gone quite well. He had managed to deliver his message, and there was nothing Honoria could do to cause mischief while under house arrest, especially now that the wretched clerk Eugenius had been sent to the army's front line on the Rhine, where he would hopefully meet a painful and richly deserved death for his part in this sordid affair. Valentinian gave little thought to his sister's final words, other than to reflect that Aetius was abroad with the army and therefore any plot between the two of them would be virtually impossible to arrange.

Standing alone at the hearth of the reception room in her apartment, Honoria continued to seethe with anger for several minutes. Eventually, she was able to compose herself and think clearly. It occurred to her that she had not seen Eugenius for several days and she assumed, rightly, that he had been despatched to some form of exile, if not to his death, for daring to share her bed. Not that he had been given much choice in the latter; Honoria had a voracious sexual appetite and, as the emperor's sister, she was used to getting what she wanted. But the affair had been an irrelevance, one of many over the years, and now that he was gone, she had no interest in his fate. Much more important was the reaction of her brother, so feeble for so long that she had come to ignore his views entirely. For once, however, it sounded as if he really would carry out his plan of action, although she wondered why this particular liaison should have prompted such uncharacteristic decisiveness. She was damned if she would be married off to some flaccid old senator against her will, but she recognised that she must act swiftly if she was to avoid the alternative of prison. Help was needed from outside her brother's court circle in Ravenna, and one possible avenue would be to make contact with Flavius Aetius. She was well aware of the rumours regarding the chief minister's ambition and had not been entirely frivolous in her threat to align herself with him. But he was already married, and more to the point she doubted whether the rumours were really true. There had been countless opportunities for him to oust her brother over the years since Valentinian had become emperor, and given that Aetius was effectively running the empire anyway, there was little reason for him to change his stance now. In any case, aside from his exceptional abilities as a soldier and administrator, he was an austere and prudish man, and she suspected he disapproved of her well-known love life. No, she needed another source of support, someone with both the desire and the leverage to persuade her brother to change his mind.

As she considered the various options open to her, she suddenly remembered she still held the engagement ring from Bassus Herculanus in her hand. Inspecting it closely for the first time, she realised that even though the prospect of being his wife made her flesh crawl, the ring itself was a beautifully crafted piece of jewellery. Three thin loops of silver had been interwoven into a single band, delicately inscribed with a garland of flowers. The ring was highly polished and sparkled in the bright spring sunlight that streamed in through the apartment windows. It had a curious lustre, and Honoria would have liked dearly to keep it, but given the circumstances, she wondered whether it could instead be put to use as a bargaining chip in extracting herself from the senator. Placing it carefully in a dish on the mantelpiece, she turned her mind again to her predicament and how best to outmanoeuvre her sapless brother. Confinement to her quarters, as the emperor had put it, was unlikely to be a problem. Several of her servants had shown their loyalty in the past by covering up her bedroom escapades, and she had no doubt they could be relied upon to carry messages beyond the palace walls. But to whom? That was the issue.

Two days later Honoria was standing in the same room, listening idly to her maid gossiping as she cleared away her mistress's lunch tray. The palace was buzzing with the news that Aetius had entered into an alliance with Attila the Hun in order to attack the Visigoth kingdom of Toulouse in southern Gaul. The maid was asking why any sensible Roman would trust a barbarian who had spent decades ravaging the eastern empire, and although Honoria was inclined to agree, she was becoming mildly irritated by such disrespectful chatter on court business. She was on the point of scolding the girl when she noticed the silver ring lying on the mantelpiece, and it dawned on her that a military alliance with Attila meant he would be open to messengers from Ravenna. She had heard enough about the Hunnish king to know that, as well as being a ruthless fighter, he had a reputation as a wily and opportunistic leader. Despite the temporary partnership with Aetius, he might see a message from the emperor's sister as a means to winning more valuable tracts of the empire in due course. Honoria cut the maid short and called for her secretary.

Publius had served Honoria for several years after losing an arm fighting the Huns in the provinces of the Danube and being decommissioned from the army. Employment for crippled soldiers was difficult to find, but he had come to the emperor's palace with a letter of recommendation from Aetius and had quickly proved his worth as Honoria's secretary by being efficient and discreet. His allegiance to his mistress had been augmented by regular invitations to sleep with her, which he accepted enthusiastically but without jealousy for her other lovers. In Honoria's view he was the ideal person to act as emissary to Attila, since he had retained contacts amongst his fellow officers in the army and would be well placed to gain access to the king. When he arrived in the room, Honoria dismissed the maid, told Publius about the arranged marriage planned by the emperor and explained the message she wished to send. At dusk that evening a one-armed figure slipped out of a palace side door and headed towards the docks. Publius had already organised a boat to take him north to Tergestum at the head of the Adriatic Sea, and he would have no problem finding a horse there to carry him onwards in search of the Hun army.

The spring snow-melt was largely complete by the time Publius entered the passes leading over the alpine mountain range towards the land-locked province of Raetia. Army friends garrisoned in Tergestum had confirmed to him that Attila's forces were stationed in the forests there, and he estimated he had little time to spare before they moved west to the Rhine to join Aetius for the invasion of southern Gaul. Riding hard, he arrived at the Huns' encampment as preparations were beginning for their departure, and with the help of one of Aetius's lieutenants acting as an interpreter between the two armies, he was granted an immediate audience with the king. Tired and dirty from his long journey, he was given no chance to refresh himself before he was ushered into the royal marquee. There he was surprised to find Attila sitting alone at a small table, with neither courtiers nor officers to protect him, eating a simple midday meal. Publius knew of the king's prowess as a fighting man and realised that he would deem bodyguards both unnecessary and insulting to his prestige. Attila beckoned to him, and he launched into the speech he had learnt word for word from his mistress.

'Your Majesty, I come with an urgent message from Ravenna, from Honoria, sister to the emperor Valentinian. She has been told by her brother that she must marry a senator and live in Rome, but she considers the match a poor one for a lady of her standing. She admires your power and influence and begs you to intervene on her behalf. I have with me a scroll carrying her seal, and as a sign of goodwill and further gifts from the Roman empire, she also asks me to give you this ring. I am instructed to bring your answer to her as soon as possible before the proposed marriage ceremony next month.'

Publius held out the scroll and the silver ring that Honoria had received from Bassus Herculanus. A long silence followed as Attila scrutinised the envoy from beneath hooded eyelids. Small and dark-skinned, his lips a gash of pink under a dense growth of untamed beard, there was a stillness about him that belied the force field of energy Publius had felt as he entered the tent. Acutely aware of the Hun's brutal reputation, he worried, not for the first time, that his mistress's plea might be considered petty and girlish, with the king's response being taken out on him as messenger. Having already lost his arm to the Huns, he had no wish to give his life to them, but he guessed that a firm and respectful attitude would serve him better than submissiveness, and he waited patiently with his hand outstretched.

At last, the king took the scroll and ring from him. 'You were a soldier?' he asked, pointing at the empty sleeve pinned to Publius's shoulder.

'Yes, Your Majesty. I lost my arm fighting your men on the Danube six years ago.'

'And you brave them again by coming here now?'

'Yes, Your Majesty. It was in the heat of battle, and I understand now that there is an alliance between our armies. Also,' he hesitated, not wishing to tempt fate by overstating Honoria's case, then continued, 'my mistress is well known to the general Flavius Aetius, and she assured me I would receive safe passage from you.'

Attila rocked back on his chair and laughed uproariously. 'You Romans never cease to amaze me. I've killed thousands of you, and yet you think that a temporary agreement with Aetius will protect an unknown messenger bearing a request from a woman I've never met.' He drank from a water glass in front of him and went on. 'But I have to admit it's the first time I've been asked to provide marriage guidance, so for that alone, soldier, I will let you live. It must have taken guts to come here amongst the men who ruined you,' he gestured again at the empty sleeve, 'and I will indeed send you home with an answer. Leave me now, and return at the same time tomorrow. The interpreter will find you somewhere to sleep. Now go.'

Once Publius had departed, Attila sat replaying the envoy's words in his mind, the scroll and ring lying on the table next to his half-eaten lunch. He had heard rumours of Valentinian's sister and could well understand why the emperor might wish to have her married off and removed from Ravenna. Despite the military alliance with Aetius, it was in Attila's interests for her to remain at her brother's palace, undermining Roman dignity with her irresponsible behaviour and opening doors to future attacks on the weakened empire by the Huns. Intervention in some form to halt the arranged marriage was therefore attractive, but surely there was greater and more immediate gain to be had from this unlikely request. He picked up the silver ring and placed it on the signet finger of his left hand, musing as he held it up in front of his face. Honoria's message seemed to him intentionally vague, and he suspected this was deliberate since its delivery by Publius had sounded carefully rehearsed. She had not specifically invited him to marry her in place of the senator, yet she had sent him a gift which, from a cursory inspection, appeared to be an engagement ring. Even if it was not intended, he could reasonably argue that this was a marriage proposal, which as an ally of Rome he would be pleased to accept. It mattered little, since Valentinian was too faint-hearted to defy him, and the sister would have to accept the consequences of her action. All that remained was to decide how big a dowry to press for. Half of the western empire seemed a fair demand and a much quicker way to gain territory than a long campaign alongside Aetius in Gaul. Once more he laughed aloud at the Romans' foolishness.

At noon the following day, Publius presented himself again at the royal marquee. Attila called him in and gave him two scrolls, one addressed to Honoria and the other to the emperor. 'I am delighted to accept your mistress's offer of marriage in place of the senator,' he said. 'I have written to her and to her brother, thanking them both for the proposal and the betrothal ring and setting out my terms.' Publius began to reply, dismayed at the king's interpretation of the message he had delivered, but Attila cut him short with a growl. 'Do not presume to speak until asked, soldier. You will leave immediately and return to Ravenna with all haste. Out, before I take your other arm off.' Publius knew better than to argue and bowed low to the king before pushing open the tent flap and heading to find his horse.

It took him nineteen days to ride back to Tergestum and a further two to find a boat for the short sea journey to Ravenna. The interview with Honoria when he returned to the palace was an uncomfortable one, but both of them recognised that the scroll addressed to Valentinian must be delivered and the background to Attila's dowry demand explained. Privately, Honoria was not in the least disconcerted by the king's terms; it was not her empire to lose, and with her brother at the helm it seemed the barbarians would have much of it in a matter of years anyway, with or without Aetius commanding the army. The emperor, on the other hand, was appalled.

*

March 453 – The Hungarian Plains

The wedding feast had all but run its course, the majority of the guests having left and only a score of Attila's hard drinking friends remaining in the dining hall. They had matched him, cup for cup of the rough local wine, but his capacity for alcohol was as legendary as his appetite for war, and few could now stand up. The king surveyed the scene around him, drumming his fingers on the banqueting table and wondering whether the time had come to join his new wife in the bridal bed. She was beautiful, a catch for anyone, and his lust for pretty women was undimmed even at the age of forty-six. But compared to him she was virtually a child, and in any case, there was no denying the marriage was for political advantage rather than love. The girl, Ildico, was a princess of the Burgundian tribe in Germanica, with whom he had entered a pact to attack the Romans, and part of that had been a matrimonial alliance. He was no stranger to such arrangements, having been married five times already. Only one woman had eluded him, and as the silver ring on his signet finger caught his eye, he thought back to the events of the last three years.

In response to his demand for a half share of the lands governed from Ravenna as dowry for wedding Honoria, the emperor Valentinian had written to him claiming that his sister had neither proposed marriage nor been entitled to do so. That privilege was the emperor's alone, and he would not consent to the king's terms. Attila had expected the rebuttal, which gave him an excuse to call off the forthcoming campaign into southern Gaul alongside Aetius. In its place, he had sent a messenger back to Valentinian stating that he would invade Rome's territories to collect what was rightfully his. An advance into northern Gaul two years ago had been blocked by the redoubtable Aetius, and the invasion of Roman heartlands south of the Alps had faltered last year at the river Po due to poor supply lines and disease amongst his troops. Nonetheless, it had led to a negotiated peace on satisfactory terms, without the need to marry the western emperor's tiresome sister. Attila had returned to his stronghold beyond the River Danube, free to plot an assault on the eastern empire in Constantinople, using the Burgundians to support him. In short, he concluded, the failed attempt to marry Honoria was no great loss, particularly when he had Ildico waiting for him in bed. He tugged the silver ring off his finger and, still holding it in his palm, he stood to walk out of the dining hall, the few men able to notice his departure shouting out ribald suggestions for what he should do next as he left them to their cups.

In the weak candlelight of his sleeping chamber, he could make out Ildico's shape under the bedclothes. He locked the door, in case any of his fellow drinkers felt inclined to offer further advice on how best to consummate the marriage, placed the ring on a side table and began to undress. Reaching down to remove his shoes, he saw drips falling onto the floor, and it was a few moments before he realised his nose was bleeding. He wondered blearily how long it had been going on and what could have caused it. As he rose, the drips became a steady rivulet, and he pulled off his shirt to dab at his face. Suddenly the rivulet turned into a torrent, blood haemorrhaging from his nose and mouth and spraying over the sheets as his lungs gasped for air. His head swam, and he collapsed onto the bed next to his new wife. Half asleep, and frightened as much by the prospect of losing her virginity as by the fearful noises coming from the savage old king, Ildico said nothing and turned her back on him, hoping that he had simply fallen into a drunken stupor. Only when the dawn came did she reawaken, to find her husband's stiffened corpse lying in a welter of his own blood beside her.

Despite having witnessed the horrors of war ever since she could remember, as her brothers and friends returned from the Rhineland battlefields bloodied and beaten, Ildico was in no state to cope with what she had woken up to. Alone amongst the Huns, so recently her tribe's sworn enemies, she was unable to explain the king's death on their wedding night, and she realised suspicion would immediately fall on her. Sickened and terrified by the sight of the blood-drenched body, she sobbed uncontrollably. Servants could hear her wails through the locked door but did not like to intervene in their master's business with his young wife. It was not until mid-morning that they dared enquire what was happening, and in the absence of any response, they finally brought hammers to knock their way into the room. In the uproar that ensued, no one noticed a young soldier slip the ring off the side table and into his pocket. The silver band had played a part alongside Attila the Hun, one of the most ferocious leaders in European history, in bringing about the demise of the mighty Roman empire. Now its journey would continue into the Middle Ages.

*

And then...

The ring is bought and sold repeatedly over the next four hundred years, much prized for its beautiful design and craftsmanship. During this time, it moves first from the Hungarian plains down to the mouth of the River Danube, where it is acquired in a Black Sea port by an Arab soldier in the failed siege of Constantinople (674–8).

Thereafter, it is taken with the invading Arab army to Spain (711) and on into France by Moorish forces, where it falls into the hands of a soldier serving Charles Martel, King of the Franks, at the Battle of Tours (732).

Now on the western seaboard of Europe, the ring finds its way to Denmark and then across the North Sea to Britain on the finger of a Viking invader (865).

*

Author's Note

The Huns were a nomadic tribe which migrated into central Europe from the other side of the Volga river in the second half of the fourth century, displacing Germanic tribes such as the Goths, Visigoths, Vandals and Burgundians and pushing them across the boundaries of the Roman empire. Attila was their leader for a twenty-year period until his death in 453 on the night of his marriage to Ildico, a Germanic princess and his sixth wife. During his reign he gained a fearsome reputation for war against Rome, for which he is best known, but the few records available also indicate that he was a talented strategist, able to unite other tribes under his banner as necessary, and even to negotiate treaties and alliances with Rome when it suited his purpose. The empire at this time was split in two, the western part being governed (by Valentinian III) from Ravenna on Italy's Adriatic coast and the eastern part being governed from Constantinople (modern-day Istanbul).

The story of Honoria's promiscuity, her forced engagement to Bassus Herculanus in 450, her plea to Attila for help and his demand for marriage, plus half the western empire as dowry, is true. She did indeed send her engagement ring to the Hunnish king, and although Valentinian wrote to him refuting the legitimacy of any marriage proposal, Attila insisted that he would claim his wife and dowry by invading Roman territories. He broke off an intended campaign with the Roman general Flavius Aetius against the Visigoths based at Toulouse and invaded northern Gaul in 451 instead. For simplicity I have excluded this part of the story, since his army was blocked by Aetius and the Visigoth king Theodoric I in an inconclusive encounter known as the Battle of the Catalaunian Plains (in the Champagne region of France). The following year, however, he turned his attention to northern Italy, advancing as far as the River Po. There he agreed peace terms with a Roman delegation before returning to his principal base on the Hungarian plains. The precise location of this is uncertain but is thought to be somewhere east of Budapest between the Danube and Tisza rivers.

Accounts of Attila's death vary, but it seems that after his wedding feast he suffered severe bleeding, possibly from the nose and mouth as a result of an oesophageal haemorrhage brought on from years of heavy drinking. One version of events suggests that he was stabbed by his new wife Ildico, but this is generally discounted by historians. The site of his tomb is unknown, as is the fate of the ring sent to him by Honoria.

Seven

Alfred the Great

January 871 – Ashdown, Wessex, England

In the late afternoon of deepest winter, nightfall is swift. A blanket of darkness had enveloped the battlefield, hiding the bodies strewn across the valley and the small hill beyond. The cries of injured men could be heard, agonised moans for help in the language of both armies, but there was little to be done for them as they lay abandoned where they had fallen in the frenzied fighting. Most of the surviving Danes had fled, streaming away in the twilight to the safety of their stockade at Reading. However, stragglers remained, their bloodlust undimmed by the slaughter, making it too dangerous to send out stretcher-bearers to fetch the wounded before sunrise. In the meantime, weary soldiers were still trickling into the West Saxon camp in small clusters, exhausted after chasing their enemies away from the ridge where much of the battle had raged but cheering and laughing as they joined their comrades.

The victory celebration around the camp's central firepit was well underway when a larger group emerged from the shadows, mounted and armed. The leader, a richly dressed man in his mid-twenties, had a body strapped across his horse behind him, and as the riders came to a halt, he shouted to the soldiers at the fire to take his reins. They responded with alacrity, despite the combined effects of an afternoon's fighting and an hour or more's drinking. Excited voices welcomed him, and hands reached up to help him from his saddle while others began to untie the body from the horse's rump. 'Careful,' he said, 'he may be a Dane, but he's an important one.'

A thin, pallid young man moved through the press around the riders and wrapped the leader in a fierce embrace. 'We thought we'd lost you,' he said. 'Thank the Lord you are safe. Come and warm yourself and show us who you've brought back with you.' He stepped back and beckoned the rider towards the firepit, shouting 'Make way for the king,' and shoving a handful of drunkards to one side. Only when the body had been dragged into the pool of light cast by the fire's flames did he stop in astonishment. 'Bagsecg!' he exclaimed. 'You killed him!'

Aethelred, King of Wessex, answered tiredly, 'Yes, brother, it's Bagsecg, but he's no use to us dead. We caught him in the pursuit from the ridge, wounded but still able to talk. I hoped that if we brought him back here, we could squeeze him for information about their defences at Reading and maybe retake it tomorrow while they're disorganised. But we had to fight our way through a bunch of Danes on the way back, and the bloody man died on us.' The king seldom swore, but it had been a long day.

His brother, the aetheling prince Alfred, burst into laughter. 'Aethelred, you're safe, and we won. That's what matters. We've killed one of their two commanders and hundreds of others. But most importantly, we've proved the Danes can be beaten. Think what that means!' He clenched his fists and punched the air with excitement. 'They've won every battle since they invaded five years ago, and now we've shown that they're not invincible after all. It took the men of Wessex to do that, and once the news gets out, Mercia and East Anglia will join your standard to drive the pagans into the sea where they belong.' He paused.'Anyway, that's for another day. Come and celebrate with the others.'

Alfred's exuberance was unusual for him. A natural ascetic, fonder of prayer and contemplation than carousing with his soldiers, he recognised nonetheless that if ever there was a time to be seen sharing ale around the firepit and swapping war stories with the men, this was it. He had led one half of the army in a brutal advance onto the ridge where the Danes had massed early in the day, commanding the shield wall and fighting shoulder to shoulder with his men until the Danes buckled and ran. His bravery had earned their respect, and an evening's drinking would win their goodwill too. Only he understood how close an encounter it had been. Splitting the Wessex army into two squadrons had been a deliberate tactic, the plan being for the king to attack the Danes on the valley floor while Alfred's men charged the ridge above. For some reason Aethelred had not launched his assault at the same time as Alfred, and the prince had feared he would find himself facing the combined might of the heathen forces alone. Luckily, his brother's troops had come to the rescue in the nick of time, and between the two of them, they had won a resounding victory. An explanation for the king's delay in engaging the enemy was needed, but it would wait for the morning. He called for a soldier to check the pickets guarding the approaches to the camp and then returned to the fire where his brother was being regaled with personal tales of the battle, drinking mug in hand and Bagsecg's corpse lying close by him.

The following morning Alfred awoke to grey skies and a steady drizzle. Unused to alcohol, his head hurt, and his guts squirmed. He made his way into the bushes beyond the perimeter of the camp, wondering whether he would ever be rid of his stomach problems, and squatted. On his return to the firepit, he felt better and thought once again about the import of the Wessex army's victory.

His animated welcome to Aethelred the previous evening had been no exaggeration. Ever since the heathen army had landed in East Anglia five years before, the Anglo-Saxons had been outwitted and outfought by them. After taking York and overwhelming East Northumbria, the Danes had moved southwards, occupying Nottingham and wresting control of Mercia from its weak-willed king, Burghred. Then, two years ago, they had invaded East Anglia again and killed its king, Edmund, leaving only Wessex to be conquered before all of Anglo-Saxon England was in Danish hands. In late December, they had at last made their move on Aethelred's kingdom, advancing up the Thames and constructing fortifications at the town of Reading in order to establish a base there. King Aethelred and his younger brother Prince Alfred had brought the Wessex army up to attack the town five days ago but had been firmly repulsed in a skirmish below the walls. They had regrouped at Windsor and advanced again yesterday to the village of Ashdown, a few miles south of Reading, where the larger battle had been fought in the late afternoon. It had been a rout, and the death of the enemy commander Bagsecg was a huge bonus. Alfred knew from accounts of the campaigns in East Anglia and Mercia that the other Danish leader, Halfdan, was a capable general in his own right, but nonetheless, the loss of Bagsecg would be a material loss to the invaders' impetus and morale. And, as he had said to his brother, the Wessex army had proved the Danes could be defeated. This was a turning point in the war, and a strategy to build on it must be devised quickly.

Looking round the makeshift camp the Wessex soldiers had made at the battle's end, he spotted his brother, still lying on the ground where he had begun celebrating the previous evening. Without the usual retinue of staff and wagons in their hurried advance from Windsor, the army had not brought tents with them, and despite their rank, the king and prince had been obliged to sleep in the open with the rest of their men. As seasoned soldiers, this was no great hardship, even in the winter, although it amused Alfred that while tents were an impossible luxury, ale never seemed to be in short supply on such occasions. He walked over to Aethelred and realised that the figure lying next to him was the corpse of Bagsecg. He shook the king awake and waited for him to gather his wits before speaking. 'Brother, we need to move. There's no food for the men here, and we are exposed if the Danes come looking for us. What do you want to do with this?' He prodded the dead body with a toe.

Aethelred groaned and rose to his knees, peering groggily about him. 'Dear God, I feel horrible. Get me some water, and then I can think straight.' Alfred shouted to a soldier behind them, and a clay pot was produced. The king splashed water over his face, drank several mouthfuls and then stood. 'That's better. You're right – we must get going. There will be plenty of food at Basing, which is only half a day's march from here, and we can send for the wagons from Windsor to join us there.' He gazed for a moment at the ridge overlooking the camp where the battle had been won and smiled broadly at the prince. 'We did it, Alfred. We beat them at last!' Then he looked down at the body of the Danish leader. 'It's a pity he died. But launching an attack on Reading today was probably unrealistic, with so many men lost and no provisions here. We must give him a Christian burial and make sure Halfdan hears about it. They need to be taught that we honour the dead and that this war is about religion as well as land. We'll win at that too.' He stooped suddenly and raised the Dane's left arm to inspect a silver ring on the signet finger.

The ring was muddied and blood-stained, but the craftmanship of the silverwork was striking. Three interwoven bands of the precious metal were etched with a garland of flowers, the decoration rubbed thin from many years' wear but still clear to see. It was an unusually delicate and beautiful item for a heathen to own, even a leader such as Bagsecg, and Aethelred found it strangely unsettling. He pulled it from the stiffened finger and held it up to the light to see it better.

'I understand why you want to honour the dead, but I didn't think you would want to rob from them,' Alfred said drily. 'We can bury him at Basing. I'll give orders to strike camp and round up any survivors from the battlefield. It doesn't matter now, but out of curiosity, why did you take so long to launch your attack yesterday? I was in real danger of being outflanked until you began.'

Aethelred turned to face him, still holding the ring in front of him. 'I was praying, brother. And it worked, so don't hold it against me. Our victory was God's will, and we must thank Him, not just by giving Bagsecg a proper burial.' He tossed the ring up in the air and caught it with a flourish. 'When we get to Basing, I'll have this melted down at the forge and recast as a crucifix. Then I will wear it as a sign of God's answer to our prayers, as we continue to take the fight to our enemies in the coming months. With the Lord on our side, the heathens will shrink before us, just as they did yesterday. Now, let's get everyone organised and on the road.'

*

April 871 – Wilton, Wessex, England

Three months later, any talk of the great fightback was a distant memory. Alfred sat in the hall of the royal lodge at Wilton, looking at his brother's body in its open coffin, wondering what to do next. He could scarcely believe Aethelred was dead, yet the wound had been a severe one and, in reality, it was a minor miracle the king had survived this long.

The brothers had worked closely in formulating their plans to save Wessex from the Danes since the victory in early January. As king, Aethelred had understandably had the final say in decision-making, and Alfred was uncertain whether he could have done any better. As it was, their efforts to build on their initial success had been an unmitigated disaster. The Danes had followed them to the hunting grounds at Basing and fought a second battle only two weeks after Ashdown. In terrible weather, and with many of their men still recuperating from the effects of the previous engagement, the Wessex army had been unprepared and had been forced to flee westwards from the invaders. After eight weeks, the armies had met for a third time, at a village called Merton near the south coast, and once again the Danes had won the day. It was there that the king had received his wound, a savage sword cut across his neck and shoulder, and with the loss of blood caused by hard riding to escape the battlefield, death had been inevitable. Incredibly, he had lingered a further four weeks in the refuge of Wilton, but yesterday he had finally taken his last breath, and Alfred was now king in his place.

A noise in the corridor beyond the hall disturbed him, and he looked up to find Aethelred's armourer standing at the door. 'Sire,' the man said hesitantly, and Alfred nodded at him to continue. 'The king... I mean, the old king... not that he was old...' He stopped and blushed in confusion.

'Don't worry, Selwyn,' Alfred said gently, 'I'm as unused to it as you are. What do you want?'

'Your Majesty, when I was preparing your brother's body for the coffin, I found this round his neck.' He held out a silver crucifix, hanging on a thin chain looped round his index finger. Alfred recognised it immediately as the cross that the metal worker at Basing had beaten out from the ring Aethelred had taken off the Danish leader Bagsecg. He noticed for the first time a dent on the upper part of the pendant and recalled his brother panting as they fled the Merton battlefield that the crucifix had saved him from having his head cut off. A bleak joke, as it turned out, he thought sourly.

The new king stood to take the cross from the armourer and slipped the chain over his head. 'Thank you', he said, 'it was important to my brother. It's the emblem of victory, and I will wear it every single day as a reminder of what is possible. It will help us win our country back from the pagans. Trust me on this.'

*

January 878 – The Somerset Levels, England

Ten riders moved in single file through the scrub bordering the marshes. No one spoke, and any sound from the horses' hooves was muffled by the sedge covering the boggy ground. A heavy mist rolling in off the open water had reduced visibility to just a few paces, and the only noise to be heard was that of drips falling from the branches of low, stunted trees laden with moisture. Neither breeze nor sunlight penetrated the murk, and it was impossible to be sure of direction. The path was little more than an animal track meandering through the featureless wasteland, occasionally petering out in a muddy puddle. Several times they had wandered off its course, blundering across it again by chance, and although nobody had said as much, they were hopelessly lost. They were also dog tired, hungry and soaked to the skin. For all that, the king thought to himself gloomily, they were at least hidden from their pursuers.

They had been on the run from Chippenham for three days now. In the chaos of the early morning attack, the armourer Selwyn had come to the royal sleeping quarters and raised the alarm. Within minutes it had been clear to Alfred that staying to fight was pointless. The Danes had breached the wooden stockade around the small town and killed scores of men before the Wessex soldiers could organise any effective form of defence. By the time the royal family had been woken, the heathens were rampaging through the streets, putting a torch to any building that offered resistance and hacking down anybody – man, woman or child – that tried to escape the flames. It had gone against all his instincts to abandon his troops, but to linger had invited certain death, and he had never been interested in martyrdom. Better to run and live to fight another day. The problem was, he and the men of Wessex had been doing just that for the last seven years, in ever declining numbers. Now, after issuing orders for them to scatter in all directions from the burning pyre of Chippenham, his army was reduced to a mere handful of soldiers alongside his wife Aelswith, their two small children and his armourer.

The escape itself had been harrowing enough. Selwyn had found rough peasant cloaks for each of them, and with hoods up to conceal their identity, they had galloped through the smoke-filled streets, charging down marauders that sought to bar their way and hurtling through the shattered remnants of the town gates. Then they had ridden south-west in driving rain for two full days, changing course repeatedly to avoid enemy patrols and halting only briefly to rest their horses and eat the meagre supplies that the armourer had been able to snatch up as they prepared to flee. Each night they had slept rough, in near-freezing temperatures, and before dawn on the third morning the persistent rain had come to a climax in a brief but torrential downpour. Now, as they edged their way into the marshes, Alfred knew that although the chase had been temporarily suspended, they were all at the limit of their endurance. Aelswith and the children, Aethelflaed and Edward, were deathly pale from exhaustion and fear; they had no food, no protection from the elements and no idea where they were. The last bastion of Anglo-Saxon defiance against the pagan invaders had been reduced to a pitiful state indeed.

The little group continued in silence, Selwyn leading the way. He and Alfred had always intended to head towards this part of the countryside in their scramble from Chippenham. The armourer had been born in the west country and, although he could not claim detailed knowledge of the marshes, he knew them to be difficult to penetrate and therefore a safe place in which to hide. In the dying light of the previous day, they had halted on raised ground overlooking a river, and he had pointed to a small elevation in the flat wetland basin upstream. It was one of several islands, he had said, on which the marsh-people eked out an existence. In dry weather it was possible to approach it on foot, so they might be able to wade across to it and set up camp. Alfred had commended him at the time, but now that they had descended into the swamp, they were unable to see their target and he worried that, even if it were to be found, it would be inaccessible after the heavy rainfall. He decided to keep faith in his dependable servant for an hour or two more, not least since he had no better alternative to offer, and was turning his mind again to the shameful loss of Chippenham when Selwyn's horse reared up ahead of him.

After the hush of their journey through the mist, the noise from the horse caught Alfred unawares. Reaching for the sword at his hip and shouting a warning to the other soldiers, he leant out of his saddle to look beyond the armourer, expecting to find Danes blocking the path. Instead, he saw a single diminutive figure, shrouded in greased animal skins, peering up at him through a lank mop of hair. It was impossible to tell the creature's sex or to read the expression on its grimy and mud-spattered face. It simply stood observing him, with neither animosity nor fear, its only possible weapon a sharpened stick at its side on which a dead fish was impaled.

Selwyn nudged his horse to one side of the path, allowing Alfred to come up alongside him. The two of them stared back at the strange apparition, and for a brief moment Alfred found himself imagining it was one of those bog-dwelling imps he had suffered nightmares about as a child. He pulled himself together with a start and, sheathing his sword in a show of friendliness, he spoke.

'Let me apologise if we disturbed your fishing. We are lost and need your help. Can you tell us where we can find dry ground to camp on and food to buy? We will make it worth your while.'

The figure surveyed the line of horses on the path behind the two men and grunted as it caught sight of Aelswith. Both children were perched on the saddle in front of her, and all three of them were looking towards the cause of the abrupt halt, their distress readily apparent. After another long moment inspecting Alfred, the figure muttered, 'Follow me,' and began to jog away along the path. Alfred took the lead, and the others broke into a trot behind him.

They rode for some twenty minutes, twisting and turning between water-logged stands of willow and alder trees and pockets of dense undergrowth, plunging ever deeper into the marsh. The path was wide enough for one horse, but no more, and only the king could see their guide as it scampered along in front of him. At last, they emerged on the bank of a sizeable mere, in whose middle stood the island they had seen the previous day. Turning to Alfred, the creature gestured with its stick towards a collection of huts there, then clambered up onto the rear of his horse and tapped him on the shoulder to advance. With a mixture of trepidation and curiosity, Alfred and his followers began to wade, the icy water reaching up to the horses' bellies at the deepest point.

Restored to dry land, it became evident that there was more to the island than Alfred had been able to make out previously. The huts themselves appeared to accommodate a number of families, women and children breaking off from their tasks to inspect the newcomers as they rode into the centre of the village. Animal pelts were stretched out to dry on racks; fishing nets lay bundled on the ground; and from the piles of cut reeds and half-constructed wicker baskets outside doorways, it was evident that weaving was an occupation for many of the residents. On the far side of the knoll, Alfred could see tethered goats and ponies grazing on an expanse of pasture running down to the mere's edge, where several flat-bottomed boats had been dragged up out of the water.

As they came to a halt, the village women shouted a welcome to the guide, who slid from the king's horse, still clutching the stick, and began to reply at great speed. The tone was so harsh and the words so unfamiliar, Alfred was unsure it was even English, until he found himself being addressed more slowly. 'Get the mother and her children here. We can give them shelter inside and warm clothes. The rest of you, wait over there, and we'll find you all some food.' A grubby hand was thrust in the direction of a patch of ground at the top of the pasture.

It was evident that their saviour had some level of seniority in the little community, but Alfred was still none the wiser as to who he or she was. He called to Aelswith to bring the children forward, and while they approached, he said, 'I am deeply grateful to you for rescuing us. Once my family and men have been fed, I will explain why we are here, and—'

The guide interrupted him, with a gruff shake of the stick, the skewered fish trembling on the upturned point. 'You can explain to my husband when he gets back this evening. He's the head of the village. He's taken the other men on a hunting expedition, and he won't be too pleased when he finds you all here. But don't worry, I can see you need help, whoever you are, and I'll sort him out.' Then she grasped Aelswith by the elbow and led her and the children into one of the huts.

Over the next few days, Alfred came to believe they were in good hands. The headman of the village, Cuthwulf, had made no attempt to hide his anger when he returned to the island that first evening to find ten extra mouths to feed. There had been a ferocious argument with his wife, whose name had eventually been divulged as Elva, due to her elfin stature. But, as predicted, Elva had prevailed, and the West Saxons had been allowed to stay. The seven men had been able to sleep out of the rain under lean-to shelters of branches thrown up alongside the huts and to dry their clothes on fires within. More importantly to the king, Aelswith and their seven-year-old daughter Aethelflaed had recovered in full from the rigours of their journey, although the boy, four-year-old Edward, remained a concern after developing a streaming cold and cough. Alfred's ear had become attuned to the strange west country dialect of the marsh-dwellers, and he had been able to confirm Selwyn's report that there were several village communities on nearby islands within the wetland basin, living on a simple diet of fish and deer and trading their pelts and reed baskets for grain from their neighbours downriver towards the north Devon coast. Discovery and attack by the Danes was extremely unlikely, given the secluded and defensive nature of their hideaway. Even more remarkable was the realisation that Cuthwulf and Elva had no idea who Alfred was.

After a week, when all bar Edward had fully recuperated, Alfred took Cuthwulf to one side and explained that he was the King of Wessex, that the invading Danes had destroyed his army and that he needed a base from which to rebuild his forces and reclaim his kingdom. He planned to stay on the island and send out messengers to rally his troops. Only when a sufficient number had been mustered would he be able to move eastwards and attack the enemy. In the meantime, he would need the villagers' continuing protection and increasing amounts of food as his men came to join him. He had already handed over the small amount of money that he and Selwyn had been able to stuff into pockets as they fled Chippenham, and he could only offer his promise that in return for their further help the villagers would be richly rewarded in due course. From his surly response it was unclear whether Cuthwulf truly understood Alfred's story, but luckily Elva was listening in and came to his rescue once again.

'Of course you can stay. You will pay us with Danish gold when the time comes. First you need a healthy son, in case they kill you.' Despite her feral appearance, Elva was clearly much more aware of the world outside the marshes, and the ways of kingship, than her husband.

With evident reluctance, Cuthwulf nodded, and Alfred shook them both by the hand in wordless gratitude. Then he set off to share the good news with Selwyn and Aelswith, touching the silver cross around his neck in a reflex movement as he whispered a prayer of thanks under his breath.

*

June 878 – Athelney, The Somerset Levels, England

The marshes in midsummer were a lot more appealing, verging on habitable, Alfred thought to himself as he and Selwyn rode slowly upstream from the river. The familiar path was firm and clearly visible; wildflowers carpeted the soft ground to either side; and the occasional glimpses of open water sparkled in the bright sun. Even the trees, so hunched and dismal when he had first come here, looked cheerful in their vibrant green of full leaf. So much change, so much to give thanks for, after the most extraordinary five months of his seven years as king.

That morning he had witnessed something he would never have believed possible. Guthrum, Halfdan's successor as leader of the Danes, had been baptised into Christianity at the church of Aller, a small town on the edge of the wetlands, together with twenty-nine of his men. It was part of the terms of surrender after the Danes' emphatic defeat by the West Saxons at the battle of Edington six weeks previously. That success had been achieved thanks to the mobilisation of the militia across south-west England, thousands of men answering the Wessex king's call to arms in the early spring and gathering on the downs north of Wilton to face the heathen army. The fighting had lasted all day until the Saxon shield wall had finally broken through the enemy's defences, terrible casualties being sustained by both sides. Then the Danes had fled back to Chippenham where Alfred had besieged them for a fortnight before peace terms were negotiated.

It had been a momentous occasion, a double victory in the war for his kingdom and his religious faith, just as his brother Aethelred had foretold after the battle of Ashdown. And as he and Aethelred had also discussed all those years ago, another turning point in the decades-long struggle against the Danes had been achieved, only this time it was built on much stronger foundations. Now there was one last duty to perform before he headed east to the royal lodge at Winchester which he planned to make his capital going forward.

The battle at Edington had been won, undeniably, by the soldiers of Wessex, and Guthrum's baptism had been arranged by the priests. But Alfred knew that none of it would have been possible if he and his little band of fugitives had perished during their flight into the marshes five months previously. Death had been perilously close for them all, especially his wife and children. But they had been able to restore their strength on the island of Athelney and then to gather and equip a core unit of soldiers before mustering the countryside militias. Ultimately, it was Elva who had been responsible for the real turning point in their fortunes, first by leading them to shelter and safety and then by persuading her husband to let them stay on and organise their fightback. During those three months, she and Alfred had become firm friends, their relationship severely tested only once, when he was left in charge of the baking oven for a few minutes and the villagers' bread supply was reduced to ashes. His plea that he had been distracted by his son's coughing had fallen on deaf ears as Elva chased him out of the hut in fury.

His reverie in the warm sunlight was broken as they emerged from the shrubbery onto the mere. The water level had subsided in the dry conditions, and they splashed their way across to the island without trouble. Villagers hailed them as they trotted up towards the huts, even Cuthwulf raising a hand in welcome. They reined in beside him and dismounted.

'Hello, Cuthwulf,' Alfred said. 'It's good to see you again. It all looks very different from the first time we came here!' He glanced around him, smiling at the familiar faces that had gathered to listen. 'I know Selwyn came back last week to pay you what we owed for our long stay, but I wanted to come here myself and thank you personally. You'll have heard that we defeated the Danes in a big battle last month, and we couldn't have done that without everyone's help here in Athelney during the winter. I particularly wanted to thank Elva because without her, my wife and children could have died. Is she here?'

Before Cuthwulf could answer, there was a commotion at the far end of the village, and Elva appeared, holding a milking pail. 'I'm here, Alfred,' she shouted and bustled up to him, still as grubby as the day they had first met.

'Elva!' the king laughed, 'I don't suppose you will ever call me Your Majesty, will you?' The combined smell from her greased clothing and the pail of warm goat's milk made him want to gag, but he controlled himself and pressed on. 'Elva, as I was saying to Cuthwulf, I owe you a special thanks for rescuing us from the marshes and nursing my family, particularly little Edward. I have a gift for you. It's been very precious to me, and I hope you will treasure it as much as I have.'

He reached up to his neck, pulled the chain with the silver crucifix over his head and placed it in the woman's imp-like hand. 'It is the sign of victory. Thank you, with all my heart.'

*

And then...

Over the next two centuries the silver crucifix heads north from the Somerset marshes in a series of trades, as Anglo-Saxon forces win back Danelaw territory from the Viking settlers. By September 1066 it is to be found round the neck of Ealdred, Archbishop of York.

Ealdred gives the crucifix to King Harold Godwinson in

thanks for Harold's victory over the invading army of Harald Hardrada at Stamford Bridge.

King Harold wears the crucifix at the Battle of Hastings the following month, where he is killed. The cross is taken from his dead body by the victor Duke William of Normandy, who wears it to his coronation as King William I of England on Christmas Day in London's Westminster Abbey.

*

Author's Note

The story of Alfred, King of Wessex, is known to us principally thanks to the records of a Welsh monk and bishop Asser, commissioned by Alfred to write his biography. The son of King Aethelwulf, Alfred, was the youngest of several brothers, three of whom reigned before him, and he continued the fight that they and their father had waged against the Viking invaders for several decades before he ascended the throne.

The battles of Ashdown (or Aesc's Hill), Basing and Merton all took place in the early months of 871, although their precise locations are unknown. The Great Heathen Army, made up mostly of Danes, had landed in East Anglia in 865, and by 869 the kingdoms of Northumbria, Mercia and East Anglia had all fallen under the invaders' control. Only Wessex remained in Anglo-Saxon hands, and if Aethelred and Alfred had not resisted the Danes' attacks between 870 and 878, the history of England might have been very different. The battle of Edington (or Ethandune, considered to be somewhere near Westbury in Wiltshire) in early May 878 really was the turning point in the war, allowing Alfred to force Guthrum's army out of Wessex and, over the next twenty years, to begin the unification of the four English kingdoms into the single entity we recognise today.

As for the episode in the Somerset levels, this also took place, roughly as described. In the summer of 877, after besieging the Danes in Exeter, Alfred had agreed a truce with their leader Guthrum, whereby the Danes would retreat to Gloucester in Mercia. Alfred spent Christmas in Chippenham, and Guthrum broke the truce with his surprise attack in early January 878. The king fled to the village of Athelney in the marshes, where he was able, over a period of three months, to organise a resistance movement. The mobilisation of the fyrd, or local militia, in Somerset, Wiltshire and Hampshire allowed him to amass a sizeable army for the battle at Edington, where his troops are thought to have outnumbered those of Guthrum. The Danish leader and his men were indeed baptised at Aller in Somerset as part of the subsequent treaty. The story of Alfred burning the bread (or cakes, as it is commonly told) is, however, just a popular legend, with no contemporary evidence to support it.

The part played by the crucifix in my version of events is also a fiction. Nonetheless, Alfred and his brother Aethelred were devout Christians, and Aethelred's delay in joining battle at Ashdown because he was taking mass is understood to be true. Alfred went on to found abbeys at Athelney and Shaftesbury and to promote religious learning throughout his reign. He died in 899 but did not come to be known as "the Great" until the Reformation in the sixteenth century. He is the only English king to have been given such a title.

Edgar Aethling Family Tree

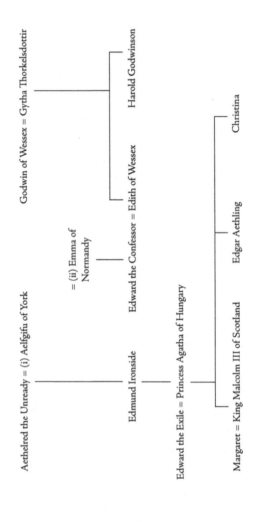

Eight

Duke William of Normandy

May 1072 – Abernethy, Perth, Scotland

'So, tell me about him, Bartolf. I mean, I've heard all the stories about what he's achieved in battle, but what's he like to deal with face to face? You spent time with him in Normandy, so you must have seen him up close, not just with a sword in his hand.'

Bartolf looked at the other man in surprise and considered the question before answering.

'Yes, Your Majesty, I was at his court for over six months, but of course I was there as an attendant to Queen Margaret and her mother Princess Agatha. Most of Duke William's dealings with our household were with the queen's brother Edgar, who was effectively a hostage there, so we didn't see much of the duke himself. Obviously, he has an enviable record as a general. He's always been ready to act quickly when he needs to, and he can be brutal at times, as you saw from Northumbria two years ago.' He stopped, to choose his next words with care. 'But he's a hard-headed politician too. He will negotiate when it suits him. Remember how he paid the Danish mercenaries to sail away from York, rather than having to fight them and Prince Edgar together.' Bartolf pointed to the fleet of ships sailing towards them. 'What you're seeing on the water down there is just a show of strength, before he sits down to talk with you.'

The two men were standing in a watchtower high above the village of Abernethy on the south side of the Tay estuary, downstream from Perth. They were evenly matched in height, but otherwise very different in appearance, Bartolf being lean, dark and clean-shaven while King Malcolm III of Scotland was barrel-chested, with a shock of blond hair, ruddy cheeks and a thick beard. The king was an experienced soldier and leader, who had waged war against Duke William of Normandy's armies by invading northern England twice in the preceding three years. But he had never met the duke – now King of England for the last five years – and he was uncertain how the next few hours might unfold.

'The lessons from Northumbria worry me. The Normans burnt everything and killed everyone in their path for six months. What's to stop William doing the same across Scotland?'

Again, Bartolf paused before speaking, conscious not only that he was merely the chamberlain to the king's wife Margaret, rather than a senior aide to Malcolm himself, but also that his response might have disastrous consequences. He was not used to the king seeking his opinion and was still coming to terms with the unexpected request to join him at the lookout point.

'Your Majesty, I don't believe Duke William wishes to rule in Scotland. He has enough on his hands already in Normandy and England. Ever since he defeated Harold Godwinson at Hastings, he's been suppressing outbreaks of rebellion by the Anglo-Saxons all around the country, as well as having to look over his shoulder across the channel.' He hesitated, wondering how to continue. 'What he wants, I think,' he said slowly, 'is to know that his northern border is secure and that you won't support your brother-in-law Prince Edgar in any more uprisings. My guess is that he's come here looking for peace. It will be a tough negotiation, but he won't want another war so far from London and Normandy.'

'Let's hope you're right,' said Malcolm pensively. 'It's a very large fleet. Now, we'd better go down to the waterfront and welcome him, one way or the other.'

As the Scottish king clattered down the spiral staircase inside the stone tower, Bartolf took a final look at the Norman ships on the river and then turned his gaze to the countryside upstream. It was a broad floodplain, offering easy access to the centre of government at Scone, beyond Perth, as well as to the town of Dunfermline, which Malcolm had made his home after marrying the Hungarian princess, Margaret, two years ago. If the duke chose to attack rather than negotiate, his army could be in control of the principal seats of Scottish power within twenty-four hours. His soldiers had already occupied Edinburgh, and Bartolf had no illusions as to the likely outcome of a battle with King Malcolm's troops. Some fifteen hundred Scots were gathered on the plain, a reasonable show of force considering how little time there had been to assemble them, but they would be no match for the battle-hardened Normans in a pitched fight. He prayed his estimate of the duke's intentions was correct and began to descend the staircase behind his king.

Despite his lack of experience as a soldier, Bartolf had acquired a keen sense of strategic awareness in his time as royal companion and, more recently, as chamberlain to Queen Margaret. Born to wealthy parents in Hungary, he had been attached to the court of Princess Agatha and her husband, the exiled Anglo-Saxon prince, Edward, from an early age. When

Edward died in 1057, the princess and her three children had been allowed to move from Hungary to live in England, but their lives had changed dramatically when King Harold was killed in the battle at Hastings in 1066. Since one of those children, known as Edgar Aetheling, had been a competing candidate for the English throne on Harold's death, the new king Duke William had removed him and the rest of Princess Agatha's household to Normandy the following year. Bartolf had accompanied them and had remained with them on their escape to Scotland seeking asylum six months later. There, he had watched King Malcolm grasp the potential value of being associated with a successful Anglo-Saxon challenge to Duke William's crown. Not only had the Scottish king supported Edgar's efforts to stir up rebellion in northern England, but he had also married the aetheling's sister Margaret as well. In Bartolf's opinion, Malcolm was just as wily as Duke William in terms of political manoeuvring, even if he did not have the military power to go with it.

At the bottom of the tower, two equerries were waiting with horses. As they mounted, Malcolm told Bartolf and the other men to follow him, and they rode slowly out of the village centre towards the estuary in silence. The king had a decision to make, and he needed to weigh up the advice of his army commanders, who were itching for a fight, against the Hungarian courtier's appraisal. By the time they reached the river, with the Norman fleet in plain view, he had made up his mind.

'Gentlemen,' he said, 'we have a dilemma. If Duke William has come to negotiate, we should only have a small welcoming party here to meet him, in case the sight of a larger force provokes him to attack. But if we do that and it turns out he has come to fight, he'll destroy us, in which case we'd be better to bring the entire army to the waterfront.' He turned to Bartolf. 'I agree with you. It's a risk, but I think he's here to negotiate. Since he knows you, I want you to stay here with me. That way,' he gave a humourless laugh, 'if you're wrong, you will die with me too.' Then he gestured to one of the equerries.

'Angus, you must ride to the generals and tell them what I have decided. On no account must they bring the army up here, however much they grumble. Are you clear?' The equerry nodded, and the king continued. 'Then I want you to collect my bodyguards and the royal standard and bring them back here.' He pointed to the second man. 'Euan, you will go to Dunfermline and tell Queen Margaret to ensure that her brother, Prince Edgar, is kept there. Tell her to lock him up if she has to. I don't want him showing his face here and antagonising the duke. Go now, both of you, as fast as possible. And do not fail me.' The equerries were used to the king's brief and simple orders and wasted no time in spurring their horses away.

Malcolm turned again to Bartolf and looked at him thoughtfully. 'I daresay you are wondering why I took you to the top of the tower. My generals are warriors. They see the world in black and white and, occasionally, blood red. In their eyes, William is an invader, and therefore we should simply engage him in battle and beat him back over the border. Maybe they are right, but the duke is a difficult man to defeat, and anyway, I think they sometimes lack perspective. I've watched you recently in conversations with Queen Margaret and her brother, and you seem to have that skill.' The king looked out over the river and then continued.

'If we fight the Normans and win, we gain nothing more than we already have, but if we lose, then all Scotland is at stake. The alternative is to try to negotiate a treaty, whereby William leaves us in peace. If your assessment is correct, William will be open to that, and in the process, we may be able to win back land in northern England which was historically ours, with no blood being shed. We'll know within the hour whether you are more sensible than the generals.' He smiled at the Hungarian. 'How lucky are you feeling?'

Bartolf shrugged. 'Your Majesty, I've served the queen and her family for over fifteen years. I owe everything to her, and now to you, and I wish to make this country my family home for generations to come. I believe I am right, but I will gladly die alongside you, if that is the way this turns out.' The king snorted with laughter at the solemn response. 'How reassuring!' he said in a sarcastic tone.

Thirty minutes later, the equerry named Angus rejoined Malcolm and Bartolf, carrying the royal standard and accompanied by eight bodyguards dressed in the king's bright blue livery. Malcolm ordered all helmets to be removed, and the group of eleven men formed a line on the riverbank, the standard fluttering prominently in the warm midday breeze. From their saddles they watched the Norman ships approach up the estuary on the tide. There were twenty in all, little more than an arrow's flight away now on the shallow expanse of water, with scores of soldiers in chain mail clearly visible on each vessel, those at the gunnels holding bows at the ready. Bartolf estimated the duke's army at around twelve hundred men, slightly fewer than the Scots, but he knew they would be well armed and disciplined. He shivered, despite the sun on his back, and thought what a meagre and defenceless group the Scottish king and his attendants must seem.

There was no doubt that they had been spotted, and the Scots waited as the ships' crews began to furl sails and cast anchors. Then three vessels detached themselves from the flotilla and were rowed in towards the small village harbour. At the prow of the leading ship was a burly middle-aged man wearing a mail vest and a sword, and carrying a shield in his left hand, ready to fend off an ambush from a hidden bowman. His head was unprotected, and he stared at the group on the waterfront, evidently measuring the risk of disembarking. Malcolm did not need Bartolf to tell him this was Duke William, the King of England. He edged his horse forward with his knees and raised his arms in a gesture of friendship. It was ridiculously dangerous behaviour by both kings, Bartolf thought, but they were each known for their bravery, and he supposed it was at moments like these that reputations were forged.

As the oarsmen brought the ships alongside the harbour wall, the Scottish king called out, 'Duke William, welcome to Abernethy. Be assured that we greet you in peace. Please join me here on dry land.' The duke said nothing but handed his shield to a soldier and climbed nimbly into the rigging around the mast to bring himself level with the mounted Scots.

'King Malcolm, our meeting is long overdue,' he said in a guttural and heavily accented voice. 'You have caused me considerable trouble in Northumbria over the last three years, and I understand you are harbouring my enemy, Edgar Aetheling. Why should I not kill you here and now?'

'For the same reason that I have not brought my army here to kill you,' Malcolm replied calmly. 'We could have met you in battle wherever you tried to land, and we would outnumber you two-to-one. As for Prince Edgar, he is my brother-in-law, and I have no reason to bar my wife's family from my country. But I am interested in talking with you, rather than fighting.'

'You're bluffing,' said William harshly. 'My scouts from Edinburgh tell me your army is nowhere near that size. I could crush you, just as I crushed Harold Godwinson at Hastings and Edgar and his Danish mercenaries in Northumbria. Your soldiers wouldn't stand a chance.' He ran his eye down the line of Malcolm's men and then pointed aggressively at Bartolf.

'You,' he rasped, 'I remember you. You came to Normandy with Edgar and his mother and sisters. Why are you here?'

Bartolf was about to reply when Malcolm answered for him. 'He came to me with Princess Agatha, and now he is my wife's chamberlain. He's no spy, if that's what you were thinking. If anything, he seems to be on your side, since it is thanks to him that we are talking here rather than fighting.' In contrast to the duke, his tone remained friendly, and he went on. 'Now, what I would suggest is that we continue this discussion over some food in the village. If you and some of your men wish to follow us, we will walk there together.' He dismounted and signalled to the other Scots to do the same. Then they waited while the duke jumped down from the rigging and summoned a handful of men to join him on the riverbank.

There was an uneasy silence as the two groups walked the five hundred paces to the village. Malcolm had sent one of his bodyguards ahead to warn the innkeeper of their arrival, and by the time they had reached the tavern, tables and seats had been arranged outside the front door in the sun. Malcolm invited the duke and one of his men to sit with him and Bartolf, while jugs of ale were brought and food ordered. To the casual onlooker it might have been a summer picnic rather than a state meeting between two monarchs. The Scottish king raised his drinking mug in a toast to his visitor, and the negotiation began.

It was not until dusk that terms were finally agreed. The discussion had been broad-based, and largely good-natured, focusing initially on the strategic interests of each country before turning to the details of an agreement. Bartolf's assessment of the duke's stance was accurate. He appeared to have no appetite for an attempted conquest of Scotland and would agree to retire his army over the border provided Malcolm undertook not to launch further attacks into English territory. In particular, any attempt by the Scottish king to foment Anglo-Saxon rebellion would be considered an act of war. As a demonstration of his commitment, Malcolm would be required to give up his eldest son Duncan to Duke William, to be held indefinitely as a hostage at the English court, and in return he would be granted estates in Northumbria.

Malcolm had anticipated the demand for a hostage, such a condition being a familiar term of treaties around Europe. He had no concerns over the treatment that Duncan would receive in London. The boy was the son of his first wife Ingibjorg, who had died several years earlier, and now that the king had two new sons from his recent marriage to Margaret, his interest in the older boy was diminished. Scotland would be safe, and he was retrieving land across the border which had been the subject of dispute between the two countries for more than a century. He feigned reluctant acceptance and offered his hand in final agreement to the deal between them. The duke looked at him steadily across the table, his arms remaining folded across his chest.

'There is one last thing' he said flatly. 'Edgar Aetheling must be sent in exile to the continent. I will not have him on these shores.'

'Why should I agree to this?' Malcolm frowned in surprise. 'You are asking me to banish my wife's brother without any assurances regarding his likely fate once he leaves us. I have pledged not to support any acts of rebellion, and I have agreed to give you my son. Surely that is enough.' It was a statement, not a question.

The duke thumped the table in irritation and stood up. 'Remember what this boy Edgar is to me,' he growled, stabbing the air with an index finger. 'Since Harold's death at Hastings, the aetheling has been a persistent thorn in my side. He has dared to challenge my right to the English crown and, as long as he remains at large, he will be the centre point of any Anglo-Saxon resurgence. He is my enemy. If you try to keep him here, then you are my enemy too, and I will do to Scotland what I did to Northumbria.' He made a visible effort to relax and sat down again. 'I recognise there is a family bond to consider. I will guarantee Edgar safe passage, and I will give you this.' He reached into a pocket and flung a silver crucifix onto the table between them.

The Scottish king picked up the cross and inspected it. It was dented and tarnished and simply crafted. Nonetheless, it had a curious allure, and he was intrigued as to why William should consider it a bargaining chip. He looked enquiringly at the duke, who answered bluntly. 'It belonged to Harold Godwinson, and I ripped it from his neck as he lay dying at Hastings. It is rumoured to have been owned by his kinsman Alfred, the first king to defend England from the Danes. That means nothing to me, but if it is an Anglo-Saxon relic then I will trade it for the last of Alfred's line. From now on, Normans will rule England, and the aetheling can consider himself lucky to escape with his life.'

Malcolm continued to make an appearance of being upset, although in reality he was pleased with the outcome. Edgar's repeated efforts to oust William from England in the last few years had come to nothing, and Malcolm was certain, from all he had heard and now seen for himself, that the duke was a more reliable and worthwhile ally. After a suitable pause, he looked to Bartolf. 'You are a witness to this agreement between our two countries, which shall be known as the Treaty of Abernethy.' Then he reached out again, and the two kings shook hands firmly.

*

September 1072 – Scone Palace, Perth, Scotland

Bartolf looked across the hall to his bride, as she laughed at a joke from one of his parents. He suspected she had no idea what had been said, for his parents' grasp of English was limited, to put it mildly, and Beatrix had struggled to understand them ever since they arrived. But she was doing her best, and he loved her for it. Equally incomprehensible was how he had managed to land such a wife. Events had moved fast since Duke William's visit, and he still could not quite believe his good fortune.

King Malcolm had been pleased with the terms of the treaty thrashed out with the duke at Abernethy, and for some reason considered Bartolf to have been a key contributor to it. As chamberlain to the queen, the Hungarian continued to manage her household, but in addition he had found himself drawn increasingly into the king's council discussions. He was at pains to remind Malcolm that he was no soldier and was told that this was precisely why his opinions were valued. Not all the nobles at the council seemed so enthusiastic.

One evening in early July, the king had taken him aside and asked him what his ambitions were for marriage and children. Bartolf had been caught out by the question, since there was only one person he had been attracted to since coming to Scotland, but she was clearly unattainable, and he had learnt to live with his disappointment. He had given a suitably vague reply, hoping that the conversation might move on, but the king had persisted. 'You are over thirty, aren't you, and it is high time you were married. As it happens, I know just the girl for you, and I'm going to arrange the wedding. Then you can settle down here in Scotland, as you said you wanted to, and have a bunch of children!' He had chortled with laughter as he watched Bartolf struggling to hide his confusion. 'Don't worry,' he had said, 'the girl is my little sister Beatrix, and don't pretend you haven't lusted after her for the last three years. It's been as plain to see as the nose on your face.' He had punched Bartolf's shoulder playfully and added, 'The real surprise, though, is that she's in love with you too. I've no idea why.'

So the couple had been formally betrothed and a wedding date set. Then Queen Margaret had suggested that Bartolf's parents be invited, and a messenger had been sent to Hungary to collect them. They had arrived only three days before the ceremony, and now they were enjoying the wedding dinner in the great hall of Scone, the very room in which Malcolm and so many earlier Scottish kings had been crowned. Bartolf continued to gaze at Beatrix, his daydreaming interrupted only by a rush of noise next to him as the king stood up, banging a shield with the hilt of a dirk.

'Ladies and gentlemen, a moment's quiet, please. This is my sister's day, and I do not wish to be remembered as the older brother who stole the limelight by talking too much. There will be toasts and speeches from others shortly, and I have only two things to say. First,' he looked fondly at Beatrix, 'I wish her great happiness and many children.' He waited as the guests cheered, and she blushed pink with embarrassment.

'And secondly, I have a small wedding gift for my new brother-in-law. As you know, a treaty was agreed with Duke William of Normandy earlier in the year. Bartolf was instrumental in saving Scotland from invasion. Unfortunately, one of the conditions was that the queen's brother Prince Edgar must leave us, and he is now in the Low Countries. In return, however, Duke William gave me this.' He held up the silver crucifix, sparkling with polish, for all to see. 'It belonged to Edgar's relation by marriage, Harold Godwinson, and long before that, to one of the earliest English kings, Alfred. It therefore seems fitting that, having lost one brother-in-law from Scotland, I should welcome another with this token of the treaty.' The guests roared their approval once again, as

Malcolm leant down to pass the crucifix to Bartolf. 'May it honour you and protect you,' he whispered.

*

November 1093 – Alnwick, Northumbria, England

Robert de Mowbray stood on the bridge spanning the River Aln, the imposing ramparts of Alnwick Castle looming behind him. The clear skies promised a chilly night, and he had no intention of being detained in the cold longer than absolutely necessary. Most of the enemy soldiers were either lying dead in the killing fields beyond the river or were fleeing in panic northwards to the border. Those few unlucky enough to have been captured had been interrogated in an unsuccessful search for ransom prospects and then executed without ceremony – a merciless business using swords already blunted from the earlier fighting. But Mowbray was not known for his generosity of spirit. As Earl of Northumbria, acting on behalf of the new English king, William Rufus, since Duke William's death, he had the power of life or death in the region, and his orders had been carried out with relish by his men in response to the invasion by the Scots. The corpses had been piled in a heap in the water meadow, awaiting mass burial, while behind him, out of sight in a wagon below the bridge, lay two other bodies, the only two that really mattered to the Norman commander. Now there remained just one man to dispose of, someone of rank by the look of his clothes and armour, who had been found unconscious on the riverbank in the fading autumn light as the victors scoured the battle ground for booty.

The captive was showing signs of coming round, and Mowbray waited impatiently as he was revived with a helmet full of water and several slaps across the face. A few minutes later he was dragged onto the ramp of the bridge, held upright between two Norman soldiers and presented for questioning. Mowbray inspected him with distaste.

'Give me a reason why I should spare you,' he barked. 'I neither know nor care who you are. To me you are simply another troublemaking Scot, and we would do well to be rid of you all.'

The prisoner raised his head painfully, fresh blood seeping from a deep slash across his cheek, and appeared to take in his surroundings for the first time. He looked up at the castle and guessed at the identity of the man in front of him. 'My Lord,' he gasped through cracked lips, 'forgive me, I fell from my horse and was knocked unconscious. I am not a Scot, in fact, but I serve King Malcolm with pride. My name is Bartolf, Thane of Lesselyn, and I also have the honour of being chamberlain to Queen Margaret.' He stopped, the effort of speaking too much to bear, but continued to hold his head high.

'Then I have news for you, Thane of Lesselyn, now that you have woken up. Your king is dead, and his son too. You will very likely join them shortly, whether you are a damned Scotsman or not. Answer my question – what are you worth to me?'

Bartolf was in excruciating pain from his wound, and struggling to think straight from the concussion he had suffered, but he knew enough of Mowbray's reputation to realise that he was only seconds away from death. As a brother-in-law to the Scottish king, he would probably command a ransom, but he had no desire to place that burden on Queen Margaret or his wife Beatrix, and he had no other value to offer. 'I cannot promise you money,' he muttered, 'but…' Then he was saved the trouble of finishing his sentence by fainting again, and the soldiers propping him up let him slump to the wooden floor of the bridge. He lay there on his side, arms splayed and the breast plate of his armour skewed to one side of his body. In falling, a silver crucifix suspended round his neck had tumbled out onto his chest.

Mowbray was on the point of putting a sword to Bartolf's throat when the crucifix caught his eye. He raised it on the tip of his weapon and studied it. Like so many others before him, he was fascinated by its lustre, which prompted him to consider more carefully the Hungarian's initial response to his interrogation. It occurred to him belatedly that as victor and king-slayer, he had an important message to send to Scotland, and if the prisoner had close links to the royal family, he would make an ideal envoy. He crouched and lifted the cross from the unconscious man's body.

Once Bartolf had been resuscitated for a second time, he opened his eyes to find the cross being swung in a pendulum above him. The same cruel voice that he had heard before he passed out forced him to refocus. 'So you have no ransom to offer, yet you have this. Explain yourself.'

'My Lord, it was a gift from King Malcolm at the time of my marriage.' Bartolf was sufficiently recovered to avoid mentioning that his wife was the king's sister and went on hurriedly. 'The king was given it by Duke William of Normandy many years ago as part of a treaty between them. Before that it was owned by Harold Godwinson. It is very old, an Anglo-Saxon treasure.' He hesitated, then added hopefully, 'I'm sure the duke's son, King William Rufus, would be interested to have it returned to him.'

'That is not for you to decide, you piece of vermin,' said Mowbray. 'Listen to me very carefully. You will return to Scotland to tell the queen and her councillors that Malcolm and the prince have been killed and that we have slaughtered every other filthy Scot we could find besides you. You will make it clear that if an army dares to set foot over the border again, King William Rufus and I will invade their country and burn every city, town and village that exists. We will destroy every crop, rape every woman and kill every child we find. In the meantime, I will keep this,' he hefted the crucifix on its chain, 'and you should give thanks that it has saved your pathetic life for you.' He kicked Bartolf in the ribs in a parting gesture of contempt and turned to walk towards the castle.

Bartolf lay alone on the bridge, bleeding and bruised. He had no proof that Malcolm or young Prince Edward had died, but he did not doubt what Mowbray had told him. Before being knocked from his horse during the battle, he had seen the king being charged down by a Norman knight, the prince fighting valiantly behind him. It was a woeful end to the raid across the border launched by the Scottish king the previous month. The intention had been to take territory from King William Rufus, now that the twenty-year-old treaty with Duke William had broken down. But they had been ambushed by a large force led by Mowbray, and the battle had been a disaster. At least the cross had saved him, but he did not look forward to explaining that to Queen Margaret. Anyway, it would be a long walk home before he need do so.

*

And then…

Robert de Mowbray retains the silver crucifix until 1095 when he leads an unsuccessful rebellion against King William Rufus. Condemned to death, his life is spared when he gives the crucifix to the king, with an explanation of its history and previous owners.

King William Rufus is wearing the crucifix when he is killed out hunting in the New Forest in 1100. In the chaos of his death, it is stolen by a soldier.

The soldier remains a member of the English royal

bodyguard for the next twenty years, joining the family of William Rufus's brother and successor, King Henry I, on a voyage to Normandy in 1120. The ship is wrecked off the French coast and all the passengers, including Henry's son and heir William Adelin, are drowned. The crucifix is washed ashore on the soldier's body at Barfleur, where it is found by a local peasant. It changes hands on the continent many times in the ensuing 150 years, ultimately finding its way across the Alps to Venice, where it is acquired by a young merchant, Marco Polo.

*

Author's Note

For the sake of clarity and consistency, I have referred throughout this chapter to Duke William of Normandy, although he also became King William I of England in 1066 and has since been known colloquially as William the Conqueror.

The invasion of England by Duke William, and his accession to the throne after killing the Anglo-Saxon king Harold Godwinson at the battle of Hastings, is probably one of the most familiar stories in English history. Less well known are his struggles to suppress numerous rebellions during his ensuing reign. Many of these were constructed around Prince Edgar Aetheling, great nephew to Harold's predecessor Edward the Confessor and the man through whom Anglo-Saxon rule might be restored. Duke William took Edgar and his family with him to Normandy in 1067, but they fled to Scotland later that year. Thereafter, King Malcolm III of Scotland continued to assist Edgar, granting him asylum on several occasions between 1068 and 1071 and supporting him on at least one raid over the border. In addition, Malcolm married Edgar's sister Margaret.

As a result, the Scottish king was seen as a threat by Duke

William, who brought an army to Edinburgh in 1072 and then sailed a fleet up the River Tay estuary. It is unclear whether any battle was fought – it is possible that William also brought troops up to the Tay over land – but ultimately, terms for withdrawal were agreed at the Treaty of Abernethy. It is likely that Malcolm was eager to negotiate, to spare Scotland the savagery that Duke William had applied to Northumbria two years previously (known as the "Harrying of the North"). No record of the treaty has survived, but we know that Malcolm was granted lands in Northumbria in return for agreeing not to launch further raids into England, that his son Duncan was taken south as a hostage and that Edgar Aetheling was banished to Flanders. The round tower in Abernethy exists to this day, one of only two such stone watchtower designs in Scotland.

The character Bartolf is real. He is known to have been in the Hungarian court of Princess Agatha, Edgar Aetheling's mother, and to have accompanied the princess, Edgar and his sisters Margaret and Christina to Scotland in 1067. At some point in the next three to four years, Margaret married King Malcolm, and Bartolf, now Margaret's chamberlain (or head of household), was permitted to marry Malcolm's sister Beatrix. However, there is no evidence that he was present at Abernethy or at the Battle of Alnwick twenty-one years later. Bartolf was granted lands by Malcolm at a place called Lesselyn in Aberdeenshire and is the founding father of the Scottish Clan Leslie.

The Battle of Alnwick was an ignominious end to a distinguished thirty-five-year reign by King Malcolm. After Duke William died in 1087, relations with his son King William Rufus became strained, and Malcolm invaded Northumbria in 1091 and again in 1093. On the second foray south, after ravaging the countryside, the Scottish army were ambushed by the Earl of Northumbria, William de Mowbray, somewhere near Alnwick. Malcolm and Edward, his eldest son by Queen Margaret, were killed, and Malcolm's body was buried at Tynemouth Priory, rather than being repatriated to Scotland. There is no precise record of how the news of their deaths was brought to the queen, but she died within days of hearing it. Bartolf, on the other hand, lived to the age of around eighty, dying in 1121.

Aside from the presence of the crucifix, the "And then" facts are also true. William de Mowbray was imprisoned for life after leading an unsuccessful rebellion against King William Rufus in 1095; the king was indeed killed, probably murdered, while out hunting in the New Forest in 1100; and King Henry I's son and heir drowned on the White Ship off the coast of France twenty years later.

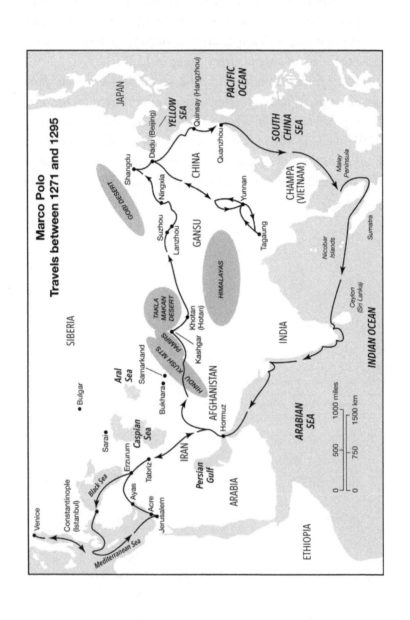

Marco Polo
Travels between 1271 and 1295

Nine

Marco Polo

February 1291 – Beijing, China

The European stepped off the junk boat onto the dockside and waved goodbye to the captain. It had been a good trip, a year-long expedition to Bagan in Burma to negotiate peace terms with the new king there. The journey home, overland to the Hong River Delta, then by sea to Hangzhou and on by the grand canal to the Mongol capital, had taken several weeks longer than expected. But it had been uneventful, and he was unharmed and back amongst friends, never something to be taken lightly on such missions.

This was Marco Polo's seventeenth year in the service of the great Mongol emperor, Kublai Khan, and even after all this time he still marvelled at the role he had been asked to perform. It was not as though he was a wiser or more forceful negotiator than any of the khan's tribal aides. However, as a European and a Christian it seemed that he was given the opportunity to discuss sensitive matters with foreign leaders in circumstances where a Mongol deputation would immediately be considered hostile. He had put it down to curiosity value more than any particular skill, and it had taken him to numerous neighbouring countries on diplomatic assignments for the khan. He was not the only westerner to have arrived in Beijing, but he had won his master's trust like no other.

And therein lay the rub. Seventeen years and still no sign from the khan that he would allow Marco to return to his home town of Venice. The European had used his access to the emperor to request permission, for his father and uncle as well as himself, on numerous occasions and had been flatly rejected. Besides being trusted, he appeared to have made the mistake of becoming indispensable. Now that he was back in Beijing, he would raise the issue again, but he could see no reason why the answer would be different, and he must be careful not to push too hard. For all the benevolence he had shown to Marco, Kublai Khan was a fearsome ruler when it suited him, and a fall from grace could be not only abrupt but fatal. He contemplated the subject as he walked up the hill from the dock, his excitement at the mission's completion tempered by the frustration that had been quietly growing over the last few years.

As he neared the crest of the hill, his thoughts were interrupted by a shout, and he looked up to see his father Niccolo standing outside their lodgings, grinning and gesticulating wildly. Marco had sent a servant ahead with his luggage, and the news of his arrival had evidently been received. He ran the last few paces to the house, and as he hugged his father, his uncle Maffeo emerged to join them.

'Father, uncle, how wonderful to see you,' he panted. 'You both look well, and I want to hear everything that's been going on since I was last here.' These reunions always made him feel like a little boy, even though he was now a grown man in his mid-thirties and considerably more important in the Mongol empire than they were.

'Oh, you will, rest assured, my boy,' said Niccolo. 'And you can tell us all about your trip too, even though we've already heard on the grapevine what a success it has been.' He ushered Marco into the house. 'But first we must feed you. You look very scrawny and dirty too. You're a disgrace to the diplomatic service!' Maffeo burst into laughter with him, and Marco knew that little had changed in the Venetian household.

After washing and changing into fresh clothes, Marco joined the others for supper and recounted the tale of his travels over the previous twelve months. When he had finished, he added that he would need to report to the khan at first light in the morning, and the brothers exchanged glances.

'Dear boy, we have some news,' said Niccolo. 'Last month, envoys arrived from Persia with a message for the emperor from his great nephew Arghun Khan. Apparently Arghun's favourite wife has died, and he's asked Kublai to send him a replacement from her family here. Kublai has agreed and has picked a young princess from Shangdu called Kokochin.' He smiled at his son. 'You're wondering what on earth this has to do with us. Think about it. This could be our chance. The emperor will be sending precious goods halfway round the world, and he'll want someone responsible to look after them on the way. That could be us three. You will have to persuade him, but this is the ideal moment, on the back of what you've achieved in Bagan. We're going home!' He gulped down a large mouthful of rice wine and slammed his drinking mug excitedly onto the dining table, as if it was all arranged.

Marco thought about the conversations he had had with the emperor over the years about returning to Venice. Never before had there been a hook like this on which to hang the request. It could just work, although it would require a delicate approach, and it certainly was not in the bag yet. 'Good news, for sure. I'll talk to him tomorrow,' he said in a measured voice. 'Don't get too excited, though. The success in Bagan can work both ways. He might want me to stay and repeat the process in some other country.' He hesitated, then raised his mug to his father and uncle and chuckled. 'But it's definitely worth a drink.'

Nine hours later, as the sun rose over the eastern horizon, Marco made his way to the palace. He knew from bitter experience that Kublai Khan was an early riser and would be expecting to see him immediately. Perhaps he should even have presented himself the previous evening, since the news of his return would undoubtedly have reached the palace within moments of him arriving at the dock. On the other hand, court business always ceased at sundown, and furthermore, the khan was scrupulous about cleanliness amongst his staff. He would surely have guessed that Marco needed to tidy himself after his long journey. Nonetheless, there was always an edge to any audience with the emperor, and especially this one. He touched the silver crucifix at his neck for good luck, as he had done so many times over the years since leaving Venice.

The imperial palace was positioned at the very centre of the city that Kublai Khan had founded twenty-five years previously. Overlooking the artificial Taiye lake created by the Jin emperors that the Mongols had displaced in their sweep southwards, it was a huge complex of state apartments and government buildings, deliberately constructed to provide visitors with an impression of power and organisation. Marco had been there many times, but he never ceased to be awed by its scale, not to mention the mix of cultures represented by the fabulous artwork, furniture and garden design. It was a perfect reflection of the empire and the emperor himself, he thought, as he was led through the corridors to Kublai's private residence, a hub of energy and civilisation but with an undercurrent of ruthless authority that one ignored at one's peril.

His guide left him facing the familiar double doors to the khan's office, and he knocked. A quavering voice answered him, and he faltered for a moment, wondering who it belonged to. He touched the silver crucifix again, then entered the room to find himself alone with the emperor. He bowed, then looked in astonishment at the man behind the gilt-edged desk, thoroughly unprepared for the change in appearance since he had left Beijing on his mission. The khan had aged several years in that time, shrinking into himself and losing that aura of vibrancy that had been his hallmark for so long. His skin was the colour of faded parchment, stretched taut across his cheekbones and hands; his hair was thin and streaked with white where previously it had been a thick pelt of dark grey, and his robes enveloped him. Only his eyes remained unchanged, their matt bronze pupils boring into Marco as he came to a halt.

'So, my European friend, what have you to say for yourself? Why has it taken so long to return from Bagan? I could have visited the place myself by now and done a better deal too.' The emperor allowed a silence to lengthen before nodding an invitation to respond, and Marco was reminded of the fierce intellect that lay behind the emaciated face. This was the man who had forged an empire across the whole of East Asia in little more than thirty years, and although he may have weakened physically in his descent towards old age, it would be unwise to think his mind was not still scimitar sharp. A cautious reply was necessary, but then again the khan was known to detest servility, preferring ministers to stand up for themselves and earn their continued place at his council. It was a difficult tightrope to walk, and Marco had mastered it better than most. He collected himself, hoping his expression had not betrayed his surprise at the khan's appearance and conscious that much of what he had to tell would have been reported already by the emperor's network of spies.

'Your Excellency, I did not think it appropriate to report to you on my arrival last night, after court business had finished. Forgive me if I have kept you waiting until now. The voyage up the coast from Haiphong was delayed by a typhoon, but the ship's captain picked up time once we were able to leave port. As for the negotiations at Bagan, the new ruler, King Narathihapate's son Kyawswa, has accepted you as overlord and has agreed to pay an annual tribute, in exchange for your troops' withdrawal. The details of the treaty are set out here,' he held out a scroll sealed with the Bagan royal crest that he knew the khan would recognise, 'and the first payment has already been made to your army's commander in the city. It only requires your approval, before the army brings the money back to your exchequer in Yunnan.'

Kublai Khan took the scroll and studied it briefly. Then he said simply, 'What of the kingdom itself? Wealth, armaments, defences? What has changed since we invaded four years ago?' The scene was set, as Marco had known it would be, for a full debriefing, and his credentials as a leading member of that spy network would be tested to the full.

His report from Bagan took most of the morning to deliver, piercing questions from the khan interspersed with tea and the occasional diversion into affairs elsewhere across the Mongol empire. Kublai was evidently pleased with what he heard and, when at last the signal came for Marco to leave, he knew there would be no better moment for his own request.

'Your Excellency, I understand that you are sending a bride to Arghun Khan in Persia. As you know, I am keen to return to my family in Europe. I wondered if you might agree to me escorting the princess to your great nephew and travelling on to my homeland from there. If it pleased you, my father and uncle would accompany me, to help ensure her safe passage, and they could also take goods to sell for you in Europe.' He guessed that the last remark would appeal to the khan, given the emperor's well-known interest in building trading links with the west.

The khan leant back in his chair and smiled. 'Always the negotiator, I see! You are good at what you do, Marco. That's the reason I have kept you in my service for so long, and it is also the reason why you should remain here. But,' he sighed, and waved a languid hand, 'I am tired. Between these walls, my work is almost done, and I shall be handing over the reins of government to my sons in due course. It would be wrong for me to deny you the chance to return home.' He stopped again and fixed his gaze on the European. 'So I will give you my permission to accompany Princess Kokochin to Persia. Subject to two conditions and one observation from an old man.' Marco had listened to the emperor attaching conditions to his terms many times, and he waited in silence.

'First, you will never speak of my plans to step down from running the empire. If I hear that you have done so, I will send warriors to hunt you down, wherever you are in the world, and you will regret the day you were born.' This was no idle threat, Marco needed no convincing of that, and he bowed his head in acknowledgement.

'Secondly, since I am giving you what you ask, you will give me something in exchange.' Another silence grew, then the khan pointed to Marco's chest. 'You will give me your silver cross. I have watched you wear it every day since you first came to my court, and it will be a token of your service to me. You will be able to find a replacement, now that you are heading back to Christian lands.' Marco nodded again, disappointed to lose the crucifix that had brought him his good fortune since leaving Europe but relieved that the price of his release was not higher.

'And, lastly,' the emperor smiled again, mischievously this time, 'I hope you are aware what you have let yourself in for. Kokochin is a beautiful and spirited seventeen-year-old, who knows her own mind. I will be interested to hear how you feel after several months on a small ship with her. I suspect the Bagan king will seem an easy adversary by comparison.'

'Thank you, Your Excellency,' Marco said. 'It has been an honour to serve you, and I know I can speak for my father and uncle in saying we will take a wealth of learning back to Europe from our time amongst your people. We will guard Princess Kokochin with our lives and will deliver her into the good hands of Arghun Khan.' He lifted the silver cross over his head and laid it respectfully on the desk in front of the emperor. Then he bowed again before retreating backwards from the room. The deal was done, but he was mystified by the khan's final comments. Surely a teenage girl, even a princess, could not be too tricky for three grown men to cope with.

*

April 1291 – Beijing, China

Kublai Khan watched as the princess turned the cross over in her hand. 'Are you sure you understand my wishes?' he asked. 'This cross belongs to Marco Polo, the youngest of the three Europeans that will escort you to Persia. He does not know that I have given it to you, but when you arrive you are to return it to him with my thanks. He is a good man who has served me well, and he will have earned a gift in delivering you safely to your new husband. It is important to him as a sign of his religion.' The khan was standing in the palace arboretum, bidding farewell to the girl before she left Beijing for the port of Hangzhou where the ships bound for Persia were waiting to set sail.

'Yes, Your Excellency, I understand. I promise I will look after it carefully on the journey, and when the time comes, I will make it clear the gift is from you.' Kokochin bowed her head in deference to the emperor, and he breathed more easily. He had dreaded a repeat of the histrionics that had occurred when he first told her about Arghun Khan's request, but she had evidently come round to the prospect of the arranged marriage and the long voyage in store with the Europeans.

'Good,' he said, 'then it is time you left the city. Your family will accompany you on the grand canal to Hangzhou, where you will find Marco and the others waiting for you. They are provisioning the ships and hope to be ready to leave in twenty days, so you will have some time to spare, but do not delay. Now go, and be sure to honour your husband when you meet him.' He kissed her on the forehead, then turned to hobble away across the gardens towards the palace.

Alone amongst the trees, the princess looked again at the crucifix. To her it represented everything she hated about the emperor's orders. She was rich, well connected, with plenty of handsome men to do her bidding in her home town of Shangdu, the old Mongol capital before Beijing had been built. She had her life before her, yet it was being ruined by marriage to someone she had never heard of until two months ago, a man twice her age who lived in a country on the other side of the world. Worse still in the short term, she would have to spend months on a boat with three Europeans, who her family had warned her to despise as ignorant, uncultured and self-serving foreigners. She had reluctantly accepted her fate regarding the marriage, knowing that she could not flout the emperor's will openly, but there was no way she was going to hand over the crucifix in thanks for the enforced guardianship. The khan would never find out whether Marco had received it, and it seemed to her that the silver could be put to much better use than a Christian cross, if she could organise it before the trip to Hangzhou. A good silver-backed glass mirror, like the ones that she had seen in the Beijing markets, would be a vital accessory if she was to look her best on meeting her damned husband and, more importantly, if she was to keep him under her thumb in future. She headed for the palace gates, wondering where to find a metalworker in the city streets beyond.

*

May 1293 – Hormuz, Persia

It was hard work cutting across the current of the channel, the tide running against them, but gradually the three junks edged their way towards land. The day's sailing had been desperately slow, a thin and fickle breeze making helmsmanship difficult, and Marco wondered whether they would even reach the port of Hormuz before nightfall. If not, they would be forced to endure yet another night's delay to their arrival, which he did not relish explaining to the princess. There had been far too many of those discussions already, and her patience had run dry many months ago.

For their voyage to have taken so long, over two years in all, seemed barely credible, yet when Marco considered the individual events that had befallen them, it was a miracle they were here at all. The journey had begun well, suspiciously well in retrospect. Kublai Khan had made fourteen ships available, each packed with goods for the Polos to trade on his behalf in India and Persia, and they had enjoyed an easy run down the South China Sea to Singapura. There they had berthed for additional supplies before venturing northwards into the Strait of Malacca. Ten days out their luck had turned, a terrifying wall of water engulfing them with no forewarning whatsoever. Half their ships had been lost without trace, and of the remaining seven that had limped into the ravaged port of Banda Aceh at the northern tip of Sumatra, another two had been deemed damaged beyond repair. They learnt later that what they had suffered was a tsunami, the worst in living memory, responsible for death and destruction on a massive scale in the region, and that their experience was by no means unusual. Refitting the remaining five vessels had taken almost six months, the single grain of comfort for Marco, as he fumed at the delay, being that Kokochin and all three Europeans had survived unharmed.

At last, they had set sail again across the Indian ocean, only to be intercepted off the north-east coast of Sri Lanka by a hostile fleet of Tamil boats and forced into harbour. The Tamils had heard enough of the Mongol advances into Burma to consider them enemies, and it had taken nine months under house arrest for Marco to persuade their king they meant no harm. Even then, only four of the ships had been permitted to continue their journey, the fifth being confiscated and its crew pressed into slavery. Following their release, further time had been expended visiting three cities on the Indian mainland to sell the emperor's wares. At least a sizeable profit had been made, on which the Europeans had been promised a healthy margin, but it was still meagre by comparison to the value of the goods that had gone to the seabed off Sumatra.

The final leg of the journey, up the west side of India and into the Arabian sea, had been relatively smooth, and as they entered the Gulf of Oman, Marco had been rash enough to think their troubles were over. After the three years and numerous hurdles he had endured travelling from Venice to Kublai Khan's court two decades previously, he should have known better. A cyclone off the coast of Muscat had ripped their sails to tatters, sweeping several crew members overboard and sinking one more ship. Again, the princess and the three Europeans had survived, by some extraordinary fluke, although in Kokochin's case it had been partly due to Marco's quick reactions. As soon as the storm had struck, he had strapped her to the central mast, while he and the other men battled to keep their vessel from capsizing. The mast itself had snapped just above her head, smashing down onto the deck behind her and crushing two Mongol sailors to death, but she had emerged unscathed bar a vicious gash above her ear from a flying wooden splinter. Thankfully, the storm had subsided as quickly as it had arisen, and in the calm that followed, they had been able to carry out the rough repairs required to take them into the shelter of the Hormuz waters. They were alive, well and now just hours away from their destination. But with only three battered ships and barely a score of crew and passengers, Marco was bound to admit they presented a sorry sight to the Persians compared to the richly furnished imperial fleet that had left Hangzhou.

A flash of light from the other side of the ship caught his eye, and he looked round to see the princess inspecting herself in a glass hand-mirror. It was a ritual she had repeated hundreds, if not thousands, of times over the last two years, and it had been a source of unreasonable irritation to him in the early months. There was no denying she was a pretty girl, but Marco and his father and uncle had found her impossibly vain and self-centred when they had first set sail. She had no concept of how to behave on board, expecting the entire crew to wait on her as servants and grumbling incessantly to the Europeans. Her bedspace was too cramped; the food was inedible; the weather was either too hot or too cold; in short she was a spoilt brat, and that was before the tsunami and the detention in Sri Lanka. Marco and she had held furious arguments about the length of the voyage, the route, the blame he should bear for their various misfortunes, and, most of all, why she was being sent to marry an unknown middle-aged man against her will. In the end Marco had simply ignored her, reminding himself daily that she was his passport out of China and how accurate Kublai Khan's last words had been.

Looking at her now, however, he realised that for once her eagerness to check her appearance was understandable. The cut above her ear had healed well, but it still showed through the hair he had cut off in order to treat it, and she was rightly concerned about how it must look. Even without that, no girl, princess or pauper, could have undergone the long journey without worrying about the reception awaiting her, and it was natural for her to want to be well groomed before they landed at Hormuz. He also had the impression that she was less antagonistic towards him since the storm off Muscat. It would be an exaggeration to say that he felt sorry for her, or that he would miss her once he had left Persia on his way to Venice, but he could appreciate her nervousness now that her journey's end was so close.

As he watched her, she thrust the mirror into a pocket and walked across the deck towards him. He braced himself for a complaint about the time it was taking to make landfall, but she smiled and leant against the ship's side next to him in companionable silence. After some moments studying the wash flaring out in the blue water behind them, she turned to him with a more serious expression.

'Marco, I owe you an apology. My eyes have been opened in the last few weeks.' Marco was unsure how to answer, and she continued. 'I am no longer the awkward teenager you took on board in Hangzhou. Naturally, this journey is not what I wanted, but it was the emperor's order, just as having you as my escort was. Without you I might have been a slave to the Tamils by now or drowned in the storm last month. I owe my life to you, and I also realise that I have not been an easy person to travel with.'

'Kokochin, it has been a long and difficult journey for all

of us,' said Marco diplomatically, unprepared for the frankness of the little speech.

'Maybe,' she answered, 'but I also have a confession to make.' She picked the hand-mirror out of her pocket and once again it glittered in the sunlight. 'You will have seen this many times, but you don't know what it is.'

Marco was mildly annoyed. 'We do have glass mirrors in Europe, you know, although I admit I've never seen one coated in silver like that before. I've watched you peering into it every day for the last two years. Of course I recognise it.'

'No, you don't,' Kokochin repeated firmly. 'I had it made in Beijing before we left. The silver came from the cross you gave to the emperor when you left his service. He asked me to return the cross to you when your mission to bring me to Arghun Khan was completed.' She lowered her eyes in embarrassment. 'It was his way of saying thank you for a difficult task, and I am ashamed to say that I had it melted down and turned into a mirror that I could use instead.' Then she raised her head again and said more brightly, 'So now I give it to you, with my thanks, as well as his. And although it is not the sign of your religion that it once was, the traders in the market told me it is a better mirror than you will ever find in Europe!'

Marco had confronted many curious and unexpected incidents in his career, but none could match this for sheer out-of-the-blue surprise. In the terror of the Sumatran tsunami and the Muscat cyclone, and the frustration of house arrest in Sri Lanka, he had often considered whether their voyage would have been different if he had been wearing the crucifix. Kublai Khan's insistence that he hand it over had always seemed an odd and peevish condition of his release from Beijing, and he had imagined it still sitting on the emperor's table, quietly tarnishing in the dust of the imperial palace. He was delighted to be reunited with it, even if the form had changed, and he guessed from his childhood memories of markets in Venice that what the traders had told the princess was true.

'Princess, it is I who should thank you, for your honesty,' he said. 'I would have been none the wiser if you had kept the mirror. As you say, the silver backing is a novelty to us in Europe, and I will take it home and show it off to everyone there as a symbol of my time with the emperor and with you. Apology accepted. And now,' he pointed over her shoulder, and she turned to look behind her, 'we are out of the main channel at last. We will be in the harbour within an hour. Welcome to Persia and to your new life.'

*

And then…

After travelling overland to Constantinople, Marco, Niccolo and Maffeo Polo return as wealthy men to Venice, which they find to be at war with the Republic of Genoa. Marco is captured in a naval skirmish and imprisoned by the Genoans for three years. As a mark of his status within Venice he is permitted certain personal effects in his cell, including the silver-backed mirror, and as a bribe towards achieving his freedom, he gives the mirror to his gaoler.

The gaoler has the silver from the mirror melted down into a disc, to avoid detection. The disc is traded many times around the western Mediterranean over the next two centuries, ultimately falling into the hands of King Charles I of Spain.

*

Author's Note

Marco Polo was by no means the first European to travel to China – amongst many others his father Niccolo and uncle Maffeo had journeyed there on the "Silk Road" and met Kublai Khan in the decade before their expedition with Marco. However, he was the first to leave a detailed chronicle of his travels. Historians have questioned whether Marco himself experienced all the events and places that he described, but his account is considered largely authentic. The Europeans took over three years to reach China, arriving at Kublai Khan's summer palace in Shangdu (or Xanadu, in Inner Mongolia) in 1274. Between 1275 and 1291, Marco served the emperor on numerous diplomatic missions, both within China and to neighbouring countries. The extent of his role is uncertain, and I have probably exaggerated it here, but he was evidently considered useful to the Mongol leader, since his pleas to return to Europe were declined on several occasions. By the time Kublai Khan released him, the emperor was suffering from ill-health and depression, ultimately dying in 1294 at the age of seventy-eight.

The story of Arghun Khan requesting a new bride from his deceased wife's family, and the emperor sending the seventeen-year-old Princess Kokochin to him, is true. It is unclear whether Marco himself prompted the emperor to let him act as escort, but the three Europeans accompanied the princess in a fourteen-ship fleet sailing to Persia, reaching Hormuz in 1293. The tsunami, the capture by Tamils and the cyclone off Muscat are fictions, but the voyage was said to have been perilous, with only a small number of the original boats and crew reaching their destination following a long weather-related delay in Sumatra and various visits to Indian cities. Thereafter, the Polos travelled overland to Constantinople, returning to Venice in 1295. On their arrival, Marco appears to have been swept up in a war being fought between the Republics of Venice and Genoa. After being captured in a naval battle in 1296, he was held in a Genoan prison for three years, where he related his story to an author and fellow captive, Rustichello da Pisa. The Travels of Marco Polo was published following Marco's release in 1299.

The first hand-held mirrors were simple discs of polished stone or metal, dating back to the Bronze Age, with low levels of reflectivity. By the third century CE, metal-backed glass was being used in Egypt, Europe and Asia, and this process was enhanced by the development of silver-mercury amalgam coatings in China as early as 500. Such technology does not appear to have been commonplace in Europe until the fourteenth century. The modern silvered-glass mirror was invented by a German scientist, Justus von Liebig, in 1835.

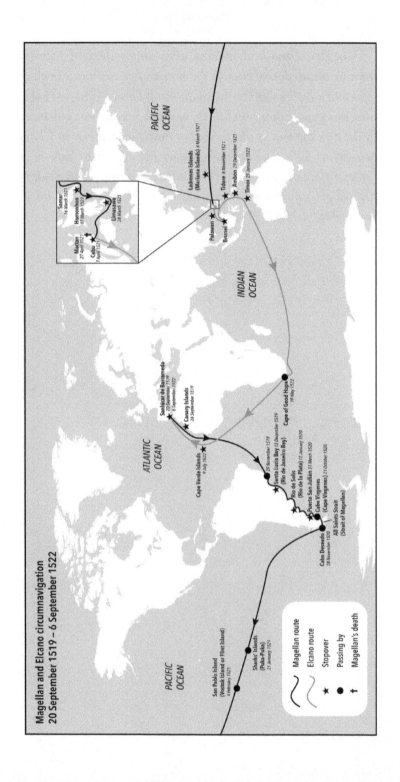

Magellan and Elcano circumnavigation
20 September 1519 – 6 September 1522

PACIFIC
OCEAN

PACIFIC
OCEAN

INDIAN
OCEAN

ATLANTIC
OCEAN

Ladrones Islands
(Mariana Islands) 6 March 1521

Tidore 8 November 1521

Ambon 29 December 1521

Timor 25 January 1522

Samar 16 March 1521

Homonhon 17 March 1521

Limasawa 28 March 1521

Mactan 27 April 1521

Cebu 7 April 1521

Palawan

Brunei

Santúcar de Barrameda
20 September 1519
5 September 1522

Canary Islands
26 September 1519

Cape Verde Islands
9 July 1522

Cape of Good Hope
19 May 1522

Rio de Solis

Santa Lucia Bay 13 December 1519
(Rio de Janeiro Bay)

29 November 1519

Puerto San Julián 31 March 1520

Cabo Virgenes 17 January 1520

Cabo Virgenes 21 October 1520
(Cape Virgenes)

Cabo Deseado
28 November 1520

All Saints Strait
(Strait of Magellan)

San Pablo Island
(Vostok Island or Flint Island)
4 February 1521

Sharks' Islands
(Puka-Puka) 21 January 1521

Magellan route

Elcano route

Stopover

Passing by

Magellan's death

Ten

Ferdinand Magellan

August 1519 – Seville, Spain

The city folk lining the square had witnessed the launch of many expeditions from the riverside wharf in the previous three decades, but never with this level of anticipation. Rumours had been brewing for several weeks, and today their truth would at last be put to the test. The five ships were waiting on their moorings in the middle of the river, bows swinging gently into the ebbing tide, and most of the crews were now on board. Only the captains and a handful of junior officers remained on shore, ready to be ferried out on the tenders tied to the wharf, and the impatience of their leader was clear for all to see as he paced backwards and forwards issuing final instructions to his team. Captain General Ferdinand Magellan had been planning this voyage for over two years, and he longed to feel the breeze of the open sea on his face again. More than anyone else on the wharf, though, he knew the importance of waiting an hour or two more, the value of a public farewell from his sponsor.

A faint fanfare of trumpets sounded in the streets leading from the Alcazar, and several minutes later, the clatter of hooves on cobbles could be heard above the buzz of the crowd. Then an ornate carriage rolled into the square, three pairs of white horses at its traces, followed by a bodyguard of a dozen riders dressed in the royal livery of blue and gold. The procession came to a halt in front of the wharf, and the crowds strained to see the occupant of the carriage as he stepped out into the midday sun. This was the first visit to Seville by their young king, Charles I, ruler of huge domains across western Europe but seldom seen around Spain other than in the ancient Castilian capital of Valladolid. The crowd burst into applause at the confirmation of the city gossip – the king really was backing this journey beyond the known limits of the New World and had taken the unprecedented step of coming to see Magellan off in person. Their opinion of the outspoken Portuguese sailor and self-styled explorer would have to be adjusted since he so clearly had the king's ear, and purse.

King Charles acknowledged the crowd with a brief wave, then stepped onto the wharf where Magellan waited respectfully to be addressed. 'Well, Captain General Magellan, the big day has arrived. Are you ready?'

'Yes, Your Majesty, we are indeed. We have a full complement of crew, 270 in all, two years' supplies and the most up-to-date charts in the world. No other expedition has ever been this well prepared. We are honoured by your visit here to mark our departure.' Magellan gestured towards the four men immediately behind him. 'Let me introduce my ships' captains. Señor de Cartagena on the *San Antonio*, Señor de Quesada on the *Concepción*, Señor Serrano on the *Santiago*, and Señor Mendoza on the *Victoria*.' One by one, the men stepped forward and bowed to the king. 'And lastly, my assistant Señor Pigafetta, who will accompany me on the flagship *Trinidad*. He is a scholar, originally from Venice, who will act as chronicler for the voyage so that you have a full record of our findings.'

'Excellent,' said the king, smiling at the captains, each of them experienced sailors many years older than him. 'I wish you all good fortune, and I look forward to your return with whatever riches the southern continent has to offer. Now, I believe you have a tide to catch. Do not let me detain you,' he looked meaningfully towards the tenders, 'but Señor Magellan, there is one small matter to discuss, if you would be so good as to stay behind another few minutes.'

The four captains bowed once again to the king, then collected their junior officers and stepped down into their individual tenders where oarsmen waited to row them out to their ships. Once they were out of earshot, the king spoke again, in a quiet and earnest voice that neither his retinue nor the crowd in the square would hear. 'Señor Pigafetta may stay. What I wish to remind you of, Magellan, is the utmost importance of this expedition, and what I say must not be shared with the other captains or crew until it is absolutely necessary. Is that clear?' Magellan nodded vigorously, and the Venetian scholar added in broken Spanish, 'You have my word.'

'As we discussed last year in Valladolid,' the king went on, 'thanks to a treaty twenty-five years ago, the Portuguese command the trade routes heading east to the Indies round the southern tip of Africa. Spain needs to control an alternative route to the Spice Islands heading westwards instead. Your commission is to find that route, a western passage through the southern landmass of the Americas. You told me that if such a passage can be found, the Spice Islands will only be a short distance beyond. On no account must the Portuguese find out the purpose of your expedition, so until you find the western passage, you are simply mapping the coast of the Americas. Understood?'

'Yes, Your Majesty,' Magellan replied with a bland expression; this was not the moment to point out that the idea of seeking a western passage, potentially so lucrative to Spain, had originally been his, not the king's, and he had set out the entire concept of the expedition in his visit to the palace in Valladolid eighteen months previously. They had struck a deal at the time whereby the king would finance the sourcing and fitting out of the fleet required for the voyage, and Magellan would take a percentage of the profits generated from any successful trade route established. He had no intention of allowing anyone, of whatever nationality, to steal the opportunity from him, and the fact that he was working for the Spanish rather than his home country was a simple matter of market forces. King Charles of Spain had agreed to fund him, whereas King Manuel of Portugal had refused.

'Good,' said King Charles. 'In which case, I will keep you no longer, other than to give you this.' He opened his hand to reveal a silver disc which he proffered to Magellan. The Captain General took it and inspected it closely, noting the familiar double-headed eagle crest of the Habsburg monarchy clearly defined on one side, the inscription *WP 1519 AD* on the other. 'You may consider it the royal seal of the commission,' the king explained, unnecessarily. 'It will remind you who you are working for, lest you are tempted to return to your Portuguese roots, and why. If your quest is successful, you will be a rich man, and I trust you will return the disc to me, since its value will be insignificant to you by then. Señor Pigafetta,' he glanced at the Venetian, 'you are my witness to this, and I charge you with the task of keeping him honest!' He gave a short laugh and added, in a loud voice over his shoulder as he walked to the carriage, 'Good luck, Magellan; be sure to bring back plenty new maps for me.'

*

February 1521 – Pacific Ocean

Seventy-seven days since leaving the shelter of the Patagonian channel, and still not a sign of habitable land. The Captain General had planned for all manner of eventualities, but he had not envisaged this. From his voyages to the Indies with the Portuguese navy a decade previously, he knew how to find the Spice Islands when approached from Singapore, and he had consulted numerous cartographers during the preparations in Spain for an estimate of their location when approached from the Americas. As a result, he had calculated a sailing time of no more than three or four days across the open water they had discovered beyond the American landmass, the calm and gentle ocean that he planned to name the Pacific. It was not so much that they were lost – he knew they were crossing the equator that day – but the Spice Islands seemed to be.

Standing on the foredeck of the *Trinidad*, Magellan scanned the horizon for the hundredth time that morning in hope of deliverance, then turned his thoughts to the practical issues facing the fleet. He had been assailed by problems almost since the start of the voyage, and the excitement of finding the western passage through the lands inhabited by the Patagones tribes now seemed little more than a brief diversion. First an attempted mutiny led by three of his ships' captains, in which two had been killed and the third had been left to rot on an island south of the River Plate estuary; then the sinking of the *Santiago* in a storm, followed by the disappearance of the *San Antonio* in what Magellan suspected was an act of desertion. Personally, he considered himself well rid of the Spanish skippers involved, since they had been fostering bad blood amongst all the crews with their open insubordination towards him. However, morale had been made worse by the loss of the two ships and, with the western passage discovery a distant memory, it was falling lower by the day now, as the remaining three vessels sailed on into the unknown with ever decreasing stocks of food and water.

In normal circumstances no expedition would have set forth with so few provisions, and Magellan cursed himself daily for the mistaken estimate of their voyage across the Pacific. The original supplies of fresh beef and pork, cheese, almonds and fruit had long since been exhausted, as had the additions taken on board in the port of San Julian at the time of the mutiny. Like many before them, the crews had fallen back on their stores of salted meat and hardtack biscuit, supplemented by seal meat obtained on the Patagonian shores. Now, two and a half months on, the salted meat was all but finished, and the seal meat had begun to spoil in the tropical heat. Only the hardtack remained, and that was infested with weevils. On the *Trinidad*, the men were reduced to eating rats caught in the ship's hold, and conditions were no better on the *Concepción* and the *Victoria*. The Captain General had been aware of this for almost a week. Today's problem was drinking water.

Copious quantities of fresh water had been taken on board from the shores of the western passage, in temperatures so low that it had turned to ice and ruptured the staves of some of the storage barrels. Even allowing for this leakage, Magellan had considered the ships to be generously provisioned for the short journey across the Pacific. Only after seven weeks did he begin to exercise caution, cutting the daily ration by half. After a further two weeks he had halved it again, confident at least that the dwindling supplies were of good quality. The previous day, the end of the eleventh week, he had inspected the *Trinidad*'s stores in person and realised that what little water remained was fouling rapidly in the equatorial conditions. He had signalled the other two ships immediately, proposing a pooling arrangement across the three vessels per head of crew, but their captains had hotly rejected his suggestion. If they were to be believed, their supplies were even more limited than his, and it was not worth the waste of time and energy to challenge them. Magellan shuddered as he remembered the rank odour and slick yellowish tinge of the liquid he had scooped from a handful of the barrels below and wondered how long they could survive on it. Several men amongst the fleet had already died, from malnutrition rather than thirst so far, but it would not take long for the numbers to rise dramatically now that the water was blighted. The solution, he thought bleakly, was to steer a middle course, halving the ration yet again so that the supply lasted longer and the men were less likely to die of poisoning in the meantime. A captain's job was all about playing the odds, and after all, land might be sighted at any moment.

Stepping down from the foredeck to the midship, Magellan summoned the officer of the watch and gave his order for the water ration to be halved on all three vessels. 'Make it clear,' he said in his usual strident voice, 'that this applies to every single person, myself included, without exception. Anyone found to be taking more than his share will be flogged.' The man swallowed involuntarily, then repeated the order to the signaller and to the quartermaster. Magellan watched as the news rippled round the decks, aware of the murderous glances he was receiving. Since the mutiny, he never forgot that, in the eyes of the largely Spanish crew, he was a traitorous Portuguese whose competence as Captain General was diminishing with every new dawn in this vast, empty ocean. He was a man of supreme confidence in his own abilities, but a knife in his guts would mean one less person for the crew to share the water supply with. He glowered back at the men, daring them to confront him, then headed to the shade of his cabin where he found the chronicler Pigafetta poring over a chart.

'Antonio,' he said, slumping into a chair, 'I fear you are wasting your time. If the chart were any use, we would have found the Spice Islands two months ago. If you want to help me, tell me how to turn five barrels of dirty water into fifteen fresh ones instead.' He sighed heavily, in a rare display of fatigue, and went on to describe his findings in the hold and the order he had just issued.

The chronicler was unused to being consulted on practical matters like this. Throughout the voyage, he had spent his time keeping a meticulous log of the fleet's progress, recording the weather, the sailing conditions, the flora and fauna found on land and at sea and the night skies used in their navigation. He had also documented the events of the mutiny in detail, although at the Captain General's instruction, he had done so in a separate, private ledger. Magellan had been concerned ever since the assumed desertion of the *San Antonio* back to Spain that a distorted version of the uprising would reach King Charles before he could explain it personally. Theft of the *Trinidad*'s log would leave him exposed to the lies of his enemies, that he had defied the king's orders and led his ships into unnecessary danger and destruction, so a secret record was required. Although Pigafetta had been hired by Magellan, he had a detached, scholarly view of life, and he prided himself on the unbiased and independent nature of his reports. Magellan trusted him completely in the role for which he had been employed but did not normally seek his advice in the business of running the ship.

There was a long silence while Pigafetta pondered the

question, his eyes wandering vaguely round the cabin in search of inspiration. The Captain General waited, well used to the unhurried nature of the man's deliberations. At last, Pigafetta spoke, in his usual sombre accented voice. 'Master, I can't think of a way to improve the water in the barrels, but I might be able to help you with your own share of it. You see the disc in there, the one the king gave you in Seville.' He pointed to a dry inkwell fixed to Magellan's desk. 'It's long been known – as far back as the ancient Greeks – that silver can act as a purifier in water. If you put the disc in the bottom of your drinking mug after you receive your ration each day, and leave it for an hour or two, it may clean the water. There would be no point dropping it into an entire barrel, but in a small container it might make a difference.'

Magellan stood up and picked the silver disc out of the pot. In the early stages of the voyage, he had kept it locked in a drawer, indifferent to the king's tokenism. After the mutiny and the loss of the *Santiago*, however, he had carried it in his pocket instead, oddly comforted by its presence next to his body. In the jubilation of finding the western passage, he had even fished it out and kissed it. But once the food supplies had begun to run out, he had thrown it into the inkwell in fury at his ignorance and misfortune. It had lain there ever since, a malevolent reminder whenever he entered his cabin of his miscalculation on the distance still to be covered. He studied it for a moment, flipping it over in his hand several times to see the crest and the inscription. 'A cleanser, eh?' he said. 'Well, I'll try anything once, and if it saves my life then I'll even give it back to the king.' Then he raised his head to look at the Venetian. 'Let's hope the Greeks knew what they were talking about. Silver can't be any more poisonous than what's in the water already. And since you've come up with the theory, you must take your chance with me. We will drink our rations together.'

'Thank you, master,' said Pigafetta lugubriously. 'My advice would be not to mention it to anyone else, in case they steal the disc. You are the person most likely to lead us towards land, so we need you alive.'

'I'm glad we agree on that,' Magellan replied, without a trace of sarcasm. 'Just remember to tell the king.'

The little fleet continued for a further twenty-one days before making landfall. By the time they were able to find fresh food and water, nineteen men had perished in the first venture into the Pacific Ocean by Europeans, and a further thirty were severely ill. The Captain General and the chronicler had survived, unharmed.

*

27 April 1521 – Mactan Island, Philippines

Dawn was still an hour away when the *Trinidad* dropped anchor in the shallow bay, two arrow flights' distance from the shore. In the dark, the pilot was wary of the sharp coral and dared not venture closer in. A tender was lowered into the water and a message dispatched to the chieftain of the island, Datu Lapulapu, in Magellan's final attempt to reach a peaceful outcome. It proved futile. As the sun rose, the messenger returned with an unequivocal response from the native leader. He would neither recognise the Christian God nor pay the tribute to the Spanish king demanded by the Europeans.

Magellan was enraged. Mactan was a tiny satellite cay to the much larger island of Cebu, whose king, Rajah Humabon, had welcomed the Europeans with open arms. He had offered to supply the fleet with food and had allowed himself and many of his subjects to be baptised as Christians. With his encouragement, almost all the chieftains nearby had followed his example, Lapulapu being the single exception. The early morning message had been his last chance. Now a less subtle form of persuasion was required.

The Captain General had assembled a force of fifty men before sailing from Cebu, in anticipation of the current impasse. Ferrying them onto the beach, a dozen or so at a time in the tender, would leave the early arrivals dangerously exposed to an ambush by Lapulapu. Instead, it was evident in the light of day that they could wade into the cay, and he led the way by jumping down into the water. He foresaw little real resistance. He and his men were wearing helmets and body armour and carrying a murderous array of muskets, axes and swords. The battle, if it came to that, would be brief and heavily one-sided.

At the front of the raiding party, halfway to the shore and still up to his waist in water, Magellan became sharply aware of two things. The men's muskets were now soaked and useless due to the foam-crested waves rolling in from the bay, and several hundred natives had suddenly appeared at the top of the beach in front of them. There was nothing to be done. He plunged on, shouting for the others to follow him and for those few who had stayed on board the *Trinidad* to begin shooting. Musket balls and crossbow bolts began to whistle overhead, but it was immediately apparent that the range was too much to make an impact.

As he splashed his way out of the surf, Magellan could see that Lapulapu's warriors were carrying lances of sharpened bamboo and close-range bows. They were yelling and waving their weapons belligerently but not as yet pressing their advantage in an attack. In the curious lull that occurred while the rest of the raiders joined him at the centre of the mile-long beach, the Captain General was able to estimate the opposition's numbers more accurately: over a thousand of them and more pouring down the sand dunes with every minute that passed. His temper boiled at their chieftain's insolence. The man needed to be taught a lesson, and if a frontal assault against such numbers was madness, then he knew an alternative.

'This way,' he called, running to his left along the sand in the direction of a group of thatched huts on a grassy knoll above some rocks at the far end of the beach. Smoke curled from their chimneys, and as he came nearer, he shouted to the sailors alongside him, 'Burn them down, all of them.' Women and children scattered in terror at the sight of the raiders rushing towards them, and Magellan's men wasted no time, hacking doors down, upturning firepits and throwing burning logs up onto the roofs. The dried reed-thatch caught fire instantly, flames devouring walls and ceilings and thick yellow-grey smoke billowing across the beach in the light breeze. The settlement was reduced to ash in minutes and, as fast as it had begun, the crackle of the inferno subsided. Only then did the Europeans hear another noise.

The Mactan warriors had watched the destruction of the huts in horror, hesitating as they waited for their leader Datu Lapulapu to join them on the beach and issue his orders. Now the chieftain had arrived, wearing his royal headdress and wielding an iron-tipped spear, and he bellowed his command. As one, over a thousand voices launched their battle cry, a blood-curdling ululation piercing the smoke that obscured the Europeans' view of the warriors' assault. Arrows began to rain down on the charred grass short of where Magellan's men stood, and he shouted at them to regroup around him. 'Stick together, and we can fight our way back to the boat. Their arrows and lances are just soft bamboo; our armour will protect us. With me!' and he began to run the short distance towards the sea, his sword drawn and ready.

He had hardly gone ten paces before he felt something smack into his leg, and he saw an arrow jutting from his calf. He reached down to wrench it out, blood spurting over his hand from the torn flesh, and was suddenly aware of the pain. He hobbled onwards, watching as other men around him were hit and remembering with dread the rumour he had heard on Cebu about the natives' weapons being dipped in poison. To his surprise, the chronicler Pigafetta appeared at his side, an unlikely soldier who the Captain General had pressed into joining the foray onto the island to ensure the event was faithfully recorded. Pigafetta put an arm under his shoulder, and the two men staggered down the knoll, Magellan panting, 'Antonio, listen to me. If I die here, be sure to tell the king in Spain I found the western passage. And take the silver disc with you, to show I'd already dodged death once.'

As they approached the rocks above the beach, the drifting smoke cleared, and Magellan realised the scale of the battle facing them. Hundreds of natives were strung out along the half-mile of sand, racing towards them, the chieftain at their head, while others could be seen circling round on the high ground behind the dunes to attack their rear. The way to the water immediately below the rocks was clear, and they might be able to cut their way through the first few warriors running alongside Lapulapu before being intercepted by the mass behind him. With Pigafetta's help, he scrambled over the rocks, the rest of his men all around him, then jumped down into the breaking waves. His injured leg folded beneath him, and he struggled to regain his footing, his chest plate and helmet weighing him down in the thigh-deep water. The brief delay was enough for Lapulapu to come within range, and he launched his heavy metalled spear.

The spear caught Magellan square on the sternum, splitting the chest plate and thumping him back down into the surf. Pigafetta pulled him upright, and as the attackers swarmed around them, another lance struck the Captain General in the neck. 'Leave me,' he gasped, collapsing under the water's surface for the third time, and the Venetian knew it was hopeless trying to save his master. On every side the Europeans were fighting for their lives, the waves churning red with blood as they washed over a score of half-submerged bodies. Pigafetta joined the remaining rabble, and they fled into the deeper water towards the boat. Only once did he look back, to see the barbarians hacking at Magellan and the other abandoned men on the shoreline in a final convulsion of killing.

*

September 1522 – Sanlucar de Barrameda, Spain

With her acting captain Juan Sebastián Elcano at the helm, the *Victoria* edged her way into the harbour, an exhausted fragment of the five-strong fleet that had set sail from Seville three years before. By most yardsticks, the expedition had been an utter disaster: four ships lost, one way or another, some 250 men dead or missing, including the Captain General, no rich cargo to sell in the bazaars, and the *Victoria* herself now barely afloat. They had found the fabled western passage, to be sure, but it was too far south and too dangerous to serve as a viable trading route to the Indies and was therefore of little commercial use to the king. And yet, as Elcano prepared to disembark, he reckoned that the momentous news he had to report would make him wealthy and famous for the rest of his life. The Basque sailor was the first man to circumnavigate the world, a dream held by seafarers and cartographers for centuries, and he was going to milk it for all it was worth. The story would need to be told with care, but that would be easily arranged. Magellan would be a mere footnote in history, especially once the events of the mutiny had been suitably revised and the loss of the four ships attributed to his incompetence. For the price of their lives, the few surviving crew members could be relied upon to support Elcano's version of events, all except the chronicler Pigafetta, who would need to be silenced. He had been Magellan's man from the beginning, and he would be dispatched quietly to the bottom of the harbour that night, before anyone was permitted to leave the ship.

As soon as the ship docked, the harbour master came on board to greet Elcano. He had a standing instruction from King Charles to tell Magellan and any other surviving captains from the expedition to report to Valladolid with all speed. Elcano received the news with delight. His plan was already working; he would have Magellan's prize money in his pocket within days, and his feat would be the talk of Europe within weeks. He explained that the *Victoria* was the only remaining vessel of the fleet and that he had nursed it home with great difficulty from the Indies. It had been a desperate business from start to finish, the death of the Captain General being just one of the many misfortunes endured. He concluded by inviting the harbour master to join him in his cabin in a toast to the king, and then he ushered the man back down the gangway. Now he must speak to the crew and, most importantly, find Pigafetta.

Antonio Pigafetta was not only a chronicler and a scholar, but he was also a keen student of human nature, and he had watched Elcano grow in stature and self-belief ever since the rout on Mactan. The Basque's original role had been as pilot of the *Victoria*, and he had been an enthusiastic participant in the mutiny under that ship's captain Mendoza. In the aftermath, with Mendoza dead, he had been forgiven by Magellan, but

Pigafetta had privately questioned his integrity from then on. When the *Concepción* had been abandoned in Cebu after Magellan's death and the loss of so many other lives, Elcano had wasted no time in seizing control of the *Victoria*, and when the new captain of the *Trinidad* had plotted a course back towards the Americas, the Basque had insisted on taking the *Victoria* west towards Africa instead. It was then that he had taken Pigafetta from the *Trinidad* to the *Victoria*, notionally to use his observation and mapping skills but really, the Venetian scholar suspected, to keep a close eye on him. As they neared Spain in the final days of their journey home, Elcano had become increasingly boastful of his success in sailing round the world. Magellan's extraordinary efforts as navigator and leader were barely mentioned, and it was evident Elcano was positioning himself to receive the acclaim that belonged to the Captain General. From there, it took little imagination to see that Pigafetta's version of events might be damaging and that he could be in mortal danger. As soon as the door to Elcano's cabin closed behind the captain and the harbour master, he eased his way across the main deck, and when the rest of the crew were distracted for a moment, he jumped up, unseen, onto the harbour wall. Walking away, inconspicuous amongst the crowds thronging the waterfront, he could feel the silver disc and his secret journal of the mutiny bumping against his ribs in the pocket of his coat. Like Elcano, he was on his way to Valladolid, to see the king.

Three weeks later, Pigafetta stood in front of King Charles in the Habsburg palace and presented his verbal report. It had been a slow journey across the Spanish mainland, complicated by his need to avoid the main roads and hostels where Elcano's spies might be looking out for him. He had arrived in Valladolid the previous evening and, sitting in the shadows of a tavern eating a long overdue meal, he had listened to talk of

Elcano's great deeds. It was clear that the captain had already been and gone from the city.

'So, Señor Pigafetta,' said the king, 'you tell a different story from Captain Elcano. How can you explain that? As I understand it, the rebellion in the early stages of the expedition was justified by Magellan's refusal to follow my orders, and the loss of the *San Antonio* and the *Santiago* was down to his incompetence as a navigator. As for the deaths of so many men in the ocean beyond the Americas, and the scuttling of the *Concepción*, it seems to me that he should bear direct responsibility for all of that too. I have no wish to speak ill of the dead, but it sounds as though he brought his fate on himself.'

'Your Majesty,' the Venetian replied in his usual doleful manner, 'with respect, Captain Elcano has not given you all the facts. I have here a private journal of the mutiny which the Captain General asked me to keep.' He pulled a dog-eared booklet from under his coat. 'And towards the back of the journal you will also find a full record of the rest of the voyage, covering the loss of each of the ships, the discovery of the western passage and the events surrounding his death.' He placed the booklet on the desk between them, and as the king picked it up and flicked through the pages, he continued.

'I was taken on as an independent chronicler, Your Majesty, and I have no reason to lie. It is true that Captain Elcano brought the *Victoria* safely back to you in the first circumnavigation of the world, but he would not have been able to do that without the work of Captain General Magellan in finding the western passage for you. The Captain General succeeded in the commission you gave him, and before he died, he asked me to return this to you, as you requested in Seville.' He reached into his coat for a second time and brought out the silver disc. 'As it says,' he put the disc on the desk and pointed to the inscription *WP 1519 AD*, 'it is a mark of his life's greatest achievement, and you will read that it also saved his life in the Pacific Ocean when we used it to purify the drinking water. It is only right that I should bring it back to you.'

The king gazed at the disc for a long moment, then looked up at the Venetian and said, 'You are an honest man, señor, and a modest one too, since you are also one of the first circumnavigators. I did not expect to see this again.' He picked up the disc and inspected it for a second time. 'You have fulfilled your duty, and I will read your journal with an open mind. Meanwhile, I shall keep this in honour of Magellan,' he held the disc out between his index finger and thumb, 'and it will be used as a seafaring talisman for others serving the Habsburg crown in future. You have my word on it, as King and Holy Roman Emperor.'

*

And then...

The silver disc remains in the hands of the Spanish royal family, until it is given by King Philip II to the Duke of Medina-Sidonia, admiral of the Spanish navy, as a mark of good fortune for the proposed invasion of England in 1588.

In the ensuing rout of the Spanish Armada, the disc is taken by Sir Francis Drake, the commander of the English fleet, and refashioned into a small silver spoon with which "to sup the taste of victory many times over".

It continues to be owned by Drake's family for the next eighty years, ultimately passing to Sir William Courtenay, whose grandfather had married Drake's widow after the naval commander died of dysentery at sea in 1596.

*

Author's Note

The events set out in this chapter of Ferdinand Magellan's doomed expedition to the Moluccas (or 'Spice Islands'), the mutiny against him by the Spanish captains, the fate of the various ships and the role played by Juan Sebastián Elcano, were described in the journal written by Antonio Pigafetta. The chronicler had been taken on by Magellan personally and was one of only eighteen Europeans to return to Spain with Elcano on board the Victoria. When Elcano was invited to report to the king in Valladolid, he was permitted to bring two colleagues with him but chose to ignore Pigafetta, apparently in order to provide a biased account of his role in the mutiny. As it happened, King Charles had already received a report of the failed uprising, unfavourable to Magellan, from crew members of the San Antonio, which had sailed back to Spain prior to Magellan's discovery of the western passage between Patagonia and Tierra del Fuego. Pigafetta nonetheless made his own way to Valladolid to present a handwritten copy of his notes to the king, and in later years he also published a diary. His account of the voyage, generally considered by historians to be reliable, served to counter the misinformation spread by Elcano and the San Antonio crew and helped restore Magellan's reputation.

For simplicity, I have excluded the details of the journey westwards from the Philippines after Magellan's death. In short, the decision was taken to scuttle the Concepción due to lack of crew following the voyage across the Pacific, the skirmish on Mactan and the poisoning of several men by Rajah Humabon of Cebu in a belated act of hostility towards the Europeans. The remaining ships, the Victoria and the Trinidad, sailed to the Spice Islands (so named due to their native growth of nutmeg, cinnamon and clove plants), as originally contracted, whereupon the new captain of the

Trinidad *attempted to return to central America. The* Trinidad *was captured by the Portuguese and eventually sank in a storm. Elcano took control of the* Victoria, *sailing westwards to Spain across the Indian Ocean, and is rightly recorded, in one sense at least, as having captained the first circumnavigation of the globe.*

Magellan suffered from being a Portuguese commander of a largely Spanish crew. In accepting a commission from another country's king, he was simply following in the footsteps of other explorers, notably the Italian Christopher Columbus who had been employed by King Charles of Spain's grandparents, King Ferdinand and Queen Isabella, to find the New World. The rivalry for trade routes between Spain and Portugal was intense, and King Charles (also elected Holy Roman Emperor in 1520) would have welcomed the opportunity to hire an experienced sailor and navigator such as Magellan.

As for the part played by the disc, the cleansing properties of silver have been known since at least the second millennium BCE, when the Phoenicians stored water and wine in silver vessels. Writing in the fifth century BCE, the Greek historian Herodotus noted that Persian kings would carry water in silver jars on long military campaigns to ensure it remained fresh. In modern times, silver compounds have been used as an antibacterial agent in a multitude of applications such as water filtration systems in hospitals, swimming pools and other public buildings and even in the International Space Station currently orbiting earth.

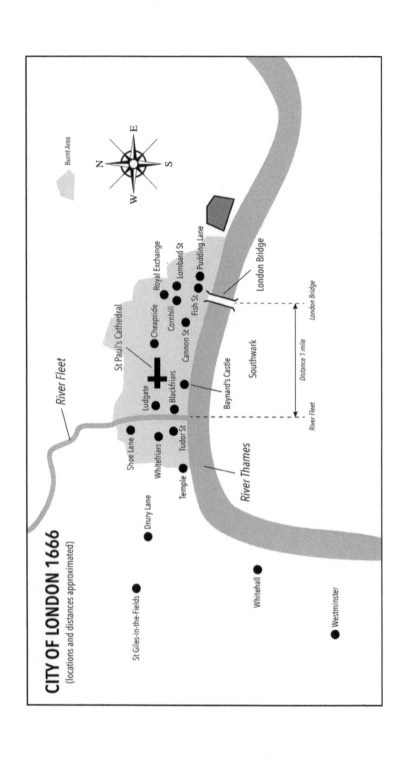

CITY OF LONDON 1666
(locations and distances approximated)

Burnt Area

River Fleet

River Thames

St Paul's Cathedral

Cheapside
Royal Exchange
Cornhill
Lombard St
Cannon St
Fish St
Pudding Lane

Ludgate
Blackfriars
Baynard's Castle

London Bridge

Southwark

Distance 1 mile

London Bridge

River Fleet

Shoe Lane
Whitefriars
Tudor St
Temple

Drury Lane

St Giles-in-the-Fields

Whitehall

Westminster

Eleven

The Great Fire of London

Saturday, 1 September 1666 – London

Sir William Courtenay wore a grim expression as the carriage advanced slowly towards the church of St Giles-in-the-Fields. He sat in silence, unmoved by the excited chatter of his family. He had no wish to upset them, and any worry about becoming infected was long gone, if the news reaching Devon over the past few months was to be believed. Even so, he could not help wondering whether the plague still lurked in the buildings around them. This was the parish where it had all begun, in the early summer of the previous year, the disease running amok for five months throughout the city and killing nearly seventy thousand people. The Courtenays had been hundreds of miles away from the danger, at their country home, and this was their first visit to London since the outbreak had died down. Surely it was safe to be here now – even the king, Charles II, had returned – and yet Sir William could not erase the memory of those weekly reports during the height of the epidemic, the dreadful symptoms of the disease, the indiscriminate and terrifying speed of transmission, the brutality of the mass burial pits. Seven thousand dead in a single week at its peak, whole families wiped out in a matter of days, and then it had tailed away, disappearing with the onset of winter as mysteriously as it had arisen. Was he mad to have brought his wife and the children up from Devon with him now?

A piping voice interrupted his brooding, and he looked round at his daughter, four-year-old Jane, who was pointing out of the window on the far side of the carriage from him. 'Father, why have those houses got red crosses on their doors?' He threw a sidelong glance at his wife Margaret, who gave an almost imperceptible nod of encouragement, and he began to frame a response, only to be beaten by the inevitable follow-up question from the little girl. Like many small children, she was delightfully curious, especially on a trip such as this with so many sights to take in, and far too impatient to wait for answers.

'What does the writing on the doors say? Is it a message? Who lives there?'

'One at a time, Jane, please,' Sir William managed to stem the breathless interrogation. 'Last year there was a terrible disease in London, called a plague, and lots of people became ill. It spread very fast, and no one really knows how. But if one person in a house was sick, the house was boarded up and everyone inside had to stay there for a while so they didn't go round infecting others in the streets.' Jane tried to interrupt, and he overrode her, searching for the words to stop his explanation becoming too complicated or distressing. 'The houses with red crosses are the ones where people were ill. While they were locked inside, they had the words "Lord have mercy upon us" written on the door. So you're right,' he smiled at her, 'it was a sort of message, like a prayer.'

'People died in there?' Jane's older sister Elizabeth asked, wide-eyed with horror. At the age of six, she had a better grasp of what death meant. 'What happened to them? Do you think their ghosts are waiting behind the doors?' Both girls pressed their faces to the carriage windows, staring at the passing houses, and Sir William knew that their sleep that night would be tormented by nightmares if he did not turn the conversation quickly towards a more cheerful topic.

'Yes, some people did die,' he said, 'and they were buried in church graveyards, just like people are at home in Devon. And because they were given a proper burial, the houses won't be haunted by their ghosts.' He wished the carriage would move on faster from St Giles's church graveyard, over the wall on his side of the street, where he remembered reading that several thousand victims had been flung into unmarked pits. 'But that was last year, a long time ago, and now everyone is fine. People who left London because they were worried about catching the disease have all come back, and it's perfectly safe for us to be here now.' Thankfully, the carriage was picking up speed, and as it lurched round a corner, he saw that they had turned into Drury Lane. 'Anyway, never mind all that. At the bottom of this street is a brand-new building called the Theatre Royal. King Charles allowed it to be built, and he often comes here to watch plays.' There was a pause as they passed the theatre, and the children craned their necks to inspect it. Then Jane said brightly, 'Did people die in there too?', and Sir William let out a burst of genuine laughter. He wanted to reply, 'Definitely, six days a week, and twice on Saturdays,' but decided the torrent of further questions was not worth risking.

Ten minutes later, they drew up at the house in Tudor Street, a modest but well-appointed town dwelling in the Whitefriars district which had been in Sir William's family for almost a century, thanks to his grandfather's study of the law in the halls of Middle Temple nearby. As they climbed down from the carriage, the caretaker emerged from the front door to greet them, a spidery, stooped man of about seventy who had served three generations of Courtenays and knew more about the house than anyone else alive.

'Hello, Godfrey,' said Sir William. 'How good to see you. It's been a long time.'

'Aye, Sir William, almost two years, I'd say. You've done well to stay away all that time. And look at you,' he crouched down to the level of the two girls. 'You must have doubled in size, Miss Elizabeth, since I last saw you. And you were barely walking, Miss Jane. You're fine-looking ladies now.' The sisters beamed, clutching their mother's hands, and she smiled too. 'Thank you, Godfrey. We wanted to come up to London months ago but decided to wait until we had a good reason. It's been a long journey, so I'll take the girls in, if you would be kind enough to unload the luggage.' The caretaker tipped his hat to her and began to help the driver bring the trunks down from the carriage roof.

Once Margaret and the girls were safely out of earshot, Sir William spoke again. 'Godfrey, London is greatly changed since we were last here. I received reports about the plague, but it was difficult to understand how bad it was without being in the city myself. Tell me about it.'

'It was truly terrible,' Godfrey replied soberly. 'They reckon almost a fifth of the folk here died. After a month or so, the ill were kept locked up indoors, but before that I saw some people who had caught it. Their skin came up in great black spots, and they got huge boils here and here,' he pointed to his armpit and then his groin, 'and their tongues swelled up and some of them were coughing blood. During the day you could hear the cries for help behind all those doors with red crosses, and you knew they were done for. And at night-time, you could hear the carters going round the streets shouting for people to bring out their dead, and you just had to lie there wondering if you were going to be next.' He shuddered. 'It was no place for you and the family, honestly. And then, suddenly, in October, it stopped, and in a way that's the scariest thing, because no one knows whether it will flare up again, or why.'

'That's why we left it so long before returning,' said Sir William. 'But I have business at Court, and Lady Margaret wanted to come up to do some shopping, so we decided it was the right moment. Thank the Lord you are safe and that the house is in good order.' He clapped the caretaker on the shoulder and turned towards the front door.

*

Sunday, 2 September 1666 – London

The Courtenay family was gathered for lunch, awaiting the arrival of Sir William, who had stayed on at the Temple church after the morning service to share long-overdue news with neighbours and friends. Sitting in the garden at the back of the house with the girls, Margaret was aware for the first time of the faint smell of smoke. Earlier in the day she had seen the fumes rising from the far end of the city by the Tower of London and drifting across the river towards Southwark, and she realised that the wind must now have swung round in the direction of Tudor Street. It was not an unpleasant smell, and she thought little of it as she heard her husband come into the house and call for her.

They sat down in the dining room and discussed the sermon, which had been about the grace of God in times of suffering and loss. 'Very apt,' said Sir William, 'especially for those poor souls in the east end of the city. Apparently, there was a fire in the middle of the night in Pudding Lane, near

London Bridge, and it's burnt down about three hundred houses already.'

'That's dreadful,' Margaret said. 'I saw the smoke and wondered what had happened. How will they put it out?'

'Oh, they're quite used to these things, I'm told. The houses there are all crammed into narrow streets, and I gather there's been no rain for ages, so every building is bone dry. But there's a water tower at Cornhill, which gets pumped full on every tide using water wheels under the bridge. They'll have plenty of water to put the flames out with. And the breeze will take the fire out over the river, so it should burn itself out soon enough.'

Unbeknown to Sir William, his information was at least two hours out of date and badly misguided. The fire had indeed started in Pudding Lane, a spark from a bakery oven, and it had moved quickly southwards onto Fish Street. From there it had spread into warehouses at the river front, sheds which were stocked with a fateful array of flammable materials – timber, rope, tallow, pitch, gunpowder – and by mid-morning it had turned from a serious but manageable blaze into a fireball. Buildings on London Bridge itself were now alight, and the pump wheels underneath for the water tower had been burnt out. Worse still, the wind, which his wife had rightly noticed to be coming from the east now, had strengthened, fanning the flames westwards along the waterfront in an uncontrollable inferno. As the family sat eating their lunch, chaos reigned in the streets leading from the city's east end, merchants and households fleeing with whatever goods and belongings they could extract before their properties were consumed. The inhabitants of Whitefriars and Temple, over a mile away, were blissfully unaware of the destruction unfolding, and in Tudor Street the Courtenays' concern continued to be about the dangers of plague rather than fire. They had taken particular care to bring their silver service up from Devon, having heard that eating off silver plates and cutlery helped to avoid disease. Even the youngest member of the family, Jane, was using a small silver spoon at the lunch table. She was not to know that it had once belonged to the famous admiral, Sir Francis Drake, as she crammed food into her mouth while simultaneously firing off a string of questions about fires, water wheels and London Bridge.

Late in the afternoon, Sir William and Lady Courtenay left the children in the care of Godfrey's wife Mabel and strolled down to the bank of the River Fleet which separated them from the city. From there it was only two hundred paces downstream to the point where the Fleet emptied into the River Thames, and they looked in astonishment at the scene on the wide reach of water in front of them. Despite the thick smoke now obscuring the view of London Bridge, they could see scores of boats ferrying passengers and cargo away from the east end of the city. The word from passers-by was that the king and his brother James, Duke of York, had come down the river from Whitehall an hour earlier to inspect the disaster for themselves and were planning to take control of the firefighting process from the Lord Mayor. Whole houses were to be pulled down in order to create gaps which would stop the fire from spreading, and of course, there was no better firebreak than water itself, in the form of the two rivers. As they walked back up the slope towards their house, Sir William reassured his wife that they would not be troubled by the blaze. It was still a long way off, and the River Fleet, running into the Thames between them and the fire, would protect them if it continued its advance. By the morning the commotion would be over; he would be able to present himself at the king's court in Whitehall as planned; and she could visit the shops in Cheapside.

*

Monday, 3 September 1666 – London

The following day Sir William awoke to a world very different from the one he had anticipated. Judging by the pall of smoke hanging over the city, it was evident that the fire was still raging, and this was confirmed by Godfrey who arrived at the house during breakfast, full of the latest news from the streets. The wind had shifted once again and was now driving the blaze north-west into the heart of the city rather than just along the riverfront. Houses were being pulled down in their dozens to create firebreaks, but the flames were simply jumping the gaps on the gale-force gusts generated by the inferno, helped by the tinder dry state of the largely wooden buildings after a long, hot summer. The Duke of York was now in charge of operations, the Lord Mayor Sir Thomas Bloodworth having proved unequal to the task and apparently now unable to be found at all. By the duke's order, command posts were being set up at various points around the city walls, and all Court business in Whitehall had been temporarily suspended by the king.

Sir William was frustrated. He could understand the need for the duke to take over from Bloodworth, whom he knew to be pompous and wholly ineffectual. But the entire reason for his visit to London was to see the king to discuss the matter of Sir George Sondes, and every day's delay in doing so was potentially damaging. Sondes was the member of Parliament for Ashburton in Devon, having taken over the position when Sir William stepped down after the restoration of the king in 1660. Now Sondes was said to be fatally ill and certainly not in a fit state to take his seat at Westminster Palace in mid-September when Parliament reconvened for the first time since the outbreak of the plague. Sir William had no great appetite for a full-time return to politics, but there were a number of property and commercial matters in Devon which affected him and needed to be dealt with promptly. Without Sondes in harness, they were drifting dangerously, and the purpose of his audience with the king, therefore, was to obtain permission to take Sondes' place in Parliament until a full-time substitute could be found. Naturally, Sir William would ensure that the new man would be to his liking. Parliament was due to meet on 18 September, and it would take two weeks for the necessary approvals to be documented once the king had given Sir William's proposal his blessing, hence the urgency to visit Whitehall. He had every reason to believe the king would be supportive; after all, the Courtenays had been staunch royalists during the civil war, to the point where their principal Devonshire home at Powderham Castle had been so badly damaged by Cromwell's troops that it was now uninhabitable. If ever there was a moment to call in a favour from King Charles, this was it.

Sitting at the breakfast table mulling over how best to force a meeting with the king, he was joined by his wife. He remembered that she wanted to visit Cheapside, home to the smartest shops in London, to buy new clothes and home furnishings after their long absence from the capital. Between them, they decided to go into the city in the early afternoon, by which time the duke's firefighting teams would surely have tamed the blaze. Cheapside would be safe enough for her, being well away from the riverfront, and he would track down the duke at one of the command posts, for a quiet word in his ear about Sondes. The duke could then be relied upon to speak to the king and set the parliamentary appointment process in motion.

At 3.00pm, Sir William and Lady Courtenay left the children with Mabel once again and walked the short distance to the bridge across the Fleet that would allow entry through the city walls at the Ludgate. At the river, Sir William bade his wife farewell and headed towards the command post in Shoe Lane, where Godfrey had told him the Duke of York could be found. Had he accompanied Margaret over the bridge and through the Ludgate, he would not have abandoned her. Within the city walls, it was bedlam. At the far end of Cheapside, the fire was now burning fiercely at the Royal Exchange, the centre of commercial and financial activities in London, and it was only a matter of minutes before it would spread into the shopping district. All order had broken down, the streets clogged with people struggling to carry what few possessions they had been able to snatch up in their flight from threatened buildings. Horses were running wild, maddened by the heat and noise of the inferno, and looting had begun. For those with money to spare, frantic efforts were being made to find porters and wagons, the cost of which had risen a hundredfold or more. At the Ludgate itself, there was gridlock, fights breaking out between cart drivers raging at the delay to pass through the gate, the same scene being repeated all round the city walls. Against this seething mass of humanity, Lady Courtenay battled her way as far as St. Paul's Cathedral and then turned round. She was home by 5.00pm, deeply shaken by what she had seen and yet still ignorant of the true ferocity of the fire itself.

The command post at Shoe Lane was located in a public house, the Mitre, and as Sir William approached, he could see the duke through a window issuing orders to a series of messengers queuing in front of him. Sir William pulled the door open and joined the back of the queue. After ten minutes, it became clear that he would have a long wait, as the duke entered a debate with each of the messengers in turn. Twitching with impatience, he could bear it no longer. He strode to the front of the line and cut across a man providing a report on the fire at Lombard Street.

'Your Grace, forgive me, but I have a matter of importance to discuss. I would be grateful for a private word with you.'

The Duke of York looked at him questioningly. 'Which district are you from? How bad is the fire and what lies in its path on the current direction of the wind?'

'No, Your Grace,' Sir William said, 'I need to talk to you about a different matter, nothing to do with the fire. I'm sure you remember me, William Courtenay, from Powderham Castle in Devon.'

'What the devil do you mean by this, Courtenay?' the duke spoke tersely. 'Can't you see we have a major disaster on our hands here? I have no interest whatsoever in what's happening in Devon.'

'You misunderstand me, Your Grace. It's to do with the opening of Parliament in two weeks' time...' He trailed off as he saw the thunderous expression on the duke's face.

'There won't be a Parliament in two weeks' time, or a Palace of Westminster to hold it in, if we don't stop the fire. Don't lecture me on what I understand, you imbecile. Now get out of my sight so I can talk to someone who will actually help.' The duke grasped him by the shoulders and shoved him out of the way to emphasise his annoyance.

Sir William retreated, furious at this public humiliation but still, like his wife, oblivious to the extent of the catastrophe engulfing the city. He returned home, only minutes after her, and they recounted in disbelief the problems they had encountered in achieving their separate objectives. They agreed that they would each try again the following day, when calm had been restored. In the meantime, an early night was called for, and they retired to bed after a prompt dinner, safe in the knowledge that they were protected from the spreading fire by the natural firebreak of the River Fleet.

Before she joined her husband in their bedroom on the first floor, Margaret checked on the children, up a second flight of stairs in a room at the back of the house. Both girls were fast asleep, and she lingered only to tidy up a tooth mug by Jane's bed. In it was the small silver spoon that Jane had been sucking on as she finished her tea and headed upstairs. Margaret slipped it into the pocket of her dress, intending to return it to the kitchen in the morning, and thought nothing more about it. Outside and unseen by the Courtenays as darkness descended, the sky was lit up in flickering colours of orange and red, the fire crackling and hissing as it continued its march westwards, gouts of flame soaring hundreds of feet into the air and clouds of sparks showering sideways on the wind. St Paul's Cathedral was now being devoured, window glass exploding and molten lead pouring off the roofs into the streets below, as the cauldron of heat intensified still further.

*

Tuesday, 4 September 1666 – London

At 4.00am, the first spark blew across the River Fleet from the burning pyre of Baynard's Castle, the medieval palace close to St. Paul's marking the south-western extremity of the walled city. The spark landed on the wooden roof of a warehouse standing between Tudor Street and the bank of the Thames. Others followed, and the building was soon alight. Because the warehouse was empty, the fire was able to gather pace, unnoticed and unchecked, and within minutes it had spread on the wind to the first house in Tudor Street. By the time Sir William and Lady Courtenay had been roused by neighbours, the front of their house, midway down the street, had begun to burn, and they stood outside the open door, stupefied by what they were witnessing. Half asleep, they had had time only to scramble into the clothes they had been wearing the previous evening, before being hustled onto the street. Suddenly Margaret clutched her husband's hand and let out an anguished cry, 'William, the girls, we have to get them.' Even as she spoke, they could see smoke beginning to curl from the reed matting on the lower steps of the staircase within the house.

'Stay there,' Sir William shouted and ran into the hallway. As he arrived at the foot of the stairs, a wall of fire flared up in front of him, the matting and the wooden side panels bursting into flames and blocking the way to the upper storeys. The heat was appalling, searing his eyeballs and badly singeing his hair and eyebrows. He had no choice but to retreat, staggering back half-blind and gasping with pain into the street where his wife sobbed. There was no other way into the house, and their daughters were trapped on the top floor. Mercifully, his burns were superficial, and the couple stood amongst their neighbours, aghast at the fire they believed could never reach them, beyond rational thought.

Around the side of the house, out of sight, the caretaker Godfrey was racing against time. As soon as the front of the building had begun to burn, he had instructed his wife Mabel to help the neighbours extract the Courtenay parents, while he went looking for a ladder. Each house in Tudor Street stood apart from the ones on either side, with only small gaps between them. To climb up two storeys from the garden was impossible, but Godfrey guessed that if he could gain access to the second floor of the adjacent building, he could stretch a ladder from one of its side windows to the side window of the girls' bedroom. The fire had not yet reached the back of the Courtenays' house, but it was spreading rapidly.

With the illumination of the blaze across the sky, finding a suitably sturdy ladder was not a problem. The Courtenays' neighbours were standing on the street, their front door open, and without asking, he plunged into their house and dragged the ladder up the two flights of stairs. He found the room facing across the gap between the two houses and smashed out the window frame. Then he laid the ladder over the void below onto the sill of the girls' bedroom and crawled across. Remarkably, the girls were still asleep, only wisps of smoke leaking into the room under the closed door, but he could hear the roar of the flames on the other side and he knew he had only moments to save them. He climbed through the open window, scooped up the smallest, Jane, and carried her back along the ladder to the safety of the other building. As he turned to repeat the journey, she began to scream, but there was nothing more he could do to help her until he had rescued her sister.

The second trip was more perilous in every way. The door to the bedroom was now on fire and thick, pungent smoke was belching out through the window. Acting by touch rather than sight, he was able to find Elizabeth and drag her to the ladder. Being two years older than Jane, she was too heavy for him to carry under his arm, so he had to crawl backwards over the ladder, pulling her with him. Gagging from the smoke and terrified by the flames advancing across the room, she clutched at the window frame and then at each rung of the ladder. Godfrey despaired that her nightclothes, or even the ladder itself, would catch light from behind, but at last he was able to coax her across to the other building, where she hugged her sister in relief, little knowing how close to death both of them had been. Then Godfrey shepherded them down the stairs and out onto the street, conscious that the neighbours' house would begin to burn at any minute.

Surrounded by the crowds in the open air, the caretaker and the little girls were lost at first. Firefighters were everywhere, buckets of water being passed from hand to hand all the way from the Fleet in a hopeless attempt to douse the flames at a dozen houses. At the age of seventy, the exertions on the ladder had taken more out of Godfrey than he had realised, and now that the girls were safe, he collapsed onto the cobbled ground. Elizabeth and Jane knelt by his side, trying in vain to revive him, and it was only when water splashed from a bucket overhead onto his face that he could summon some energy. He stood and, holding the children's hands, he went searching for their parents. He found them in the shadows cast by the fire, still stunned by what they believed to be their loss, and he stepped back to allow the tearful family reunion. It was being repeated, in one form or another, all along the street, and he himself was joined by Mabel who had come from the line of water carriers.

Two hours later, when it was clear that there was nothing to be salvaged from the burning carcass of their house, Sir William Courtenay announced that they must walk towards Westminster for shelter and food. They had friends there who would take them in and allow them to gather their thoughts for the future. He turned to Godfrey, checked that he and Mabel also had somewhere to go and thanked him one last time for his bravery. The caretaker was embarrassed, muttering that he had simply been doing his duty, and Lady Courtenay came to her husband's side, the children at her skirts.

'Godfrey, you have saved the two people most precious to me in the whole world. Our friends in Westminster will help us, and once we have settled the girls in Devon, we will come back and make sure you and Mabel are all right. But in the meantime, I want to give you this, the only thing Sir William and I possess here now, apart from the clothes we're standing in.' She grasped his ash-streaked hand and pressed a small silver spoon into his palm. 'It's all I have. It used to belong to

Sir Francis Drake. He was England's saviour, and you have been ours.' Then she burst into tears, leaving Godfrey even more uncomfortable than he had been before, and the family walked away into the grey dawn light.

*

And then...

When the caretaker Godfrey dies ten years later, his wife Mabel sells the silver spoon to raise money to support herself.

Over the following sixty years, the spoon is bought and sold several times in the capital, ultimately being acquired by the Laird of Mackintosh, who takes it from London to his family home in northern Scotland.

*

Author's Note

The path and impact across London of the plague in 1665 and then the Great Fire in 1666 were reported by numerous eyewitnesses, notably in the diaries of Samuel Pepys.

This was the last major outbreak of plague in Britain and the worst since the Black Death in 1348. The official number of deaths recorded was 68,596, but the real number is estimated at nearer a hundred thousand, some 15–20% of the capital's population. The cause of the infection was not understood at the time and was only identified in the late nineteenth century as a bubonic bacterium spread amongst humans by the bite of fleas carried on black rats. Some deaths were also caused by a pneumonic, or airborne, version of the same germ. The plague is thought to have arrived in London on bales of cotton and other fabric imported from Amsterdam, where over thirty thousand inhabitants had died in the previous two years. It escalated rapidly from May until September, during which there was a massive exodus of the wealthy from the capital, including King Charles II who moved his court and Parliament to Oxford. In October it began to wane and was largely over by the onset of winter.

The Great Fire of London the following September raged for five days, destroying over thirteen thousand houses and rendering some one hundred thousand people homeless. Virtually all civic buildings in the city were destroyed, including eighty-seven of the 109 churches. The king took a personal interest and put his brother the Duke of York (later King James II) in command of the firefighting operations, as described. By the end of the third day (Tuesday 4th) the blaze had spread westwards from London Bridge almost as far as Whitehall, prompting the king to evacuate to Hampton Court. However, the wind then dropped and, by dawn on the Thursday, the fire had burnt itself out. Parliament was able to convene on 18 September as planned, the first session to be held in Westminster Palace since April 1665. Sir George Sondes, MP for Devon, and the Courtenays of Powderham Castle were real, although the former's illness and Sir William's attempt to take his place in Parliament are a fiction.

Efforts to ward off infection during the plague included smoking, carrying nosegays or herbs, the use of perfume, the cleaning of coinage in jars of vinegar and, for those who could afford it, the use of silver cutlery and crockery at meals. The medicinal properties of silver had been noted as early as 400 BCE in ancient Greece by Hippocrates (alongside its use as a purification agent – see Chapter 10). By the early twentieth century, its antibacterial use in the world of medicine had been extended to applications such as surgeons' stitches, eyedrops for the treatment of ophthalmic infection and wound dressings in World War I. More recently, it has been developed into antibiotic coatings for a variety of medical instruments such as needles, catheters and breathing tubes and into amalgam fillings for dental work.

Twelve

The Werewolf of Moy

Mid-September 1743 – Moy Hall, Inverness, Scotland

The hill path from the ancient village of Cawdor to Loch Moy involves a long, gentle climb up to the watershed, followed by a steep descent into the upper tributaries of the River Findhorn. On a still autumn day, it is a pleasant walk, with good views north-west across the Moray Firth to the Black Isle and south-west into the deep trench of Loch Ness. Above the treeline, the little-used track passes through low heather, skirting occasional patches of soggy moss, and at its peak, a brief scramble over bare rocks and scree is called for. It is a nine-mile journey in all, an easy stroll for anyone familiar with the route and fit enough for the mild exertion required. Eileen Fraser knew it better than most. Every Saturday, she was allowed to leave her job in the kitchen of Moy Hall, on the shore of the loch, to visit her mother in Cawdor. Normally, she would make the trip there and back in a day, but this weekend she had taken her children to visit their grandmother and had been permitted to return on the Sunday afternoon instead. She enjoyed the routine of the remote weekly excursion, and in the three years that she had been working at the Hall, she had never had reason to consider it unsafe. That Sunday, however, she and the children were not alone on the hill.

It had been a beautiful day, and Eileen had stayed on with her mother longer into the afternoon than usual. Now, as the family crested the ridge and began to pick their way down the slope towards Loch Moy, the shadows were lengthening, and she realised that they would struggle to be back at the Hall before dark. She was not worried; the children, eleven-year-old twins called Callum and Isobel, were still full of energy, and they would have no trouble following the path in the twilight. As they left the last of the smooth, weather-beaten rocks behind them, she stopped to admire the full moon, high in the cloudless blue sky above, then turned her attention to the peat hags on the flatter ground ahead. These soft earthen depressions in the heather were not dangerous, but they could be misleading in both depth and dampness. It was sometimes necessary to climb down six or eight feet in order to cross them and not unknown to find an ageing red deer sunk up to its flanks in the marshy bottom of a hag after heavy rainfall. The summer had been exceptionally dry, so they were unlikely to get their feet wet, but nonetheless it was an effort after the long walk to clamber in and out of the hollows.

With the Hall now visible in the distance, little more than two miles away, Callum and Isobel were running forward, their heads bobbing in and out of view as they scampered through the peat hags. Eileen let them be, taking the opportunity to enjoy the autumnal colours of the Findhorn glen before returning to her evening shift in the Hall kitchen. By force of habit, she tested the bottom of each hag with her walking stick before stepping onto it, and gradually the gap widened between her and the children. It was only when she came to a flat, unbroken stretch of heather that she noticed they had disappeared altogether. She walked on, guessing that they were hidden in an unseen fold in the ground, waiting to ambush her in a game they never seemed to tire of. She smiled to herself and prepared to play along with the joke by pretending to be surprised. There was a narrow peat hag spanning the path some forty yards away; that was where they would jump up in front of her, shouting and laughing.

When she arrived at the lip of the cleft, she was genuinely surprised not to find the children. She could see their footprints in the soft peat and indistinct scuff marks leading off to the right as though something had been dragged away. She hesitated, listening intently but hearing nothing, and was aware of an odd, rank smell which she could not place. Then she walked sideways along the top of the hag, peering down into it as it twisted away from her, readying herself for the ambush. Nothing could have prepared her for what happened next.

Beyond a curve in the embankment, she heard a low, savage growl. She advanced, still believing this to be part of the children's game, and found herself looking directly down into the pale amber eyes of a rangy grey-black animal. It was an enormous beast, which she recognised from old pictures in the Hall to be a wolf, and it stood motionless, staring at her ferociously as it guarded its prey. In her shock, Eileen took a moment to fully absorb the scene below her, and then she spotted the clothes amongst the bloody mess on the peat in front of the animal. Callum's throat had been torn out, and his entrails ripped from his stomach. Strips of flesh hung from the animal's mouth, and its snout was red with gore. The boy was clearly dead, and his mother began to scream, galvanising the wolf into action. It leapt at her, clearing the six-feet wall of the peat hag in one bound and snapping at her lower legs. Her skirts protected her from the vicious teeth, and before it could launch itself at her upper body, she was able to raise her stick and thrash it across the head. It snarled in fury and backed away out of range, spit drooling from its red-rimmed jaws as it resumed its implacable stare. Eileen advanced on it, still brandishing the stick and shrieking incoherently, and after taking a hefty blow on one of its ears, it jumped back down to gnaw at Callum's body, evidently preferring to continue gorging on its original kill rather than risk injury chasing a second.

Eileen was made of stern Highland stuff, and once the initial horror had washed over her, she was able to gather herself. There was nothing to be gained by following the wolf into the base of the hag – she would be attacked again, and Callum was beyond help. From her elevated position, she began to search for her daughter instead, running further along the embankment and calling out for her. It did not take long. Burrowed into a crevice in the far wall, hidden from the wolf, Isobel lay face down in the peat, catatonic with fear and unable to speak. Eileen climbed down and pulled her to her feet, and after a brief embrace, they scrambled back onto the flat heather above and ran for their lives. A hundred paces on, Eileen glanced over her shoulder and saw that the wolf had come to the top of the hag to watch them go. Even at that distance, she was again struck by its monstrous size and malevolent gaze. Then it disappeared from sight once more, and she knew she would never see her son's body again.

Half an hour later, just as the sun was setting, mother and daughter arrived at the back entrance of the Hall and gabbled their tale to the kitchen staff. Isobel still shook violently at the memory of the attack but was able to describe how she and her brother had surprised the wolf in its lair as they sought a hiding place in the peat hag. There had been no time to cry out. In an instant, it had leapt at Callum's face, raking its front claws down his cheeks and sinking its teeth into his neck. Blood had erupted from his wounds, and Isobel had run on along the hag in silent terror. As she finished her account, she began to sob, and Eileen looked on helplessly. The cook, who had worked at the Hall for over thirty years and was fond of the Fraser family, soothed the young girl and took control. 'Isobel, you need a hot, sweet drink and then bed. I'll organise that, but first I'm going to take your mother to the laird. He'll know what to do about the wolf.' She summoned one of the scullery maids and told her to look after the girl while she led Eileen through the house to the front rooms.

Angus Mackintosh, Laird of Moy Hall and the twenty-second chief of the clan, was sitting in his study when he heard the cook calling for him. He could see immediately from the women's expressions that something dire had occurred, and he beckoned them into the room. They stood in the doorway, and the cook explained that they had terrible news to report. The laird nodded in encouragement and Eileen launched into her story. As soon as she mentioned the wolf, he was tempted to interrupt, but he let her finish and offered his condolences for her son, before questioning her account.

'Eileen, I know you believe the animal to have been a wolf, but to be honest, that seems very unlikely. The last wolf to be seen in Scotland was killed over sixty years ago, the other side of the Drumochter pass in Perthshire. There hasn't been a wolf in this area for more than a century.'

'That's as may be, Laird,' Eileen said. 'But I know what I saw. It was a huge beast, twice as tall as a deerhound and heavier. It would need to have been big to get the better of Callum, and there's no way an ordinary dog would do that to a person.' She trembled at the memory of the shreds of skin and guts falling from its mouth as it raised its head to stare at her, and swayed against the door frame.

'Never mind,' said Mackintosh hurriedly. 'What matters is that we kill it, whatever it is. There's nothing we can do in the dark, but in the morning, I will arrange for a hunting party to track it down, and we'll collect your son's body. For now, the best thing you can do is get some rest, so that you can find the site of the attack for us.' He watched the cook lead Eileen away and wondered how much of the excitable tale was really true.

*

Mid-October 1743 – Moy Hall, Inverness, Scotland

Thirty days later, at noon, two woodcutters presented themselves at the Hall and asked to see the laird. He emerged from the front door and recognised them both as members of the team he had assembled to hunt the animal responsible for Callum Fraser's death. No sign had been found of the wolf when Eileen took them to the peat hag, nor of the boy's body, although there had been clear evidence of something meeting a bloody end there. Eileen had been distraught, howling in grief as she relived the horror of the previous afternoon, and the laird had arranged for her to be escorted back to the Hall. Then he had instructed the huntsmen to fan out across the moor and continue the search. All of them were armed with muskets, and keen to avenge the Fraser family, although in truth they shared the laird's belief that they were hunting a wild dog rather than any wolf resurrected from centuries before. They had failed in their task, and after three days, the search had been called off.

The woodcutters were brothers, Donald and Hamish Munro of Kyllachy, who Mackintosh knew to be sensible men, not prone to exaggeration. He listened with increasing concern as the spokesman, Donald, described what they had found in the forestry between Loch Moy and the Findhorn. Earlier that morning, they had been cutting timber, and they had come across the freshly killed carcass of a red deer. It was a mature stag, weighing some three hundred pounds, with no sign of disease or injury, apart from the savage tear to its throat and a gouging laceration across its belly. Its attacker had apparently been disturbed by the men shortly after the kill, as they moved deeper into the forest. Experienced stalkers, they had inspected the wounds and wondered between them what sort of animal was capable of bringing down a healthy deer of this size. It was only when they heard a fierce growl from the undergrowth beyond them that they had realised they were being observed. They had walked forward, axes raised, and the growl had risen to a terrible snarling sound. As they stepped over a fallen tree trunk, they had found themselves face to face with a massive dark beast, poised on its haunches to spring at them, and they had turned on their heels and run. The abiding memory, for both of them, was the merciless stare of its pale amber eyes.

'It was a wolf, Laird, I'm sure of it, and a big one at that,' said Donald, 'the same one that killed the Fraser boy. No dog in all Scotland could have killed a fully grown stag like that. And the wounds – you should have seen them. Whatever animal it was would have needed teeth as sharp as a razor.'

Mackintosh had hoped the story begun by the Fraser woman had gone away since the failed search. He did not doubt the disappearance of the boy Callum, and he trusted the Munros, but it still seemed absurd that a wolf should be roaming the neighbourhood. Many years ago, he had met Sir Ewen Cameron of Killiecrankie, widely acknowledged to have killed the last wolf in Scotland in 1680. There had been occasional scare stories of sightings since then, but nothing substantiated, and certainly not in the low-lying region around

Inverness. He was about to say something of the sort, couched diplomatically to avoid appearing scornful of their account, when Hamish, the more laconic of the brothers, spoke for the first time.

'There's another thing, Laird. Remember the full moon last night? Well, it's exactly a month on from when Eileen's son was attacked. There was a full moon that night as well. Now there's talk in the village that the beast is a werewolf. By the size of it, that could be right.'

'Oh, Hamish, listen to you!' said Mackintosh heartily. 'First a wolf, and now a werewolf, neither of which exists here. There's a disease in Europe called rabies which is spread amongst dogs. Sometimes they go mad, attacking people for no reason. Maybe that's what you saw, although I've never heard of it in Scotland. Come on in and have a dram, both of you, and put this nonsense behind you. We'll organise another search party, and this time I'll get Murdo MacQueen of Pollochaig to join us. If anyone can track the beast down, he will.'

The brothers looked at each other uncertainly, but the offer of whisky was too strong to turn down, and they followed Mackintosh into his library where a decanter was found. Thirty minutes later, their nerve was restored, and they left the Hall to help round up the other huntsmen, the laird's insistence that they stop the spread of the werewolf rumour ringing in their ears.

The hunting party was slow to assemble that afternoon, as each man had to be called away from his job, some of them in remote parts of the glen. In the end, the light began to fail, and Mackintosh was obliged to defer the expedition until the following morning. Shortly after dawn, twenty estate workers, including the head stalker MacQueen, set out from the Hall and scoured the moors and riverbanks around Loch

Moy. They searched all day, and every other day that week, to no avail. Eventually, the laird stood them down, all but MacQueen, whom he instructed to continue for another few days. By the end of a fortnight, with no spoor to track and no fresh kills to suggest the beast was still at large, he ordered the stalker to return to his farm. A worrying thought had begun to take seed, and he had decided a visit to Inverness was required.

In keeping with his status as head of the clan, Angus Mackintosh had wider experience of the world beyond the Highlands than many of his neighbouring lairds. He had travelled extensively in Europe as a young man, and more recently he had spent two years soldiering there, part of the British army fighting against its age-old enemy France. He had been a captain in the Royal North British Fusiliers, an infantry regiment that had originally attracted him due to his interest in musketry. After the Battle of Dettingen in June that year, where the Fusiliers had played a key role, it had been announced that the regiment would move from Bavaria to winter quarters in the Netherlands. At the age of forty-two, Mackintosh had decided to resign his commission and return to Scotland, stopping off at various points in the Rhine valley, and then in London, as he headed home.

Three things had happened on his journey, all of them helping to prompt the plan he now had in mind. Firstly, as he made his way through Rhineland, he had listened to fellow travellers' tales of the werewolves said to frequent central Europe, and the local folklore that these animals emerged on a full moon, converting for twenty-four hours from human to animal form and attacking anything that crossed their path. Although he had initially scoffed at Hamish Munro's suggestion, the presence of a werewolf would explain the savagery of the beast around Moy and the fact that it could not be found once it had resumed its human shape. The stalker MacQueen had never failed before, so there must be some extraordinary phenomenon at work.

Secondly, Mackintosh's understanding of firearms had taken a material step forward. In the city of Koblenz, on the banks of the mighty Rhine river, he had visited a gunsmith to admire the latest designs in weaponry and had seen for the first time the effect of rifling in a gun barrel. Having witnessed first-hand at Dettingen the limitations of the smooth-bored musket, accurate up to fifty yards at best, he had grasped immediately how spiralled grooves in the barrel might stabilise a bullet's trajectory in flight, thereby retaining its accuracy over much greater distances. This promised to transform an infantry soldier's lot from murderous salvos at close quarters to longer range marksmanship, and he could see how it would also apply to hunting deer and other animals in the Scottish Highlands. The concept was still in its early stages of development, but he had bought one of the new rifles with alacrity.

The final matter was a combination of the first and second. According to the Rhineland folklore, werewolves were impossible to kill using ordinary weapons and vulnerable only to silver objects. In London he had bought a small silver spoon as a gift for a child to whom he had been invited to be a godparent. In his absence in Europe the child had died, but Mackintosh had only received the news on his return to Moy. With no children of his own, he had no need of the spoon, and it had occurred to him that it could be melted down into a silver bullet for his new rifle. He knew of a gunsmith in Inverness, ten miles to the north, who would do this for him without asking tiresome questions, but it was essential that the work was done before the next full moon. He had fifteen days, which he estimated to be more than enough.

*

Mid-November 1743 – Moy Hall, Inverness, Scotland

It was a crisp, cold day when Mackintosh rode out to Murdo MacQueen's farm at Pollochaig, a desolate smallholding standing on a spur above the Findhorn river. The first snow of the winter had fallen the previous night, and small drifts had formed across the road leading up to the steading. As he approached, he could see the man rounding up sheep into a makeshift pen, and he thought, not for the first time, what a harsh existence it must be for the local farmers outside the summer months. MacQueen himself was a rough, cantankerous fifty-year-old, more able to cope than most, and Mackintosh suspected he fed well on venison poached from the Moy estate. The laird did not begrudge him that – there were plenty of deer about – and if the stalker could perform the job required the following day, he could have all the meat he wanted. But this task needed to be done Mackintosh's way, and he worried that MacQueen would bristle at such a suggestion.

'Good morning, MacQueen,' he shouted across the paddock as he dismounted and tied his horse to a stunted rowan tree by the farmhouse. The stalker raised a hand in acknowledgement and then ignored him for ten minutes as he chased the last of his flock into the pen. Mackintosh waited patiently, suspecting that this was partly for show, to establish that MacQueen was his own man and no servant to the laird. At last, the sheep were contained, and the stalker walked slowly over to the house.

'I need your help again, MacQueen,' said Mackintosh. 'I'm guessing you heard the rumour last month that the beast we were looking for is a werewolf.' The stalker nodded, but said nothing, and the laird continued. 'Personally, I think it is unlikely, but with the full moon coming round again tomorrow, I think we should be prepared, just in case. I'm planning to raise the hunting team again, and I'd like you to join us, if you would. This time, though, I want to organise it differently. You're the best marksman here, and my plan is for the others to sweep the moor and drive the animal to you, so that you can shoot it.' He paused, knowing that his next words were crucial. 'There's a theory that werewolves can only be shot dead with a silver bullet. You may think me superstitious, but I have had such a bullet made for my gun,' he gestured to the rifle strapped to his horse's side in a leather case, 'and I would like you to use it, instead of your own musket. Would you be happy with that?'

The answer he received was not the one he expected. 'Aye,' MacQueen grunted, 'but nae how you've suggested it.'

'Why not?' said Mackintosh, slightly piqued at the simple rejection of his plan. 'We need to make sure that the man with the silver bullet gets within range to shoot. We'll manage that by driving the beast straight to you.'

'Right enough,' replied the stalker, 'and what happens when the beast turns on the drovers instead? It could kill all twenty of them, with nae harm to itself, and still nae come near me.' He pointed down to the snow-covered ground. 'There's your answer.'

'I'm sorry,' Mackintosh frowned in frustration, 'I don't understand you.'

'Tracks,' said MacQueen brusquely. 'We'll know exactly where the beast is, from its footprints. Get five men from round the estate to look out for its tracks, then fetch me. I'll stalk it from there myself, with no one else getting in my way, and I'll kill it with yon gun.' He jerked his head at the rifle and added, 'I'll be needing a few ordinary bullets to practise with.'

Mackintosh could appreciate the simplicity of the suggestion and agreed to it readily. He slipped the rifle out of its case, passed it to the stalker and explained why its accuracy could be relied upon over two hundred yards or more. MacQueen looked unimpressed, and Mackintosh decided to let him find out for himself when he tested the rifle. Then he rummaged in a pannier and dropped a handful of bullets into the man's hand – four of lead and one of silver. The round silver ball sparkled in the bright November sunshine, and the laird could not resist asking the question that had most intrigued him. 'So you believe in werewolves, then?'

'Oh aye,' said MacQueen. 'There's all sorts in the Highlands.' Then he walked into his house, without another word, leaving Mackintosh more confused than ever.

*

Early the following morning, MacQueen set up a target in the paddock and knelt in the snow, resting the rifle on a crossbar of the stock-pen. It was another beautiful, clear day, the white orb of the full moon still visible in the western sky. He fired the first of his four lead bullets at seventy yards, walked over to inspect the result and was pleased to find that he had hit the bullseye. He repeated the test at a hundred yards, and again at a hundred and fifty yards, increasingly surprised by the accuracy of the weapon. He decided to try the final bullet at two hundred yards, and as he reloaded, he thought about the difference such a gun would make to stalking. Bringing down a stag at that distance would be like stealing from a blind man, and poaching would be almost effortless. He finished tamping the bullet down the barrel and leant the ramrod against the wooden upright next to him. The sheep behind him in the pen were bleating, but he thought nothing of it as he brought the rifle up to the aim for the last time.

Suddenly the noise from the sheep rose to a deafening clamour, and he looked round, the rifle cocked and ready at his cheek. With a countryman's instinct, he knew something was seriously amiss but could not make out the cause of the flock's distress. Then the sheep bolted in terror, some jumping at the walls of the pen, others streaming towards him in their flight from the far side of the enclosure. As they came closer, MacQueen could see beyond them, and a terrible chill ran through him. A huge, grey-black wolf was devouring a ewe, ripping the flesh from its neck and shoulders in savage bites, scraping the entrails from the lacerated stomach cavity with its hind paws. Blood soaked the snow around it, and already a dismembered limb had been stripped to the bone. The speed at which the animal was savaging the carcass was beyond anything the stalker had ever witnessed, and he let out a bellow of horror.

The beast stopped its frenzied eating instantly and looked straight at MacQueen. He had enough time to register the intensity of its amber eyes before it lunged towards him, its slavering jaws still dripping blood, its vicious yellow teeth bared. He could smell the stench of its body on the breeze, and he fired just as it sprang at him in a final bound. The lead bullet caught it in the chest, flinging it back onto the snow, and MacQueen wasted no time in grabbing the ramrod and running out of sight behind the steading. He reloaded with shaking hands, aware that this was his last bullet, the silver one.

Any normal animal, even a fully grown stag, would be stone dead from a wound like the one the wolf had sustained. Despite the shock and the danger of the attack, MacQueen was much too experienced a huntsman to have panicked, and he had aimed for the heart. But if the beast was indeed a werewolf, and the rumours of their invincibility were true, then his job was not yet done. He thanked God for having had the presence of mind to snatch up the ramrod as he ran, then braced himself, raised the rifle and peered round the steading wall.

The blood-stained snow where the ewe had been mutilated was deserted, apart from the single limb that had been torn from it, a pathetic remnant of the crazed attack. MacQueen wondered for a brief moment whether he, the famous stalker, was now the prey but took comfort from the fact that the ewe's body had been dragged away. He scanned the hill beyond the paddock, and there, on an outcrop some two hundred and fifty yards away, was the werewolf, standing stock still and watching him. He would not get a better chance, and he did not hesitate, trusting the remarkable weapon at his shoulder and the silver bullet in its barrel. In a single movement he stepped out from behind the wall, adjusted his aim and pulled the trigger. The beast went down immediately, blood dribbling from the second bullet hole over its heart, and this time it stayed down.

*

And then…

The stalker MacQueen retrieves the silver bullet from the werewolf's body and returns it to the Laird of Mackintosh. It is kept in Moy Hall as a keepsake of the werewolf's demise, until a visit by Bonnie Prince Charlie prior to the Battle of Culloden in 1746. In the laird's absence, his wife Lady Anne Mackintosh gives the prince the bullet as a good-luck token for the battle ahead.

The prince's army is defeated at Culloden, and he spends several months on the run in Scotland, with the bullet in his pocket, before he is able to escape to France.

Once in France, he travels to Paris, where he loses the bullet to the eminent writer and philosopher Voltaire in a wager over a game of cards.

The bullet remains in Voltaire's ownership for the next thirty years.

*

Author's Note

According to official records, the last wolf to be killed in Britain was in 1680 at Killiecrankie in Perthshire, by Sir Ewen Cameron. However, local legend has it that MacQueen of Pollochaig, stalker to the Laird of Mackintosh at Moy Hall estate near Inverness, killed the last of the species in 1743.

The myth of the werewolf has featured in European folklore for several centuries, alongside a belief in witchcraft. In a process known as lycanthropy, a human is transformed into a wolf, often on the night of a full moon, due to a curse or an affliction such as a bite from another werewolf. The idea that werewolves are immune to harm from ordinary weapons, and vulnerable only to silver, appears to be a relatively modern concept, attributed to German seventeenth-century legend and (in the case of silver bullets) twentieth-century fiction.

There is no record of Angus, Laird of Mackintosh and twenty-second chief of the clan, participating in the Battle of Dettingen in Bavaria (in June 1743) or visiting a German armourer, although he did captain a company in the government regiment of the Black Watch during the '45 Rebellion. As such, he was effectively on the opposing side to his wife Lady Anne, who hosted Bonnie Prince Charlie at Moy Hall in February 1746 while the laird was garrisoned in Inverness. There is also no record to suggest that Lady Anne gave the prince a good-luck token, of silver or any other material, before he left the Hall to continue the campaign against the English which ended so disastrously at Culloden two months later.

The reference to the invention of gun barrel rifling in Rhineland is at least partially true. Rifled barrels first appeared in the early/mid-1700s in Pennsylvania, developed by gunsmiths such as Martin Meylin, who had emigrated there from western Germany. Initially, the rifle's long-range accuracy was of appeal principally to settler-hunters, but by the 1750/60s, it was being put to military use in the colonial battlegrounds of the Seven Years War and subsequently in the American War of Independence.

Thirteen

Marie Antoinette

March 1778 – Paris, France

The Théâtre des Tuileries was abuzz with excitement. The latest play of the great writer and philosopher Voltaire was to be premiered there that night, and it was rumoured that the man himself would attend. Voltaire had not been seen in Paris for almost twenty years, and this would be a momentous return to public life after his self-imposed exile from the capital. His absence had only served to heighten his fame, and large crowds had gathered in the streets to catch a glimpse of their national hero. The performance was due to begin in ten minutes, and all the ticket holders were already in their seats, awaiting his arrival.

In the darkness outside, a wave of cheering rippled along the Cour Royale, and a carriage forced its way through the throng to the front steps of the theatre, its blinds drawn. A footman moved to open the carriage door, and a hush fell. Then an ivory-slippered foot emerged on the top step, followed by voluminous skirts and, finally, the head and shoulders of a lady, bowing under a magnificent, feathered headdress. She descended slowly to the pavement, looking around her with an imperious expression, and there was an audible sigh of disappointment. Tonight, at least, Queen Marie Antoinette was a poor second to Monsieur Voltaire.

The queen was escorted into the theatre, her lady-in-waiting bustling around her to arrange the train of her dress as she advanced up the steps. In her wake, a spokesman began to address the crowd. Shouting to make himself heard over the rising bubble of noise, he explained that the playwright had been unwell since his journey to Paris and was therefore unable to attend in person. However, it was hoped that Monsieur Voltaire would be sufficiently recovered to receive Her Majesty later in the evening to hear her opinion of his new work, and he would certainly be coming to watch another performance later in the month. The crowd were mollified, and calls went up for his good health as people settled down to await news from within, about the play itself.

Two hours later, the double doors to the theatre forecourt were thrown open, and the rapturous applause of the audience swelled out into the night. The play's eponymous leading character, "Irene", had killed herself in a tragic clash between love and duty, and even Marie Antoinette had been seen dabbing her eyes at the dramatic denouement. As the curtain came down on the assembled cast for the third and final time, she swept out of the royal box and down the stairway to her carriage. This time the crowd were more amenable, having been fed updates of Irene's unfolding predicament by theatre staff at the end of each act. They were still yelling their approval of the play as the carriage made its way back down the Tuileries, its blinds now raised so that the queen could acknowledge them with a regal wave, as if they were cheering for her rather than for the plot.

It was only a matter of minutes before the carriage turned into the Rue de Beaune and drew up at the front door of the residence where Voltaire was staying. The laborious process of extracting the queen from the vehicle and ushering her into the building was repeated, and in the main reception room the host, the Marquis de Villette, welcomed her to his humble abode. 'Your Majesty, it is an honour to have you here. Allow me to introduce my guest and longstanding friend Monsieur Voltaire.' He gestured to a wizened old man with piercing blue eyes propped up by cushions on a sofa at the far side of the room.

At the age of twenty-two, Marie Antoinette had been only vaguely aware of Voltaire before his return to Paris the previous month. But she had quickly grasped the extent of his reputation and had made it her business to ensure she attended the premiere of *Irene*. Any popular support was welcome in these troubled times for France, and by aligning herself to the writer, she hoped that some of the Parisians' approval might be extended to her. The riots in the capital over the last three years had made it an awkward place for the royal family to visit, and she had also perceived, belatedly, that her extravagant spending at Versailles was not endearing her to the people. Nonetheless, she was the queen, and as such she considered it her duty to be seen in public, preferably alongside one of the country's most treasured citizens. She took off her headdress and laid it carefully on a seat, then walked across the room towards Voltaire, somewhat put out to find that he was not rising to his feet to greet her. It was only as she drew closer that she realised how ill he looked, his thin body hunched in pain and his skin dangerously pallid.

'Monsieur Voltaire, I am delighted to meet you, having heard so much about you for so many years,' she lied. 'Your return to Paris is long overdue, and my husband and I hope very much that we can persuade you to visit us at Versailles as well.'

Voltaire cleared his throat with a wheezing cough before answering. 'You are too kind, Your Majesty. Let me first apologise for not standing up, but as you will have heard, I have been unwell, and my legs have deserted me. My head is still clear though, clear enough to worry about my critics, anyway. Tell me about the play – I trust you enjoyed it?'

'It was excellent,' the queen replied with genuine enthusiasm, sitting down next to him and launching into a series of questions about the plot and Irene's ultimate fate. They talked animatedly, the conversation moving from the play to the writer's home at Ferney near Geneva, her childhood in the Habsburg capital of Vienna and her recent life at the French Court. The queen displayed a lively interest in everything he had to say, and he was pleasantly surprised by her curiosity and intelligence, so different to the reports he had received of her since her marriage to King Louis XVI four years previously.

After thirty minutes, the marquis intervened to ask whether the queen would like some food, explaining that Voltaire had eaten earlier in the evening. She shook her head and said brightly, 'What shall we do instead, Monsieur Voltaire? Do you play cards? Perhaps a hand or two of quadrille, and you can take some money off me?'

Voltaire gave a tired laugh and shifted uncomfortably on the sofa. 'You are humouring me, Your Majesty. I have heard it said you enjoy playing cards, and I suspect you would be the victor. In any case, my gambling days are behind me. I have no more need of money.' He leant forward to cough heavily into a handkerchief and sank back into the cushions. 'I'm dying, you see.'

'Surely not,' the queen protested, more cheerfully than she felt. 'The journey from Ferney to Paris has exhausted you, but in a few days, you will be up and about, ready to enjoy the new play. After all, you cannot let the public down. They are waiting outside the theatre to salute you, and I assure you they are more interested in you than me!'

'No, my dear, I wish it were true, but I am eighty-three, and my time is fast approaching.' He paused for a moment and then went on in a stronger voice.'However, I have an idea, if you will bear with me for a moment.' He turned stiffly and beckoned to his manservant hovering by the door. 'Armand, fetch my writing case please, the small one, sitting on the bureau.' They waited, discussing the attitude of the Parisian people to the royal family in recent months, and again Voltaire was surprised by the frank and self-aware responses he received. Then the servant reappeared with a battered brown leather valise, which the writer opened and balanced on his knees to pick something out of a pouch on the underside of the lid. Marie Antoinette watched with amusement, not knowing what to expect.

'I would like to tell you a little story, if I may,' Voltaire said, and she nodded.'Many years ago, before you were born, I met another monarch here in Paris, a man called Charles Edward Stuart. His grandfather had been deposed from the throne of England, and shortly before we met, Charles had tried to win the throne back. But his army had been defeated in battle, and he had spent several months on the run in Scotland before he could escape to France. He returned to Paris, and since that time, he has spent many more years plotting another invasion. It has never come to pass, for various reasons, but not for lack of passion on his part.' He looked at her steadily.'You are wondering where this is leading, of course. Well, hear me out. At our meeting, we played cards, and I won. Instead of paying me with coins, he gave me this.' He opened his hand to reveal a highly polished silver ball, pitted and dented on one side, and laid it on the sofa cover between them.

'A bullet?' the queen asked in surprise.

'Yes, indeed. But not just an ordinary one. The bullet was originally used to kill a wolf, probably the last wolf in Britain. Prince Charles was given it as a good luck token before his battle against the British army and carried it with him on his escape. To me it is a symbol not so much of good fortune, for obvious reasons, but of hope over adversity. He never gave up in his royal quest, and I have kept the bullet with me ever since I won it, in my own life-long quest for freedom of thought. Now it is time I handed it on to someone else, and since I will not let you win money from me at cards, I would like to give the bullet to you instead. If I may be so bold, I suggest you and the king use it as a reminder to take care of your crowns. As Charles and his family found, they are easy to lose and difficult to regain.' He fell silent, and his eyelids began to blink with fatigue.

Marie Antoinette was mesmerised by the strange offering, and after picking it up to inspect it more closely, she said in a quiet voice, 'Monsieur Voltaire, I've received many gifts, first as the daughter of an empress and more recently as a queen, but nothing with a history like this. I promise you I will cherish it.' She looked at the bullet once again and frowned in concentration, as if committing something to memory. 'Hope over adversity, you say? It will be my guiding light in the years to come.' Then she stood, aware that the old man's energy was fading rapidly. 'Now, it is time to leave you. But I shall look forward to receiving you at Versailles before you return to Ferney, and I don't want to hear any more nonsense about you dying in the meantime.' She dropped the bullet into a silk purse hanging at the waist of her dress and began to bid farewell to the marquis, who had been listening in astonishment to the conversation. Behind her, on the sofa, Voltaire was already sound asleep.

*

October 1793 – Paris, France

The trial had taken two whole days, the Revolutionary Tribunal sitting for fifteen hours on the first day and seventeen hours on the second, a farcical length of time considering the outcome had been decided in advance by the Committee of Public Safety. The verdict had been delivered at 4.30am, and the defendant had been returned to the Conciergerie prison, to prepare herself for execution at noon. She had been found guilty of treason against the state, amongst other lesser crimes, for which the inevitable sentence was death by guillotine. When asked by the Tribunal if she had anything to say in response, she had remained silent. What was there to add, after a process in which she had been given no opportunity to marshal her defence and a sequence of events that had begun so long ago?

Back in her cell for a few hours, Marie Antoinette sat reflecting on those events, as she had done so often in the weeks leading up to the trial. Her fate had been sealed when her husband, King Louis XVI, had been found guilty of treason the previous January. He had been executed by guillotine within a week, in front of a baying mob of some twenty thousand, as described to her in loathsome detail by her gaolers, and she knew at that point it was only a matter of time before she was subjected to the same treatment. In some ways, she was surprised it had taken so many months. Despite the lack of communication with the outside world, the imprisonment had been tolerable while her children and sister-in-law had remained with her. However, in July, her eight-year-old son Louis-Charles, strictly speaking now King Louis XVII, had been dragged from her, never to be reunited, and then in

August she had been moved to solitary confinement. There she had been kept under continuous surveillance, tormented by the ever-present guards and provided with no privacy other than a flimsy screen across part of the cell. She did not need the pretence of a trial to recognise how abject her position now was in the relentless march of the Revolution.

And yet in reality, she mused, the writing had been on the wall for at least two years. After the bread shortages and the storming of the Bastille in mid-1789, the royal family had been forced out of Versailles to be held under house arrest at the Tuileries Palace in Paris. Life had returned to some kind of normality the following summer, when the lawmaker Mirabeau had intervened on their behalf in an attempt to broker a reconciliation between the monarchy and the revolutionaries. The king had agreed to enforce laws voted by the National Assembly, and they had been permitted to visit their chateau at Saint-Cloud, just west of the capital. However, the mood had changed again in the spring of 1791, when Mirabeau died, and they lost what little leverage they had enjoyed within the Assembly. Being blocked from travelling to Saint-Cloud for Easter was the trigger for the queen to begin plotting their escape from France, and looking back, she could place the slippery slope to her death sentence on a single chaotic week.

In June 1791, she had arranged, with the king's reluctant agreement, for the royal family to flee across the northeastern border to the Netherlands, a region controlled by her brother, the Austrian emperor, Leopold II. From there the intention had been to gather an army to exert pressure on the Assembly, through the threat of invasion, to reinstate King Louis in the position of absolute power he had held prior to the Revolution. The expedition had been a disaster from the beginning. After slipping out of the Tuileries under the cover of darkness, improbably disguised as servants to a Russian baroness, they had been recognised the following afternoon at one of the staging posts on their journey through the French countryside. Detachments of royalist cavalry that were supposed to join them from the border as an escort had failed to emerge as planned, and twenty-four hours after they had set out, they had been arrested at gunpoint in a small town called Varennes. Within four days, to the abuse and ridicule of the mob, they had been returned to the Tuileries Palace and placed under close guard. They had been only three hours or so from the sanctuary of the border, but it was a lifetime in terms of the impact. The purpose of their attempted escape, to summon Austrian forces to attack France, became the talk of Paris, and Marie Antoinette had always been viewed with suspicion as a foreigner with the interests of an enemy power at heart. The people's support for the royal family, already hanging on a thread, had been irreparably damaged, and the later discovery of documents belonging to the king confirming the treasonable plan had led within weeks to his death.

The rattle of a key in the cell's door lock roused her from her thoughts, and she stood to see over the screen who her visitor might be. A last-minute reprieve was unlikely, but hope sprang eternal. The door swung open and a large, bull-like man entered, dressed entirely in black. His bald head gleamed in the early morning light coming from the small window high in the back wall, and the queen needed no introduction. 'Monsieur Sanson, we meet again,' she said dryly.

'Yes, My Lady,' said the man politely, 'I do not choose my clients, you understand, but we have an appointment at noon.'

'So I gather,' Marie Antoinette replied, 'and just nine months on since you came for my husband. Don't you have enough royal blood on your hands? I am prepared to dispense with Madame Guillotine's favours if you are.'

'Again, My Lady, I am simply following my orders. King Louis was brave to the end, and I have no doubt you shall be too. There is a practical matter I must take care of, and then I will leave you in peace before your final journey to meet me in the Place de la Révolution.' He held her gaze with no trace of embarrassment as he took a large pair of scissors from his coat pocket. 'I regret to say I must cut your hair.'

The queen had been warned of this, and there was no point resisting. She lowered her head, and in a few rough snips, the executioner cut her shoulder-length tresses to an uneven line above her neck, the hair that had turned grey overnight in Varennes, she remembered, as she saw it falling around her feet. 'Thank you, My Lady,' Sanson said once the work was done, still scrupulously polite, 'I will see you again in three hours' time,' and with that he bowed and left the cell. As the door closed behind him, she considered the irony – prison guards leering at her for three months with barely a civil word or action between them, and then a man who would kill her later that morning with better manners than she might have expected from her own family. The time for rage or anguish at her fate was long gone, and she bore no ill will to Henri Sanson. He had a job to do, and in the febrile atmosphere of the Revolution no one, not even the head executioner, was foolish enough to defy his instructions.

Ninety minutes later, Marie Antoinette completed a final letter, folded it into an envelope addressed to her sister-in-law Elizabeth and placed it on the rough table in front of her to await collection. Besides her pen and ink, the only other item on the table was her letter case, the single personal possession she had been allowed to keep when reduced to solitary confinement. She delved in the bottom of the case, withdrew a small object and rolled it thoughtfully in the crease of her palm. So much adversity in the fifteen years since she had been given it, and yet until now she had never lost hope. Like Voltaire she had chosen to keep the silver bullet with her writing materials, and remarkably, her guards in the Conciergerie had never bothered to search the bottom of the little case. The dented bullet sparkled, even in the dim light of the cell, and with it all the excitements and setbacks of her reign alongside the king came flooding back to her. The extravagances of Versailles; the frustration of house arrest in Paris; the return to public acceptance under Mirabeau; the doomed escape and capture in Varennes; the readiness of Barnave and his moderates to negotiate with her on behalf of her timid husband until the extremists took control of the Assembly; the terrifying night that the Tuileries palace was stormed and they had fled on foot into the streets; and finally, of course, the abolition of the monarchy and Louis's execution. She had kept her promise to Voltaire, to cherish the bullet and her crown, but now, like the playwright's Irene, the final act in her tumultuous life was over. Adversity had triumphed, despite all her efforts, and there was nothing more to do but wait for her appointment with Sanson and his dreaded guillotine.

When the guards came for her, she was sitting peacefully, her hands curled in front of her, ready for the ropes she knew would be brought to bind her wrists. As they led her out into the courtyard, she looked back at the dingy cell she had spent so long in, water dripping down the cracked walls, her shorn hair strewn across the filthy stone floor, the screen on one side of the room that had offered so little privacy. Then she climbed onto the tumbrel, and the journey through the Paris streets began. The mob was everywhere, hundreds lining every pavement and thousands more waiting in the Place de la Révolution where the guillotine had been plying its daily trade for the last few months. The noise was ear-splitting, wave after wave of mass jeering interspersed with individual taunts and obscenities. Only when she began to walk up the steps to the scaffold where the executioner waited for her did it subside, the people straining to hear any last words from the woman they had called Widow Capet since her husband's death on the same spot.

'Hello again, My Lady,' said Sanson, polite as ever. 'Do you have anything you wish to say to the crowd?' Marie Antoinette shook her head, and he guided her gently across the wooden platform, her head held high, her clenched hands still tied in front of her. At the base of the guillotine, she stopped to examine the scene around her, the crowd silently drinking in the delicious horror of the moment, then she swivelled back to face the executioner, inadvertently treading on his shoe as she turned.

'Excuse me,' she said, 'I did not mean to do that.' Sanson shrugged off her apology and motioned for her to go down on her knees, but she continued. 'Monsieur Sanson, allow me to do one last thing.' She opened one of her fists and showed him the silver bullet. 'This has guided me for many years, but I have no more need of it now. Unlike others, you have treated me with respect, so take it, with my thanks, and do your job swiftly.' He lifted it out of her hand without comment, then she knelt, rested her chin on the cup of the blood-stained headblock, and the blade crashed down on her bare neck. Her severed head tumbled into the basket below, and the crowd erupted with approval, shouting, *'Vive la République,'* over and over again. On the platform next to Marie Antoinette's headless body, Henri Sanson bowed to his audience, muttering instead under his breath, *'Vive l'argent'.*

*

And then…

Unaware of the bullet's curious history, and with access to state institutions such as the National Mint through his official role as head executioner for the Republic, Sanson sells it to the Mint where it is converted into a one-franc coin.

Recast on three occasions over the next seventy-five years to mark the leadership of Napoleon Bonaparte, the restoration of the monarchy under King Louis XVIII and then the launch of the Second French Empire under Napoleon III, the coin remains in circulation in Paris.

During the Franco-Prussian War of 1870–71, Paris is invaded, and the coin falls into the hands of a Prussian soldier. It is taken back to Berlin where it is exchanged for local currency at the Reichsbank, the central bank for the newly created nation state of Germany. It remains in a vault there for another sixty years.

In early 1936 Adolf Hitler, Chancellor of Germany, instructs the Reichsbank to release disused silver and gold items from its vaults for conversion to medals in readiness for the forthcoming Olympic Games in Berlin. The one-franc coin is recast as a silver medal for the women's two-hundred-metre sprint event.

*

Author's Note

Marie Antoinette, youngest daughter of the Austrian empress, Maria Theresa and the Holy Roman Emperor, Francis I, became Queen of France in 1774 when her husband ascended the throne as Louis XVI. She was only thirty-seven when she was executed on 16 October 1793. The details of her hair being shorn, her hands being tied, her journey through the streets in the tumbrel (an open cart) from the Conciergerie to the Place de la Révolution (now the Place de la Concorde) and her apology to the executioner Henri Sanson for treading on his shoe, are all true, although there is no record of her going on to give him payment in any form for a swift end.

The reference to the royal family's escape from Paris in disguise in June 1791, and their subsequent arrest at gunpoint in Varennes, is also factual. The queen and her husband had been caught red-handed in an attempt to bring foreign forces to bear on the French state, so the charges of treason at their brief and probably rigged trials were easily proven. Another charge, and a long-held opinion amongst the population, that Marie Antoinette's excessive spending was responsible for the country's economic woes, was less valid. France's financial difficulties were largely the result of several costly wars, exacerbated by a run of poor harvests which raised the cost of bread dramatically, prompting riots in Paris and elsewhere. Although she was wildly extravagant in the early years of her marriage at Versailles, and known to be fond of gambling, the queen's expenses (funded by the state) would only have accounted for a small portion of the country's huge debts. While she resisted the social and financial reforms proposed in the lead-up to the Revolution, she was neither as foolish nor as insensitive as she is often depicted. Faced with an introverted and indecisive husband, she found herself drawn increasingly into political negotiations on his behalf with the likes of Mirabeau and Barnave, both of whom were said to be impressed by her intelligence and eager to find a role for the monarchy within the objectives of the Revolution. After the failed attempt to escape in mid-1791, France's declaration of war against Austria in April 1792 and the creation of the National Convention as the ruling body of the Republic following the abolition of the monarchy in September 1792, her fate was effectively sealed.

There is at least an element of truth in the parts played by Voltaire and Charles Edward Stuart (Bonnie Prince Charlie) in this chapter. Voltaire came to Paris in late February 1778, after a twenty-year absence at his estate near Geneva, for the launch of his new play Irene at the Théâtre des Tuileries. Marie Antoinette attended the premiere, but Voltaire was prevented from doing so by illness, and he died two months later in the house of his host, the Marquis de Villette. It is not known whether he ever met Bonnie Prince Charlie, but in December 1745 he wrote a manifesto for the French King Louis XV expressing the monarchy's support for the prince's invasion of Britain, and it is therefore possible that he might have been introduced to the prince at some point after the latter's escape from Scotland to France in late 1746. Both he and the prince were likely to have been in Paris around this time.

Fourteen

1936 Olympic Games

1 August 1936 – Berlin, Germany

'How much longer do we have to wait?' Rachael Becker grumbled to herself, little realising that she could be heard amongst the din booming out through the stadium gates ahead of them. She had been standing for two hours, and her legs were aching. It would not have mattered, if those legs were not the reason she was here in the first place, and she worried that they might somehow be damaged by the inaction. It was a ridiculous notion, of course; her big race was five days off, and she was in peak physical condition, but she had not come all this way to stand still for the Germans' benefit.

'Any moment now,' said a male voice behind her, and she looked round in surprise. A tall, good-looking man was smiling broadly, and she regretted her petulant remark immediately. 'Don't worry,' he added, seeing her embarrassment, 'I'm as fed up as you, but I think the kick-off is imminent. Look,' he pointed over the walls of the stadium, as a huge airship loomed into view, swastikas emblazoned on its tailfins and the Olympic flag streaming in its wake. 'The Hindenberg. That's the signal for the officials to take their seats, and then we'll begin the march round the track.' Together with the rest of the US team, they craned their necks to admire the airship as its shadow enveloped them, and then a peel of trumpets came from the loudspeakers nearby.

'Here we go,' said the man and pointed again, this time along the spectator-lined avenue leading from the centre of the city. A convoy of open-topped cars was making its way slowly towards the stadium gates, the crowd clapping and cheering as it passed by. At the cordoned-off apron to the gates, watched by the assembled athletes from all the national teams, the vehicles drew to a halt; doors were opened by crisply uniformed chauffeurs; and a score of dignitaries stepped out onto the paving. Apart from the president of the International Olympic Committee, the Comte de Baillet-Latour, who had visited the US training camp the previous week, Rachael recognised only one of them. Emerging from the leading car to a roar of welcome down the avenue was the chancellor of Germany. You could not spend two weeks in Berlin, in the run-up to the biggest sporting event ever staged, and not know what Adolf Hitler looked like.

The group waved in acknowledgement to the crowd and also to the teams of athletes waiting to begin their ceremonial procession into the stadium. Then Hitler led the way through the massive stone-pillared gates, pausing only to receive a bouquet of flowers from a little girl. She curtseyed politely, and the chancellor bent down to pat her benevolently on the shoulder, before resuming his path onto the running track. One hundred thousand ticket holders within the stadium stood to deliver a deafening rendition of the national anthem, "Deutschland Über Alles", and the officials climbed the steps to a tier of balconies swathed in swastika flags, the uppermost reserved for Hitler and his principal government ministers.

As they took their seats, the music changed, and the crowd switched to the Nazi party anthem, "Horst Wessel Lied", the volume rising to a crescendo when Hitler stood up again to offer the stiff-armed party salute at the final bars of the song. At last, the cauldron of noise subsided, and the spectators' attention was diverted once more to the gates.

Rachael and her US teammates had been drawn up in parade form outside the stadium walls, along with all the other forty-eight national teams, in readiness for this moment. The Greeks were the first to march onto the track, in recognition of their Olympic heritage, and as they filed past the balconies, their flag-bearer proudly leading the way, the competitors saluted, as one, to the group of officials. Behind them the process was repeated in alphabetical order by every country, some giving the Nazi greeting, some the Olympic welcome sign, some, like the US, removing their hats and making an eyes-right gesture. The crowd cheered each team, the loudest applause going, inevitably, to the Germans as Hitler rose to his feet once again to return their salute. Rachael followed the example of the rank in front of her, relieved to be on the move and slightly unnerved by the noise reverberating round the inside of the stadium and the martial formality of the event. She had given little thought to the political aspect of the opening ceremony, and only now was she beginning to understand that this was more a display of German nationalism than worldwide sporting prowess. As the US team arrived in their seats and settled down to watch the remaining teams march in, she found herself next to the man she had unintentionally spoken to outside the walls.

'Quite some performance, isn't it?' he leaned down to speak into her ear. 'It's all for effect of course, to make us think the Germans are a superior race and that they'll win everything. Allow me to introduce myself. My name's David Ehrlich.' He smiled again, and they shook hands.

'Hi, David, I'm Rachael,' she replied. 'Thanks for keeping me right earlier, but how did you know about the airship and the cavalcade? Your timing was either brilliant or incredibly lucky!'

'A bit of both,' he laughed. 'A friend of mine in the press corps told me the Hindenberg was the signal for the opening ceremony to begin, and I knew Hitler would want to make a big entrance. The whole thing has been stage-managed to the last degree, to show how super-efficient the Germans are. That guy there, Joseph Goebbels, the dark, thin-faced man sitting two along from Hitler,' he pointed to the chancellor's balcony directly across the running track from them, 'he's organised it all. He's in charge of Nazi propaganda, and you have to admit, he's very good at it. He's also one of the people responsible for the treatment being dished out to the Jews here.'

'What do you mean?' said Rachael, increasingly intrigued by her teammate. Now that she had been able to see his face properly, she remembered that she had glimpsed him in the Olympic village several times in the last two weeks, although she had no idea what his sport might be.

'You know, the way Jews aren't allowed into restaurants and shops; their businesses are boycotted by the Germans; they can't hold jobs in the civil service; they're not allowed to vote, all that stuff that has been going on since the Nazis came to power.' Ehrlich looked at Rachael as if what he was saying was self-explanatory. She shook her head in confusion.

'Sorry, David, this is all new to me. I don't really know anything about Germany. I just got a late call to join the athletics squad, and I've spent most of my time training since we arrived. I have Jewish relatives in New York, but I haven't seen them in ages.'

'You really have been living under a stone!' Ehrlich laughed again. 'I'm afraid you have a lot to catch up on. I'll tell you about it back in the village. With such a racket going on, this isn't really the place for it.'

'OK,' Rachael said, 'but at least tell me who all those people around Hitler are. He's the only one I recognise.'

'Well, it looks like the march-past is about to finish, so I'll make it quick before the Germans start hollering at their idol again. On Hitler's left is Hermann Goering, President of the Parliament, looks jolly enough but a nasty piece of work, apparently.' Rachael could see a large florid figure dressed in a white uniform, clearly revelling in the attention of the mostly German spectators. 'Next to him is von Ribbentrop, the foreign affairs minister and one of Hitler's favourites, which means nobody else trusts him. Then there's Reinhard Heydrich, head of the Gestapo secret police, so you can imagine what a charming character he is. And the one on the end is Albert Speer, the chief architect for the Nazis, who supervised the design of this stadium.' Ehrlich paused as the noise swelled to mark the last national team's salute to the balconies. 'On Hitler's right is Heinrich Himmler, head of the national police force, Heydrich's boss, a real Jew-hater, apparently. Then there's Goebbels, then Rudolf Hess, Deputy *Führer* to Hitler and, lastly, Hess's sidekick Martin Bormann who seems to have winkled his way into Hitler's favour as a kind of private secretary. He knows where all the skeletons are buried, if anyone does, but hanging onto Hitler's coat-tails can be a dangerous game. So there you are, the Nazi party in a nutshell!'

Rachael continued to gaze at the nine men seated in the top balcony opposite her, uncomfortably aware how ignorant she was about the country she had arrived in over two weeks ago. Most of Ehrlich's summary had meant nothing to her, but her interest was aroused by the references to the Jews. After all, her grandfather was Jewish, a runner in his younger days from whom she guessed she had inherited her athletic genes. She owed it to him to learn more about the treatment being dished out to his people, as David had phrased it. The girl on her other side was nudging her in the ribs to draw attention to something, and before she turned to see what it was, she said, 'That's brilliant, David, but it looks like I urgently need to take a class in German current affairs. Will you be my tutor, back in the village?'

'Sure,' he answered easily, 'I'm running the marathon, and it's not for another eight days. Any time that suits you. Come and find me, and I'll look forward to lesson one.' Then he gestured to her other neighbour and began to chat with the man on his far side.

Rachael looked down onto the track where the girl next to her was pointing. An ash-blond man in white singlet and shorts had come through the gates and was now running clockwise round the circuit, holding a burning torch high in front of him. The athlete in her could not help but be impressed by his superb agility and the strength required to hold the heavy torch steady. The runner passed in front of the dignitaries and moved on to the far end of the loop, the applause rising as he neared the steps running up the side of the stadium to a wide-open stone platform. Without pausing, he began to ascend the steps, his chest heaving with effort as he climbed. On the platform stood a huge circular metal font, as tall as the man himself, and he reached up to dip the torch over its side. Flames leapt up as the oil in the font ignited, and the spectators bellowed in excitement. Then, as the runner stepped back and bowed to the officials in the balconies, Hitler rose from his seat to stand at a microphone, and the noise fell away to absolute silence. Every eye in the stadium was on him as he announced, 'I proclaim open the Olympic Games of Berlin, celebrating the eleventh Olympiad of the modern era.' The crowd went wild, nearly a hundred thousand voices in unison shouting the national call to victory: 'Sieg Heil, Sieg Heil, Sieg Heil.' All eight of Hitler's ministers joined him in a final Nazi salute to their countrymen, and the international visitors looked on in awed astonishment, never having witnessed a tribal display quite like it.

*

6 August 1936 – Berlin, Germany

The day of Rachael's final competition had arrived, and she woke to the familiar sensation of butterflies and mild nausea. These would grow, she knew, as the time of the race drew nearer, and would disappear in an instant once the starting pistol had fired. But today there was an added element of tension.

At the age of nineteen, Rachael was one of the youngest members of the US athletics squad. Raised in a village outside Kansas City, she had been encouraged by the headmistress of her high school to join a running club, where she had been spotted in sprint races by a state team coach. By eighteen she was the one-hundred-metre Kansas State champion and had caught the eye of the national talent spotters. Six weeks before the US Olympic team was due to travel to Berlin, one of the leading female runners, Matty Berenger, had broken her arm in a freak cycling accident, and the team organisers had reshuffled the race allocations amongst the squad. A new Olympic event for female competitors had been announced, the two-hundred-metre sprint, and Rachael had been selected to represent the US in this, leaving the more experienced runners to focus on the blue-riband one-hundred-metre race and the four-by-one-hundred-metre relay. With no international racing exposure, indeed having only left her home state for the first time to travel to the US team embarkation point of New York, she was hugely out of her depth. The one thing she had learnt from her new Olympic coach, however, was that she was amongst the fastest girls in the world over this new distance of two hundred metres. And her fiercely competitive nature would make up for the lack of experience.

Since their arrival in the Olympic village in mid-July, Rachael had spent most of her time at the training track. She was naturally shy and, being younger than most of her colleagues, she tended to hold back from the conversations around the dining hall and common rooms. Her roommate, an eighty-metre hurdles specialist from Pittsburgh, was as unsophisticated as she was, and between them they were blissfully ignorant of the backdrop to the Games in Berlin. It was only since her chance conversation with David Ehrlich at the opening ceremony that she had begun to take an interest in the rise to power of Hitler's Nazi party and the current situation in Germany. She had met David on two more occasions in the village and had been appalled by what he had told her. From a Jewish background himself, he was the first to admit that he might be biased, but the facts spoke for themselves.

'Think about it, Rachael,' he had said, 'the Nazis are the only political party in the country. Any opposition is illegal, so they can basically do what they like. Last year they passed laws stripping Jews from citizenship, sacking them from the civil service and stopping them from marrying so-called normal Germans. If you're a Jewish shopkeeper or business owner, non-Jews won't buy from you; if you're a Jewish doctor, you're prohibited from working in public health buildings like hospitals or surgeries. For over a year now, there have been posters in public places saying "Jews not wanted". They've even banned Jews from gyms and sports clubs. If you don't believe me, just look at what happened to Gretel Bergmann, the German high jump champion. She was expelled from her club three years ago and then booted out of their Olympic team a few weeks ago, even though she holds the national record. She was told it was due to underperformance, but everyone knows it was really because she's Jewish.'

'But that's crazy,' Rachael had protested. 'Why would they do all this? Especially when they're in the international spotlight as hosts to the Games. And why on earth would they exclude one of their likely medal winners, when you told me yourself at the opening ceremony that they want to win everything?'

'Well, that's just it. They want to showcase Germany as the master race, and the way they see it, that doesn't include Jews. But they've tried to hide what they're doing. My friend in the press corps tells me that they took down all the anti-Semitic posters in Berlin a month ago and that they promised the International Olympic Committee German Jews would be allowed to participate, even though that's clearly not true. There's plenty of examples besides Bergmann. The worst of it is the lack of international awareness. There's been a few articles in foreign newspapers like the New York Times, but it's not getting the coverage it deserves.' He had sighed heavily in frustration.

'My grandparents back in New York are Jewish, or at least my grandfather is,' Rachael had explained. 'He emigrated from Germany before the Great War. My grandmother's side of the family are Methodists, so we've kind of lost our Jewish roots. I'll tell Grandpa all about this when I get home to show him my gold medal.' They had both laughed, and the conversation had reverted to training programmes and preparation tips, as it always seemed to in the Olympic village.

Rachael had not forgotten David's description of German-Jewish oppression in the intervening days, but it had been overtaken by the excitement of events on the running track. The US sprinter Jesse Owens had caused a huge upset to the Germans' quest for supremacy by winning three gold medals in consecutive days. He had beaten the German favourite Lutz Long into second place in the one hundred metres and had gone on to win the long jump and the two hundred metres as well. According to David Ehrlich's press sources, Hitler had been incandescent with rage, not just that Long had been beaten but that he had lost to a black American. The fact that another American, Helen Stephens, had won the women's one hundred metres at the expense of Germany's Käthe Krauss had not helped matters. The American camp had been ecstatic, and the surge of patriotic enthusiasm had only served to heighten the expectations on the newcomer to the team in the untested two-hundred-metre race format. Rachael could not wait to be out on the track, and the minutes ticked by agonisingly slowly.

At last, however, lunch came and went, and she was transported to the stadium in good time for the 4.00pm start. In the changing rooms she exchanged brief greetings with the other competitors, all strangers to her from a mix of different countries. From the heats the previous day, she recognised the two her coach had told her to watch out for, the Polish girl Margot Wapiennik and a young German Ilse Reinbach, and she took careful note of their running bib colours as she shook hands with them. Then they were escorted out to face the noise of the crowd, rising and falling at the spectacle of the men's discus event taking place in the centre of the arena. They took their places on the eight-lane track, Rachael at number three, with Wapiennik next to her at number four and Reinbach two further over at number six. She shook her limbs to loosen any muscle tightness, surveyed the line of girls on either side calmly, then crouched to dig her starting blocks in the compacted cinder running surface, the world shuttering down to a twenty-five second tunnel of lung-bursting intensity. The thought of her grandfather sitting by the radio in the early morning of New York flickered in her mind, and she knew she must take a medal home to him.

'*Auf die Plätze… Fertig…*' *Bang*, the starting pistol sounded, and she was off the line like a greyhound. Rounding the curve of the first hundred metres, she could see the German girl in the lead, but that meant nothing until the straight. The Pole was just behind her, and as they kicked into the second hundred they were exactly level. The other runners were falling away, and with fifty metres to go, it was a three-way race, Reinbach still leading by almost half a second. Rachael could hear Wapiennik straining next to her, and they ran on, shoulder to shoulder. Twenty metres out, they had caught the German, and at ten metres Rachael was ahead by a fraction. Three strides… two… and she lunged for the tape with her head and chest, as her coach had taught her. It had gone, breached by the Pole less than one tenth of a second ahead of her. She looked to her right and saw Reinbach crossing the line in third, arms flailing in exhaustion, then she gathered her breath and hugged Margot Wapiennik in congratulation. She had taken Olympic silver in her first international competition and scored a personal best; she disliked losing, but she was comfortable that she had given it her all. And she had done her grandfather proud.

Thirty minutes later, the three girls stood on the podium next to the running track, waiting for the medal ceremony to begin. Hitler himself was due to present the medals, the first time he had chosen to do so since the Games began, to mark the inaugural race for women over two hundred metres. The word was that he had agreed in the expectation of a German victory, so he would be deeply disappointed. For Rachael, however, all thoughts of the country's aspirations for racial supremacy had vanished. She was still bubbling with excitement at her second place and enjoying every moment of her time on the floor of the stadium. She watched as a group of three men and a woman bearing a tray made their way towards her, recognising amongst them the German chancellor, the IOC president and the official that had fired the starter's pistol for their race. They came to a halt at the left-hand end of the podium, and the loudspeaker blared, *'Die Bronzemedaille, für Fräulein Ilse Reinbach, von Deutschland.'* Hitler picked a medal off the tray, and the German girl dipped her head for him to place it around her neck. A massive cheer echoed round the stadium, and Ilse straightened to smile her thanks and wave at the crowd. Once the noise had subsided, Hitler exchanged a few words with her, shook her hand warmly and moved to the other end of the podium where Rachael stood.

She noticed with surprise how compact he was, a square, stocky figure dressed in a neat but unremarkable brown uniform, the trademark moustache neatly clipped, his eyes hidden under the peak of his cap. She listened for the magical words from the announcer, *'Die Silbermedaille, für Fräulein Rachael Becker, von die Vereinigten Staaten von Amerika'.* Then, like the girl before her, she bent forward to receive her medal, scarcely registering how muted the cheering was from the partisan spectators. As she soaked in the atmosphere, she was surprised to hear Hitler speak in halting English.

'Congratulations, *Fräulein* Becker. You have a German name, I notice. You are from a German family, perhaps?'

Rachael had not expected to be allowed to talk to the great man, the leader of all Germany and figurehead of the Games. She had certainly not planned to make a scene. She was just a naive nineteen-year-old from the Midwest, relishing every second of her racing result. As she raised her head, touching the silver medal in front of her, she locked eyes with him for the first time, and the words tumbled out before she could restrain herself.

'My grandfather's family were Jews from Hamburg. I have inherited my running skills from him. I won this medal for him.'

In that instant, the expression of hatred, of pure and unconfined evil, was laid bare across Hitler's face, the force of it almost a physical punch at Rachael. She jerked her head back, and without another word, he turned to his left to address the gold medallist beside her. The IOC president, the Comte de Baillet-Latour, gave her a pitying glance, and the other male official brandished an oak seedling in a pot at her, the gift to all medallists at the Games. She was hardly aware of it being thrust into her hands, of the cheer for Margot Wapiennik and the sound of the Polish national anthem, such was the lingering malevolence of what she had just experienced.

*

Mid-December 1941 – Washington DC, USA ˙

David Ehrlich lifted the telephone on the table in his front hallway, surprised to have his Friday evening interrupted by the shrill bell. 'This is the operator speaking. I have a call for you from Kansas City central post office, do you wish to take it?' There was only one person it could be. 'Yes, thank you,' he replied and listened to the metallic clicks on the line as the call was put through.

'David, are you there?' Her voice was immediately recognisable. 'It's me, Rachael Becker.'

'No need to introduce yourself, Rachael, I'd know your voice anywhere. What a treat to hear you amongst all the bad news. You found my number?'

'It was on your letter heading the last time you wrote to me. Listen, I need to hurry because this is costing me a fortune. I need a favour, but I think it's one you'll approve of.'

'OK, go for it,' he said, wondering what was coming. Germany had declared war on the US the previous day, but it surely wasn't connected to that. Despite all his efforts to educate her over the last few years, he reckoned Rachael was still fairly detached from the real world. They had kept in touch regularly by letter ever since the Berlin Olympics, and she had visited him in Washington once when she was attending an interstate athletics championship there. He had brought her up to date with events in Europe, and it was evident she had taken the trouble to learn more about the Nazis' ill-treatment of Jews since 1936. Even so, her life as a primary school teacher in Kansas City was both all-consuming and at the same time very remote from the atrocities taking place on the other side of the Atlantic.

'I've made a decision,' Rachael spoke quickly. 'I've decided to hand in my Olympic medal to express my disgust at Hitler and his people, now that we're at war. I should have done it years ago. It's a tiny gesture, but if it raises awareness of what they're doing to the Jews, then it's worth it. I'm coming to Washington next week to meet the Kansas senator Arthur Capper at the Capitol Building, and I wondered if you could arrange some press coverage.'

David was amazed. His lessons, as she called them, had evidently made more of an impression than he had realised. Then he remembered her Jewish grandfather and how upset she had been after meeting Hitler in Berlin. 'That's fantastic,' he said. 'Tell me what day, and leave the rest to me. Come and stay when you're here.'

'A week today, ten in the morning,' she answered. 'The school term finishes on the seventeenth, and I need to be back home again for Christmas. I'll take you up on the offer of a bed, on the eighteenth and nineteenth, if that's OK. I'll call you when I arrive in town. Must go, see you...' and the line went dead. David stood in the hallway, looking at the handset thoughtfully. As usual, Rachael was doing things at top speed. Perhaps between them they could really make a difference.

Over the course of the next week, David talked to a variety of people in the Washington political hierarchy. Working as an advertising manager at the *Chesapeake Gazette*, one of the city's regional newspapers, meant that organising the press was the easy part, even though he was not a journalist himself. More delicate was the matter of political sensitivity around the Jewish cause. He had come across this the hard way since moving to the capital in 1939 and acting as a local representative for the World Jewish Congress. Despite all the evidence from the previous decade, there was still a reluctance in Washington to acknowledge what was happening. The barbarity of the "Kristallnacht" oppression unleashed across Nazi Germany in 1938; Hitler's speech on his tenth anniversary as chancellor proposing the complete annihilation of the Jewish race; reports in the last six months of large numbers being murdered in eastern Europe – so much to tell and yet so little being done. The president was understood to be receptive to the cause, but many of his colleagues in the Senate and Congress less so. David knew nothing about the Republican senator, Capper, and decided to leave him to Rachael. There were better angles to focus on from his list of contacts, and he worked feverishly every evening to bring them to fruition. By the time Rachael appeared on his doorstep, it looked as though all the pieces had fallen into place, subject to what she had arranged with Capper and a hefty dose of luck.

On the morning of 19 December, David and Rachael took a cab to the Capitol Building and explained at the gate that they were there to meet the Kansas senator. Their names were ticked off a list, and they were ushered into a vestibule. After several minutes, a secretary led them into a meeting room where over a dozen men were already gathered. David had briefed Rachael on who would be there, and she talked easily with each of them as she was introduced. Besides Senator Capper, there were representatives from the American Olympic Committee and the Amateur Athletics Union, some of whom had witnessed her extraordinary exchange with Adolf Hitler at the medal ceremony in Berlin. As a state-level marathon runner for several years after the Olympics, David had remained in touch with both organisations and had been able to pick up the phone to them to suggest their attendance. Also in the room were a sports writer, a political journalist and a photographer from the *Gazette*, for what David had promised them would be the scoop of the year. Only one person was missing, an invitee lined up by the *Gazette*'s well-connected chief executive, but it had not been clear whether he would find time to attend, and David had not mentioned his name to Rachael.

'Well, I suggest we begin,' announced the senator in a loud voice, cutting across the conversations around the room. 'Miss Becker here is a constituent of mine in Kansas, who many of you will remember from her medal-winning performance at the Berlin Olympics five years ago. She has something important she wishes to say, and I am delighted to welcome her here. Rachael, the floor is yours.' He beckoned her forward and, for the first time since her arrival, she looked nervous. 'Don't worry,' Capper smiled soothingly as he watched her struggling for words. 'You dealt with Hitler just fine, so don't be shy amongst friends.'

'Thank you, Senator,' she replied, blushing slightly. 'I really appreciate you inviting me here and allowing these folks along too.' She gestured at the semi-circle of men facing her. 'Forgive me, everyone, if this sounds big-headed, but very few Americans have actually met Hitler. I have, when he gave me my Olympic medal, and it was the most unpleasant experience of my life, on what should have been the happiest day ever. What I saw that day was evil personified. My friend here, David, had made me aware of what the Nazis were beginning to do to the Jews in Germany before the Olympics, and he has continued to update me ever since.' She paused at the sound of a door behind her opening and closing, then pressed on. 'It is a disgrace that the plight of the Jews in Europe is being ignored here in America. Now that Germany has declared war on us, others will hopefully see Hitler for what he really is. I have no wish to continue owning an Olympic medal that has been tainted by the hand of such a monster, and I am surrendering it to the State in a plea to the government to help stop the persecution he is responsible for.' She reached into her handbag and extracted the medal on its canvas lanyard, the silver shining brightly in the winter sunlight flooding through the south-facing windows. As she moved to pass the medal to the senator, a voice at her back broke the silence.

'Hear, hear,' said President Roosevelt. 'A great sentiment, Miss Becker, and a much better speech than most of the ones we have to listen to here in the Capitol.' He advanced into the centre of the room, grinning mischievously, then put on a more solemn expression and grasped her hand, as the photographer's camera flashed and whirred. 'I will do everything in my power to win round my colleagues in the Democratic party, and I know Senator Capper will do the same with the Republicans.' Rachael blushed again, struck dumb by the president's surprise appearance, and the little group in front of them burst into spontaneous applause as he took the medal from her. David Ehrlich smiled to himself. The *Gazette* was going to love this: sports readers, women readers, Democrats, Republicans, fellow Jews, every patriotic American in the nation, they were all going to read about it, and it was definitely going to make a difference this time.

*

And then...

After Rachael Becker's visit to Washington, and the wide press coverage that ensues, the silver medal is lodged at the US Treasury for safekeeping.

In August 1942, the US Secretary of War Henry Stimson authorises the release of large amounts of silver from the US Treasury to the Manhattan Project, a programme to create enriched uranium on a scale sufficient to produce an atomic bomb. The medal is recast as a silver coil and used in the electromagnetic separation process required to split atoms at the Y-12 plant at Oak Ridge, Tennessee. The atomic bomb resulting from this process (code-named "Little Boy") is dropped on the city of Hiroshima in Japan on 6 August 1945.

After World War II the coil is returned to the US Treasury, along with all the other silver used in the Manhattan Project.

In the mid-1960s, the silver coil is one of many released by the US Treasury to NASA for use in the development of the US space programme. It is melted down and applied in the construction of a silver-zinc battery, to be used in the lunar module Aquarius on the *Apollo 13* mission.

*

Author's Note

A brief chapter such as this cannot begin to do justice to the terrible story of Jewish oppression under the Nazi regime. It is true to say that international awareness in the lead-up to the Berlin Olympics was limited, despite efforts in the US, Great Britain and other countries to boycott the Games. The American Olympic Committee President Avery Brundage had visited Germany in late 1934 and had come away opposing the boycott, after being assured that the Games would not be politicised. Some countries chose not to send Jewish competitors, but others, including the US, did so. Within Germany, only one person with Jewish ancestry, a former Olympic gold medallist in fencing, Helene Mayer, was permitted to participate, duly winning a silver medal. The story of Gretel Bergmann's exclusion is true, and there are many more alongside hers.

The references to Jesse Owens, Lutz Long, Helen Stephens and Käthe Krauss are accurate, whereas Rachael Becker, David Ehrlich, Matty Berenger, Ilse Reinbach and Margot Wapiennik are fictional characters. Although there was a men's two-hundred-metre sprint competition in Berlin, the first women's two-hundred-metre Olympic sprint did not take place until the 1948 Games in London (won by the Dutch athlete Fanny Blankers-Koen). Even if the race had occurred in Berlin, the medals would not have been presented by Hitler, who had chosen not to take part in any of the medal ceremonies. Despite the German athletics team's disappointing performance against the likes of Owens and Stephens, the wider Olympic squad topped the country medals table after dominating the gymnastics, rowing and equestrian events. The USA was ranked second and Hungary third.

International recognition of the Jewish persecution in Europe remained subdued in the early years of World War II. President Roosevelt supported the admission of German Jews to the USA but was limited in what could be achieved by the country's restrictive immigration laws. It was only in late 1942, when news of the widespread exterminations began to emerge, that allied governments led by the president united to condemn the Nazis' actions. Arthur Capper, a long-serving Republican senator for Kansas, was known to support certain policies of Roosevelt's Democratic party administration.

As for the silver medal itself, it would have played a miniscule part in the Manhattan Project, resulting in the creation of the "Little Boy" atomic bomb. The US War Department borrowed some fourteen thousand tons of government silver, all of which was duly returned after the end of the war. The source of the silver used in NASA's lunar mission batteries is unclear, but it is not impossible that it too was drawn from the US Treasury.

Fifteen

Apollo 13 Mission

At 2.13pm Eastern Standard Time (EST) on 11 April 1970, the *Apollo 13* spacecraft was launched from the Kennedy Space Centre in Florida, USA. It was the seventh crewed mission for the Apollo space programme and the third to target a moon-landing after Neil Armstrong and Buzz Aldrin had walked on the lunar surface in July 1969. The spacecraft comprised the Saturn V launch rocket, the command and service module named Odyssey and the lunar landing module named Aquarius.

The crew was led by the mission commander, Jim Lovell, an experienced astronaut who had flown in *Apollo 8*, the first spacecraft to orbit the moon. He was accompanied by Jack Swigert, the command module pilot, and Fred Haise, the lunar module pilot, both of whom had served in the military and had experience as test pilots but neither of whom had previously been into space.

The launch and the follow-up procedures went relatively smoothly, and after some forty-six hours, with around two and a half days' flight to the moon remaining, the capsule communicator at Mission Control in Houston (known as the Capcom) was able to tell the crew, 'The spacecraft is in real good shape as far as we are concerned. We're bored to tears down here.' It sounded too good to last, and it was.

Fifty-five hours and forty-six minutes into the flight, Jim Lovell finished a filmed tour of the spacecraft, destined for broadcast on TV, saying, 'This is the crew of *Apollo 13* wishing everybody there a nice evening, and we're just about ready to close out our inspection of Aquarius and get back for a pleasant evening in Odyssey. Goodnight.' Nine minutes later, an electrical short circuit in wiring to one of the command module's two oxygen tanks caused it to explode, ripping the tank apart and damaging its neighbour.

The crew became aware that something was amiss when they heard a sharp bang, accompanied by vibrations and the illumination of a warning light. Jack Swigert immediately reported to Mission Control, 'Houston, we've had a problem here.' Further warning lights indicated the loss of two of the command module's three fuel cells, which relied on an oxygen feed, and thirteen minutes later, Lovell was able to see gas venting into space when he happened to glance out of the spacecraft window. 'We are venting something out into the… into space… it's a gas of some sort,' he told the Capcom. It was the oxygen from the damaged second tank escaping at high pressure, and as this continued it became clear that all oxygen supplies to Odyssey would soon be lost, and the third fuel cell would cease to function. In addition to the crew's need for oxygen in order to breathe, the loss of the fuel cells meant that the command module would not be able to generate electrical power for heat and light, nor to produce water for drinking and cooling vital equipment. 320,000 kilometres (two hundred thousand miles) above earth, the mission's objective had changed in an instant. The lunar landing was aborted, and the goal now was simply to bring the astronauts back from outer space alive.

One hour after the explosion, Mission Control and the crew began to consider the possibility of using the lunar landing module Aquarius as a form of lifeboat for the journey back towards earth. Aquarius and the command module Odyssey were effectively two separate crafts, connected by a short tunnel. The lunar module was equipped with fully charged silver-zinc batteries and oxygen tanks ready for use on the moon-landing expedition. It could therefore be used to house the crew for the several days required to fly back to earth, although the men would have to return to the command module prior to re-entering the earth's atmosphere, to make use of Odyssey's heat shield. Given that it had been expected to be abandoned on the surface of the moon, Aquarius had no such protection and would burn up on re-entry. With only fifteen minutes of power left in the command module, the crew shut down its systems to conserve emergency battery power for re-entry and made their way through to the lunar module. There, oxygen supplies were plentiful, but other provisions were an immediate concern.

The primary issue was power. The six silver-zinc batteries on board Aquarius had been installed to support two astronauts on the moon for up to forty-five hours, but now they would need to support three men for an estimated ninety hours. Mission Control devised a way for Odyssey's fuel cells to be charged from Aquarius to support re-entry requirements, and all non-critical electrical systems on the lunar module were turned off. This successfully limited energy consumption to one-fifth of anticipated levels, although in doing so it removed an important source of heat. As a result, the temperature in the spacecraft fell to as low as 38° Fahrenheit (3° Celsius), making sleep for the crew difficult, threatening severe fatigue and a potential reduction in their ability to operate effectively in the cold, dark conditions. Nevertheless, the batteries were equal to the challenge, and with the conservation measures in place, Aquarius still had a remarkable 20% of its power available at the end of its voyage.

Water supplies were another worry. While the fuel cells in the command module produced water as a by-product to the generation of electricity, the batteries in the lunar module did not function in the same way. The crew limited their consumption in Aquarius to just 180 millilitres (six fluid ounces) per person per day, 80% down on normal intake, but even then it was estimated that they would run out of water five hours before re-entry. They all suffered from dehydration, losing fourteen kilograms (thirty-one pounds) of body weight between them, and Fred Haise developed a urinary tract infection. However, as with the power supply, their efforts to ration water were successful, with 9% of their reserves still remaining at the point of return to the earth's atmosphere.

After thirty-six hours in the lunar module, with a further two days still to endure until re-entry, yet another problem arose. Lithium hydroxide canisters were provided in both Aquarius and Odyssey to remove carbon dioxide from the air within the spacecraft. However, in common with the provision of power, the canisters in the lunar module were designed to support two men for two days, rather than three men for almost four days. There was plenty of lithium hydroxide available in the command module, but its square canisters were not compatible with the round openings in the lunar module's equipment. When a warning light in Aquarius showed that the carbon dioxide had built up to dangerous levels, the mismatch needed to be overcome urgently. Engineers at Mission Control devised a solution using plastic bags, cardboard and duct tape, all materials carried on board the spacecraft, and as soon as Haise and Swigert had built the crude adapter in line with the instructions from Houston, the carbon dioxide readings dropped rapidly.

Aside from the numerous challenges within the spacecraft, Mission Control and the crew had to work out how to bring it back to earth once the lunar landing had been aborted. A series of "burns", or manual manoeuvres, were performed, initially to establish a return-to-earth trajectory looping round the far side of the moon, and then to adjust the angle of re-entry to speed up the journey time and ensure splashdown in the South Pacific Ocean, as originally planned. The complex calculations to achieve the revised flight path, in a lunar module that had not been designed for such a navigation, were performed under enormous time pressure in Houston and the manoeuvres themselves carried out with extraordinary precision by the crew.

Four hours before re-entry, the part of the command module that had suffered the oxygen tank explosion was successfully detached and jettisoned, allowing the crew to photograph the wreckage as it drifted away. Three hours later, the astronauts powered up the command module and crawled back into it through the tunnel from the lunar module, ready for re-entry to the earth's atmosphere. Aquarius was then jettisoned and at 1.07pm EST on 17 April 1970 the command module Odyssey splashed down gently in the ocean near Samoa, just 6.5 kilometres away from the retrieval ship USS *Iwo Jima*. Other than fatigue, dehydration and Fred Haise's urinary tract infection, the crew were in good condition, and the following day they were flown to Hawaii to be welcomed home by the US president, Richard Nixon. Unbeknown to them, their mission had attracted huge media coverage, with people all round the world following events as they unfolded and some forty million Americans watching the splashdown live on television.

As for the fate of the jettisoned lunar module, Aquarius, it was largely destroyed by burning up in the earth's atmosphere on re-entry from space. However, great care had been taken to ensure that re-entry occurred above a specific area in the Pacific south of Samoa so that any surviving parts of the module would fall into the Tonga Trench, the deepest point on the seabed in the southern hemisphere. The reason for such caution was that Aquarius carried a graphite transport cask containing 3.8 kilograms of the radioisotope plutonium-238, intended for powering equipment on the lunar surface, which NASA wanted to be buried as deep as possible in the ocean to avoid potential radioactive leakage.

The six silver-zinc batteries aboard Aquarius, which had kept the three astronauts alive for four long days and nights and provided the power for the final hour of their flight in Odyssey, were melted into their component parts as the lunar module burnt up on re-entry. In liquid form, the silver rained down into the sea above the Tonga Trench and continued to sink, cooling into thousands of small, solid metal nuggets as it went. 10,800 metres later, over 6.5 miles down, the metal finally came to rest on the floor of the Horizon Deep, the lowest point of the trench. In the pitch dark and extreme cold of the seabed, the silver nugget that had first been discovered five thousand years earlier on the other side of the world, nestled into the sediment. After its incredible journey through time, criss-crossing the globe, venturing far into space, saving lives, causing death and playing a part in all manner of significant historical events along the way, the nugget was at last restored to the earth's crust, out of human reach once more. It is still there.

*

Author's Note

The Apollo 13 story is well known, a remarkable feat of scientific and human triumph over adversity, or a successful failure, as the mission commander Jim Lovell later described it. Apart from the final paragraph, events took place much as I have related them, although I have not ventured into the detail of the huge navigational and technical challenges that Mission Control and the crew were so resourceful in addressing.

The silver-zinc batteries played a key part in the crew's survival and the spacecraft's return to earth. Weighing around sixty kilograms each, it is at least theoretically possible for the silver content in them to have survived the furnace of re-entry to the earth's atmosphere in liquid rather than gaseous form, hardening into solid metal lumps on impact with seawater. Materials reach a heat of around 2,900° Fahrenheit (1,600° Celsius) on re-entry, whereas silver's melting point is 1,763° F (962° C), and its boiling point is 3,924° F (2,162° C). The likelihood of the silver from the nugget dug out of the Anatolian rock face in 3000 BCE returning precisely to its original state is admittedly remote. If it did occur, the nugget's location at the bottom of the Tonga Trench, the second deepest point on the world's seabed after the Mariana Trench (almost eleven thousand metres deep, near Guam in the Western Pacific), is likely to remain hidden for many years to come.

Acknowledgements

I would like to thank family and friends for their encouragement in bringing this, my first novel, to fruition. Their patience, support and occasional harassment has been invaluable.